CASEFILE

Nameless opens up the files of some of his most fascinating cases in this collection of ten stories and two novelettes. Spanning the detective's fifteen-year career, *Casefile* is a page-turning pot-pourri of the P.I.'s toughest, most dangerous adventures. Here, as always, Nameless dazzles with keen solutions to seemingly insolvable crimes.

D1735956

KNIGHTSBRIDGE
EASYEYE™

THE "NAMELESS DETECTIVE"

CASEFILE

BILL PRONZINI

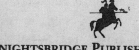

KNIGHTSBRIDGE PUBLISHING COMPANY

NEW YORK

This one is for Thomas L. Dunne of St. Martin's Press, with thanks for his continuing faith in "Nameless."

Table of Contents

Preface

Why doesn't he have a name?

This is the first question readers of the "Nameless Detective" series always ask. Well, I always answer, he's not really nameless; he has a name, just like everybody else, but I don't say what it is. Why not? they ask. Trying to capitalize on Hammett's Continental Op? I tell them no. Trying to establish a hook, a gimmick, to get people to read the stuff? they ask. I tell them no. At which point some of them become annoyed enough to demand: Then why doesn't the damn detective have a name?

It amazes me that anybody should be bothered by this. It seems to me I've made "Nameless" real enough, with enough unique and interesting character traits to set him apart from any other fictional detective. What's in a name, after all?

Anyhow, the damn detective doesn't have a name because when I began the series in 1968 I couldn't think of one that suited him. Big, sort of sloppy Italian guy who guzzles beer, smokes too much and collects pulp magazines. What name fits a character like that? Sam Spadini? Philip Marlozzi?

He stayed nameless through half a dozen stories.

Then, in 1970, I decided to do a novel. Better give him a name now, I thought. Mike Martello? Lew Archerone? With half the book completed and the character still unnamed, it occurred to me somewhat belatedly (I'm not always quick on the uptake) that *I* was also a big, sort of sloppy Italian guy who smoked too much, guzzled beer and collected pulp magazines. I was writing about myself, was what I was doing. Me at the age of fifty or so; me as a private eye instead of a professional writer.

All of the character's beliefs, hang-ups, prejudices, perceptions were pretty much mine. Whatever he did in a given situation, however he reacted, was more or less what I would do and how I would react. Which also explained, psychologically, why I had never been able to think of a suitable name for him. He was me; I was him. And I had no desire, conscious or unconscious, to rename myself.

Not too many other people figured this out until, in a 1978 collaboration between "Nameless" and Collin Wilcox's Lieutenant Frank Hastings (*Twospot*), he was publicly and for novelistic reasons given a first name: Bill. Aha! folks said then. The damn detective has the same first name as the writer; ergo, he must have the same last name, too. Right?

Right. But he has remained officially "Nameless" in subsequent entries in the series and will continue to remain so in future entries. For one very good reason.

Bill Pronzini may be an okay name for a writer, but it's a *lousy* name for a private eye.

The ten stories in this collection were all written for magazine publication—the first eight for U.S. mystery digests, the last two on commission for the Japanese slick magazine *Shosetsu Shincho*. They span the full length of "Nameless's" career, from his first recorded case in 1968 ("It's a Lousy World") to the present; and I think they reflect the changes and growth in the character and in my own style and plotting technique. (I've revised all of the early ones, to rid them of some youthful mistakes, but conceptually they're the same stories that appeared in the magazines.)

It should probably be noted that the opening segments of two of the stories, "One of Those Cases" and "Private Eye Blues," were later revised and expanded into the opening chapters of two novels in the series, *Undercurrent* and *Blowback*, respectively. A number of other published "Nameless" stories and novelettes, not included here, became the basis for such novels as *The Snatch*, *Blowback*, *Labyrinth* and *Scattershot*. Some folks don't seem to like this practice. I fail to understand the objection. Expanding one's own published short stories into novels, or splicing two or three together into a novel, has been a common practice among writers for a long time; no less a personage than Raymond Chandler made a habit of "cannibalizing" his early *Black Mask* stories for his Philip Marlowe novels, and nobody gets upset about *that*. If doing it makes a good idea better, or creates a good new idea through combination—why not?

It should also be noted here that the story "Private Eye Blues" was written for a different reason than the others. When it was published in *Alfred Hitchcock's Mystery Magazine* in 1975, and later reprinted in *Best Detective Stories of the Year 1976*, edited by Edward D. Hoch, it carried a slightly different ending than the one which appears in these pages. A full explanation is included in an afterword to the story.

One final comment:

None of these stories (and none of the "Nameless" novels) are intended as pastiches of Hammett or Chandler or Ross Macdonald or anyone else. They follow a tradition, yes, and contain certain conventions that are consciously exploited (nobody loves the old-fashioned private eye story more than I do), but "Nameless" is not Spade or Marlowe or Archer or any other detective. His vision of the world and of the detecting business is his own.

Nor were these stories written with any pretensions to "literary merit" or "genre importance"; their only purpose is to entertain. I can only hope that when you've finished reading them, you feel that "Nameless" and I have succeeded in that purpose.

BILL PRONZINI

San Francisco, California
June 1982

It's a Lousy World

Colly Babcock was shot to death on the night of September 9, in an alley between Twenty-ninth and Valley streets in the Glen Park District of San Francisco. Two police officers, cruising, spotted him coming out the rear door of Budget Liquors there, carrying a metal box. Colly ran when he saw them. The officers gave chase, calling out for him to halt, but he just kept running; one of the cops fired a warning shot, and when Colly didn't heed it the officer pulled up and fired again. He was aiming low, trying for the legs, but in the half-light of the alley it was a blind shot. The bullet hit Colly in the small of the back and killed him instantly.

I read about it the following morning over coffee and undercooked eggs in a cafeteria on Taylor Street, a block and a half from my office. The story was on an inside page, concise and dispassionate; they teach that kind of objective writing in the journalism classes. Just the cold facts. A man dies, but he's nothing more than a statistic, a name in black type, a faceless nonentity to be considered and then forgotten along with your breakfast coffee.

Unless you knew him.

Unless he was your friend.

Very carefully I folded the newspaper and put it into my coat pocket. Then I stood from the table, went out to the street. The wind was up, blowing in off the Bay; rubble swirled and eddied in the Tenderloin gutters. The air smelled of salt and dark rain and human pollution.

I walked into the face of the wind, toward my office.

"How's the job, Colly?"

"Oh, fine, just fine."

"No problems?"

"No, none at all."

"Stick with it, Colly."

"Sure. I'm a new man."

"Straight all the way?"

"Straight all the way."

Inside the lobby of my building, I found an out-of-order sign taped to the closed elevator doors. Yeah, that figured. I went around to the stairs, up to the second floor and along the hallway to my office.

The door was unlocked, standing open a few inches. I tensed when I saw it like that, and reached out with the tips of my fingers and pushed it all the way open. But there was no trouble. The woman sitting in the chair in front of my desk had never been trouble for anyone.

Colly Babcock's widow.

I moved inside, shut the door and crossed toward her. "Hello, Lucille."

Her hands were clasped tightly in the lap of a plain black dress. She said, "The man down the hall, the CPA—he let me in. He said you wouldn't mind."

"I don't mind."

"You heard, I guess? About Colly?"

"Yes," I said. "What can I say, Lucille?"

"You were his friend. You helped him."

"Maybe I didn't help him enough."

"He didn't do it," Lucille said. "He didn't steal that money. He didn't do all those robberies like they're saying."

"Lucille . . ."

"Colly and I were married thirty-one years," she said. "Don't you think I would have known?"

I did not say anything.

"I always knew," she said.

I sat down, looking at her. She was a big woman, handsome—a strong woman. There was strength in the line of her mouth, and in her eyes, round and gray, tinged with red now from the crying. She had stuck by Colly through two prison terms and twenty-odd years of running, and hiding, and looking over her shoulder. Yes, I thought, she would always have known.

But I said, "The papers said Colly was coming out the back door of the liquor store carrying a metal box. The police found a hundred and six dollars in the box, and the door jimmied open."

"I know what the papers said, and I know what the police are saying. But they're wrong. *Wrong.*"

"He was there, Lucille."

"I know that," she said. "Colly liked to walk in the evenings. A long walk and then a drink when he came home; it helped him to relax. That was how he came to be there."

I shifted position on my chair, not speaking.

Lucille said, "Colly was always nervous when he was doing burglaries. That was one of the ways I could tell. He'd get irritable, and he couldn't sleep."

"He wasn't like that lately?"

"You saw him a few weeks ago," she said. "Did he look that way to you?"

"No," I said, "he didn't."

"We were happy," Lucille said. "No more running. And no more waiting. We were truly happy."

My mouth felt dry. "What about his job?"

"They gave Colly a raise last week. A fifteen-dollar raise. We went to dinner to celebrate, down on the Wharf."

"You were getting along all right on what he made?" I said. "Nothing came up?"

"Nothing. We even had a little bank account started." She bit her lower lip. "We were going to Hawaii next year, or the year after. Colly always wanted to go to Hawaii."

I looked at my hands. They seemed big and awkward resting on the desk top; I took them away and put them in my lap. "These Glen Park robberies started a month and a half ago," I said. "The police estimate the total amount taken at close to five thousand dollars. You could get to Hawaii pretty well on that kind of money."

"Colly didn't do those robberies," she said.

What could I say? God knew, and Lucille knew, that Colly had never been a saint; but this time she was convinced he'd been innocent. Nothing, it seemed, was going to change that in her eyes.

I got a cigarette from my pocket and made a thing of lighting it. The smoke added more dryness to my mouth. Without looking at her, I said, "What do you want me to do, Lucille?"

"I want you to prove Colly didn't do what they're saying he did."

"I'd like nothing better, you know that. But how can I do it? The evidence—"

"Damn the evidence!" Her wide mouth trembled with the sudden emotion. "Colly was innocent, I tell you! I won't have him buried with this last mark against his name. I won't have it."

"Lucille, listen to me . . ."

"I won't listen," she said. "Colly was your friend. You stood up for him with the parole board. You helped him find his job. You talked to him, gave him guidance. He was a different man, a new man, and you helped make him that way. Will you sit here and tell me you believe he threw it all away for five thousand dollars?"

I didn't say anything; I still could not meet her eyes. I stared down at the burning cigarette in my fingers, watching the smoke rise, curling, a gray spiral in the cold air of the office.

"Or don't you care whether he was innocent or not?" she said.

"I care, Lucille."

"Then help me. Find out the truth."

"All right," I said. Her anger and grief, and her absolute certainty that Colly had been innocent, had finally got through to me; I could not have turned her down now if there had been ten times the evidence there was. "All right, Lucille, I'll see what I can do."

It was drizzling when I got to the Hall of Justice. Some of the chill had gone out of the air, but the wind was stronger now. The clouds overhead looked black and swollen, ready to burst.

I parked my car on Bryant Street, went past the sycamores on the narrow front lawn, up the concrete steps and inside. The plainclothes detective division, General Works, was on the fourth floor; I took the elevator. Eberhardt had been promoted to lieutenant not too long ago and had his own private office now, but I caught myself glancing over toward his old desk. Force of habit; it had been a while since I'd visited him at the Hall.

He was in and willing to see me. When I entered his office he was shuffling through some reports and scowling. He was my age, pushing fifty, and he seemed to have been fashioned of an odd contrast of sharp angles and smooth, blunt planes: square forehead, sharp nose and chin, thick and blocky upper body, long legs and angular hands. Today he was wearing a brown suit that hadn't been pressed in a month; his tie was crooked; there was a collar button missing from his shirt. And he had a fat, purplish bruise over his left eye.

"All right," he said, "make it quick."

"What happened to your eye?"

"I bumped into a doorknob."

"Sure you did."

"Yeah," he said. "You come here to pass the time of day, or was there something?"

"I'd like a favor, Eb."

"Sure. And I'd like three weeks' vacation."

"I want to look at an Officer's Felony Report."

"Are you nuts? Get the hell out of here."

The words didn't mean anything. He was always gruff and grumbly while he was working; and we'd been friends for more years than either of us cared to remember, ever since we went through the Police Academy together after World War II and then joined the force here in the city.

I said, "There was a shooting last night. Two squad-car cops killed a man running away from the scene of a burglary in Glen Park."

"So?"

"The victim was a friend of mine."

He gave me a look. "Since when do you have burglars for friends?"

"His name was Colly Babcock," I said. "He did two stretches in San Quentin, both for burglary; I helped send him up the first time. I also helped get him out on parole the second time and into a decent job."

"Uh-huh. I remember the name. I also heard about the shooting last night. Too bad this pal of yours turned bad again, but then a lot of them do—as if you didn't know."

I was silent.

"I get it," Eberhardt said. "You don't think so. That's why you're here."

"Colly's wife doesn't think so. I guess maybe I don't either."

"I can't let you look at any reports. And even if I could, it's not my department. Robbery'll be handling it. Internal Affairs, too."

"You could pull some strings."

"I could," he said, "but I won't. I'm up to my ass in work. I just don't have the time."

I got to my feet. "Well, thanks anyway, Eb." I went to the door, put my hand on the knob, but before I turned it he made a noise behind me. I turned.

"If things go all right," he said, scowling at me, "I'll be off duty in a couple of hours. If I happen to get down by Robbery on the way out, maybe I'll stop in. Maybe."

"I'd appreciate it if you would."

"Give me a call later on. At home."

"Thanks, Eb."

"Yeah," he said. "So what are you standing there for? Get the hell out of here and let me work."

I found Tommy Belknap in a bar called Luigi's, out in the Mission District.

He was drinking whiskey at the long bar, leaning his head on his arms and staring at the wall. Two men in work clothes were drinking beer and eating sandwiches from lunch pails at the other end, and in the middle an old lady in a black shawl sipped red wine from a glass held with arthritic fingers. I sat on a stool next to Tommy and said hello.

He turned his head slowly, his eyes moving

upward. His face was an anemic white, and his bald head shone with beaded perspiration. He had trouble focusing his eyes; he swiped at them with the back of one veined hand. He was pretty drunk. And I was pretty sure I knew why.

"Hey," he said when he recognized me, "have a drink, will you?"

"Not just now."

He got his glass to his lips with shaky fingers, managed to drink without spilling any of the whiskey. "Colly's dead," he said.

"Yeah. I know."

"They killed him last night," Tommy said. "They shot him in the back."

"Take it easy, Tommy."

"He was my friend."

"He was my friend, too."

"Colly was a nice guy. Lousy goddamn cops had no right to shoot him like that."

"He was robbing a liquor store," I said.

"Hell he was!" Tommy said. He swiveled on the stool and pushed a finger at my chest. "Colly was straight, you hear that? Just like me. Ever since we both got out of Q."

"You sure about that, Tommy?"

"Damn right I am."

"Then who did do those burglaries in Glen Park?"

"How should I know?"

"Come on, you get around. You know people, you hear things. There must be something on the earie."

"Nothing," he said. "Don't know."

"Kids?" I said. "Street punks?"

"Don't *know.*"

"But it wasn't Colly? You'd know if it was Colly?"

"Colly was straight," Tommy said. "And now he's dead."

He put his head down on his arms again. The bartender came over; he was a fat man with a reddish handlebar mustache. "You can't sleep in here, Tommy," he said. "You ain't even supposed to *be* in here while you're on parole."

"Colly's dead," Tommy said, and there were tears in his eyes.

"Let him alone," I said to the bartender.

"I can't have him sleeping in here."

I took out my wallet and put a five-dollar bill on the bar. "Give him another drink," I said, "and then let him sleep it off in the back room. The rest of the money is for you."

The bartender looked at me, looked at the fin, looked at Tommy. "All right," he said. "What the hell."

I went out into the rain.

D. E. O'Mira and Company, Wholesale Plumbing Supplies, was a big two-storied building that took up three-quarters of a block on Berry Street, out near China Basin. I parked in front and went inside. In the center of a good-sized office was a switchboard walled in glass, with a card taped to the front that said Information. A dark-haired girl wearing a set of headphones was sitting inside, and when I asked her if Mr. Templeton was in she said he was at a meeting uptown and wouldn't be back all day. Mr. Templeton was the office manager, the man I had spoken to about giving Colly Babcock a job when he was paroled from San Quentin.

Colly had worked in the warehouse, and his immediate supervisor was a man I had never met named Harlin. I went through a set of swing doors opposite the main entrance, down a narrow, dark passage screened on both sides. On my left when I emerged into the warehouse was a long service counter; behind it were display shelves, and behind them long rows of bins that stretched the length and width of the building. Straight ahead, through an open doorway, I could see the loading dock and a yard cluttered with soil pipe and other supplies. On my right was a windowed office with two desks, neither occupied; an old man in a pair of baggy brown slacks, a brown vest and a battered slouch hat stood before a side counter under the windows.

The old man didn't look up when I came into the office. A foul-smelling cigar danced in his thin mouth as he shuffled papers. I cleared my throat and said, "Excuse me."

He looked at me then, grudgingly. "What is it?"

"Are you Mr. Harlin?"

"That's right."

I told him who I was and what I did. I was about to ask him about Colly when a couple of guys came into the office and one of them plunked himself down at the nearest desk. I said to Harlin, "Could we talk someplace private?"

"Why? What're you here about?"

"Colly Babcock," I said.

He made a grunting sound, scribbled on one of his papers with a pencil stub and then led me out onto the dock. We walked along there, past a warehouseman loading crated cast-iron sinks from a pallet into a pickup truck, and up to the wide, doubled-door entrance to an adjoining warehouse.

The old man stopped and turned to me. "We can talk here."

"Fine. You were Colly's supervisor, is that right?"

"I was."

"Tell me how you felt about him."

"You won't hear anything bad, if that's what you're looking for."

"That's not what I'm looking for."

He considered that for a moment, then shrugged and said, "Colly was a good worker. Did what you told him, no fuss. Quiet sort, kept to himself mostly."

"You knew about his prison record?"

"I knew. All of us here did. Nothing was ever said to Colly about it, though. I saw to that."

"Did he seem happy with the job?"

"Happy enough," Harlin said. "Never complained, if that's what you mean."

"No friction with any of the other men?"

"No. He got along fine with everybody."

A horn sounded from inside the adjoining warehouse and a yellow forklift carrying a pallet of lavatories came out. We stepped out of the way as the thing clanked and belched past.

I asked Harlin, "When you heard about what happened to Colly last night—what was your reaction?"

"Didn't believe it," he answered. "Still don't. None of us do."

I nodded. "Did Colly have any particular friend here? Somebody he ate lunch with regularly—like that?"

"Kept to himself for the most part, like I said. But he stopped with Sam Biehler for a beer a time or two after work; Sam mentioned it."

"I'd like to talk to Biehler, if it's all right."

"Is with me," the old man said. He paused, chewing on his cigar. "Listen, there any chance Colly didn't do what the papers say he did?"

"There might be. That's what I'm trying to find out."

"Anything I can do," he said, "you let me know."

"I'll do that."

We went back inside and I spoke to Sam Biehler, a tall, slender guy with a mane of silver hair that gave him, despite his work clothes, a rather distinguished appearance.

"I don't mind telling you," he said, "I don't believe a damned word of it. I'd have had to be there to see it with my own eyes before I'd believe it, and maybe not even then."

"I understand you and Colly stopped for a beer occasionally?"

"Once a week maybe, after work. Not in a bar; Colly couldn't go to a bar because of his parole.

At my place. Then afterward I'd give him a ride home."

"What did you talk about?"

"The job, mostly," Biehler said. "What the company could do to improve things out here in the warehouse. I guess you know the way fellows talk."

"Uh-huh. Anything else?"

"About Colly's past, that what you're getting at?"

"Yes."

"Just once," Biehler said. "Colly told me a few things. But I never pressed him on it. I don't like to pry."

"What was it he told you?"

"That he was never going back to prison. That he was through with the kind of life he'd led before." Biehler's eyes sparkled, as if challenging me. "And you know something? I been on this earth for fifty-nine years and I've known a lot of men in that time. You get so you can tell."

"Tell what, Mr. Biehler?"

"Colly wasn't lying," he said.

I spent an hour at the main branch of the library in Civic Center, reading through back issues of the *Chronicle* and the *Examiner*. The Glen Park robberies had begun a month and a half ago, and I had paid only passing attention to them at the time.

When I had acquainted myself with the details I went back to my office and checked in with my answering service. No calls. Then I called Lucille Babcock.

"The police were here earlier," she said. "They had a search warrant."

"Did they find anything?"

"There was nothing to find."

"What did they say?"

"They asked a lot of questions. They wanted to know about bank accounts and safe-deposit boxes."

"Did you cooperate with them?"

"Of course."

"Good," I said. I told her what I had been doing all day, what the people I'd talked with had said.

"You see?" she said. "Nobody who knew Colly can believe he was guilty."

"Nobody but the police."

"Damn the police," she said.

I sat holding the phone. There were things I wanted to say, but they all seemed trite and meaningless. Pretty soon I told her I would be in touch, leaving it at that, and put the receiver back in its cradle.

It was almost five o'clock. I locked up the office, drove home to my flat in Pacific Heights, drank a beer and ate a pastrami sandwich, and then lit a cigarette and dialed Eberhardt's home number. It was his gruff voice that answered.

"Did you stop by Robbery before you left the Hall?" I asked.

"Yeah. I don't know why."

"We're friends, that's why."

"That doesn't stop you from being a pain in the ass sometimes."

"Can I come over, Eb?"

"You can if you get here before eight o'clock," he said. "I'm going to bed then, and Dana has orders to bar all the doors and windows and take the telephone off the hook. I plan to get a good night's sleep for a change."

"I'll be there in twenty minutes," I said.

Eberhardt lived in Noe Valley, up at the back end near Twin Peaks. The house was big and painted white, a two-storied frame job with a trimmed lawn and lots of flowers in front. If you knew Eberhardt, the house was sort of symbolic; it typified everything the honest, hardworking cop was dedicated to protecting. I had a hunch he knew it, too; and if he did, he got a certain amount of satisfaction from the knowledge. That was the way he was.

I parked in his sloping driveway and went up and rang the bell. His wife Dana, a slender and very attractive brunette with a lot of patience, let me in, asked how I was and showed me into the kitchen, closing the door behind her as she left.

Eberhardt was sitting at the table having a pipe and a cup of coffee. The bruise over his eye had been smeared with some kind of pinkish ointment; it made him look a little silly, but I knew better than to tell him so.

"Have a seat," he said, and I had one. "You want some coffee?"

"Thanks."

He got me a cup, then indicated a manila envelope lying on the table. Without saying anything, sucking at his pipe, he made an elaborate effort to ignore me as I picked up the envelope and opened it.

Inside was the report made by the two patrolmen, Avinisi and Carstairs, who had shot and killed Colly Babcock in the act of robbing the Budget Liquor Store. I read it over carefully—and my eye caught on one part, a couple of sentences, under "Effects." When I was through I put the report back in the envelope and returned it to the table.

Eberhardt looked at me then. "Well?"

"One item," I said, "that wasn't in the papers."

"What's that?"

"They found a pint of Kesslers in a paper bag in Colly's coat pocket."

He shrugged. "It was a liquor store, wasn't it? Maybe he slipped it into his pocket on the way out?"

"And put it into a paper bag first?"

"People do funny things," he said.

"Yeah," I said. I drank some of the coffee and then got on my feet. "I'll let you get to bed, Eb. Thanks again."

He grunted. "You owe me a favor. Just remember that."

"I won't forget."

"You and the elephants," he said.

It was still raining the next morning—another dismal day. I drove over to Chenery Street and wedged my car into a downhill parking slot a half-block from the three-room apartment Lucille and Colly Babcock had called home for the past year. I hurried through the rain, feeling the chill of it on my face, and mounted sagging wooden steps to the door.

Lucille answered immediately. She wore the same black dress she'd had on yesterday, and the same controlled mask of grief; it would be a long time before that grief faded and she was able to get on with her life. Maybe never, unless somebody proved her right about Colly's innocence.

I sat in the old, stuffed leather chair by the window: Colly's chair. Lucille said, "Can I get you something?"

I shook my head. "What about you? Have you eaten anything today? Or yesterday?"

"No," she answered.

"You have to eat, Lucille."

"Maybe later. Don't worry, I'm not suicidal. I won't starve myself to death."

I managed a small smile. "All right," I said.

"Why are you here?" she asked. "Do you have any news?"

"No, not yet." I had an idea, but it was only that, and too early. I did not want to instill any false hopes. "I just wanted to ask you a few more questions."

"Oh. What questions?"

"You mentioned yesterday that Colly liked to take walks in the evening. Was he in the habit of walking to any particular place, or in any particular direction?"

"No," Lucille said. "He just liked to walk. He was gone for a couple of hours sometimes."

"He never told you where he'd been?"

"Just here and there in the neighborhood."

Here and there in the neighborhood, I thought. The alley where Colly had been shot was eleven blocks from this apartment. He could have walked in a straight line, or he could have gone roundabout in any direction.

I asked, "Colly liked to have a nightcap when he came back from these walks, didn't he?"

"He did, yes."

"He kept liquor here, then?"

"One bottle of bourbon. That's all."

I rotated my hat in my hands. "I wonder if I could have a small drink, Lucille. I know it's early, but . . ."

She nodded and got up and went to a squat cabinet near the kitchen door. She bent, slid the panel open in front, looked inside. Then she straightened. "I'm sorry," she said. "We . . . I seem to be out."

I stood. "It's okay. I should be going anyway."

"Where will you go now?"

"To see some people." I paused. "Would you happen to have a photograph of Colly? A snapshot, something like that?"

"I think so. Why do you want it?"

"I might need to show it around," I said. "Here in the neighborhood."

She seemed satisfied with that. "I'll see if I can find one for you."

I waited while she went into the bedroom. A

couple of minutes later she returned with a black-and-white snap of Colly, head and shoulders, that had been taken in a park somewhere. He was smiling, one eyebrow raised in mock raffishness.

I put the snap into my pocket and thanked Lucille and told her I would be in touch again pretty soon. Then I went to the door and let myself out.

The skies seemed to have parted like the Red Sea. Drops of rain as big as hail pellets lashed the sidewalk. Thunder rumbled in the distance, edging closer. I pulled the collar of my overcoat tight around my neck and made a run for my car.

It was after four o'clock when I came inside a place called Tay's Liquors on Whitney Street and stood dripping water on the floor. There was a heater on a shelf just inside the door, and I allowed myself the luxury of its warmth for a few seconds. Then I crossed to the counter.

A young guy wearing a white shirt and a Hitler mustache got up from a stool near the cash register and walked over to me. He smiled, letting me see crooked teeth that weren't very clean. "Wet enough for you?" he said.

No, I thought, I want it to get a lot wetter so I can drown. Dumb question, dumb answer. But all I said was, "Maybe you can help me."

"Sure," he said. "Name your poison."

He was brimming with originality. I took the snapshot of Colly Babcock from my pocket, extended it across the counter and asked, "Did you see this man two nights ago, sometime around eleven o'clock?" It was the same thing I had done and the same question I had asked at least twenty times already. I had been driving and walking the streets of Glen Park for four hours now, and I had been to four liquor stores, five corner groceries, two large chain markets, a delicatessen and half a dozen bars that sold off-sale liquor. So far I had come up with nothing except possibly a head cold.

The young guy gave me a slanted look. "Cop?" he asked, but his voice was still cheerful.

I showed him the photostat of my investigator's license. He shrugged, then studied the photograph. "Yeah," he said finally, "I did see this fellow a couple of nights ago. Nice old duck. We talked a little about the Forty-niners."

I stopped feeling cold and I stopped feeling frustrated. I said, "About what time did he come in?"

"Let's see. Eleven-thirty or so, I think."

Fifteen minutes before Colly had been shot in an alley three and a half blocks away. "Do you remember what he bought?"

"Bourbon—a pint. Medium price."

"Kesslers"

"Yeah, I think it was."

"Okay, good. What's your name?"

"My name? Hey, wait a minute, I don't want to get involved in anything . . ."

"Don't worry, it's not what you're thinking."

It took a little more convincing, but he gave me his name finally and I wrote it down in my notebook. And thanked him and hurried out of there.

I had something more than an idea now.

*   *   *

Eberhardt said, "I ought to knock you flat on your ass."

He had just come out of his bedroom, eyes foggy with sleep, hair standing straight up, wearing a wine-colored bathrobe. Dana stood beside him looking fretful.

"I'm sorry I woke you up, Eb," I said. "But I didn't think you'd be in bed this early. It's only six o'clock."

He said something I didn't hear, but that Dana heard. She cracked him on the arm to show her disapproval, then turned and left us alone.

Eberhardt went over and sat on the couch and glared at me. "I've had about six hours' sleep in the past forty-eight," he said. "I got called out last night after you left, I didn't get home until three A.M., I was up at seven, I worked all goddamn day and knocked off early so I could get some *sleep*, and what happens? I'm in bed ten minutes and you show up."

"Eb, it's important."

"What is?"

"Colly Babcock."

"Ah, Christ, you don't give up, do you?"

"Sometimes I do, but not this time. Not now." I told him what I had learned from the guy at Tay's Liquors.

"So Babcock bought a bottle there," Eberhardt said. "So what?"

"If he was planning to burglarize a liquor store, do you think he'd have bothered to *buy* a bottle fifteen minutes before?"

"Hell, the job might have been spur-of-the-moment."

"Colly didn't work that way. When he was pulling them, they were all carefully planned well in advance. Always."

"He was getting old," Eberhardt said. "People change."

"You didn't know Colly. Besides, there are a few other things."

"Such as?"

"The burglaries themselves. They were all done the same way—back door jimmied, marks on the jamb and lock made with a hand bar or something." I paused. "They didn't find any tool like that on Colly. Or inside the store either."

"Maybe he got rid of it."

"When did he have time? They caught him coming out the door."

Eberhardt scowled. I had his interest now. "Go ahead," he said.

"The pattern of the burglaries, like I was saying, is doors jimmied, drawers rifled, papers and things strewn about. No fingerprints, but it smacks of amateurism. Or somebody trying to make it look like amateurism."

"And Babcock was a professional."

"He could have done the book," I said. "He used lock picks and glass cutters to get into a place, never anything like a hand bar. He didn't ransack; he always knew exactly what he was after. He never deviated from that, Eb. Not once."

Eberhardt got to his feet and paced around for a

time. Then he stopped in front of me and said, "So what do you think, then?"

"You figure it."

"Yeah," he said slowly, "I can figure it, all right. But I don't like it. I don't like it at all."

"And Colly?" I said. "You think he liked it?"

Eberhardt turned abruptly, went to the telephone. He spoke to someone at the Hall of Justice, then someone else. When he hung up, he was already shrugging out of his bathrobe.

He gave me a grim look. "I hope you're wrong, you know that."

"I hope I'm not," I said.

I was sitting in my flat, reading one of the pulps from my collection of several thousand issues, when the telephone rang just before eleven o'clock. It was Eberhardt, and the first thing he said was, "You weren't wrong."

I didn't say anything, waiting.

"Avinisi and Carstairs," he said bitterly. "Each of them on the force a little more than two years. The old story: bills, long hours, not enough pay— and greed. They cooked up the idea one night while they were cruising Glen Park, and it worked just fine until two nights ago. Who'd figure the cops for it?"

"You have any trouble with them?"

"No. I wish they'd given me some so I could have slapped them with a resisting-arrest charge, too."

"How did it happen with Colly?"

"It was the other way around," he said. "Babcock was cutting through the alley when he saw them coming out the rear door. He turned to run and they panicked and Avinisi shot him in the back. When they went to check, Carstairs found a note from Babcock's parole officer in one of his pockets, identifying him as an ex-con. That's when they decided to frame him."

"Look, Eb, I—"

"Forget it," he said. "I know what you're going to say."

"You can't help it if a couple of cops turn out that way . . ."

"I said forget it, all right?" And the line went dead.

I listened to the empty buzzing for a couple of seconds. It's a lousy world, I thought. But sometimes, at least, there is justice.

Then I called Lucille Babcock and told her why her husband had died.

They had a nice funeral for Colly.

The services were held in a small nondenominational church on Monterey Boulevard. There were a lot of flowers, carnations mostly; Lucille said they had been Colly's favorites. Quite a few people came. Tommy Belknap was there, and Sam Biehler and old man Harlin and the rest of them from D. E. O'Mira. Eberhardt, too, which might have seemed surprising unless you knew him. I also saw faces I didn't recognize; the whole thing had gotten a big play in the media.

Afterward, there was the funeral procession to the cemetery in Colma, where we listened to the minister's final words and watched them put Colly into the ground. When it was done I offered to drive Lucille home, but she said no, there were some arrangements she wanted to make with the caretaker for upkeep of the plot; one of her neighbors would stay with her and see to it she got home all right. Then she held my hand and kissed me on the cheek and told me again how grateful she was.

I went to where my car was parked. Eberhardt was waiting; he had ridden down with me.

"I don't like funerals," he said.

"No," I said.

We got into the car. "So what are you planning to do when we get back to the city?" Eberhardt asked.

"I hadn't thought about it."

"Come over to my place. Dana's gone off to visit her sister, and I've got a refrigerator full of beer."

"All right."

"Maybe we'll get drunk," he said.

I nodded. "Maybe we will at that."

Death of a Nobody

His name was Nello.

Whether this was his given name, or his surname or a sobriquet he had picked up sometime during the span of his fifty-odd years—I never found out. I doubt if even Nello himself knew any longer. He was what sociologists call "an addictive drinker who has lost all semblance of faith in God, humanity or himself." And what the average citizen dismisses unconcernedly as "a Skid Row wino."

He came into my office just before ten o'clock on one of San Francisco's bitter-cold autumn mornings. He had been a lawyer once, in a small town up near the Oregon border, and there were still signs of intelligence, of manners and education, in his gaunt face. I had first encountered him more than twenty years ago, when a police lieutenant named Eberhardt and I had been patrolmen working south of the Slot. I didn't know—and had never asked—what private hell had led him from small-town respectability to the oblivion of the city's Skid Row.

He stood just inside the door, his small hands nervously rolling and unrolling the brim of a shapeless brown fedora. His thin, almost emaciated body was encased in a pair of once-brown slacks and a tweed jacket that had worn through at both elbows, and his faded blue eyes had that tangible filminess that comes from too many nights with too many bottles of cheap wine. But he was sober this morning—cold and painfully sober.

I said, "It's been a long time, Nello."

"A long time," he agreed in a vague way.

"Some coffee?"

"No. No, thanks."

I finished pouring myself a cup from the pot I keep on an old two-burner on top of my filing cabinet. "What can I do for you?"

He cleared his throat, his lips moving as if he were tasting something by memory. But then he seemed to change his mind. He took a step backward, half-turned toward the door. "Maybe I shouldn't have come," he said to the floor. "Maybe I'd better go."

"Wait, now. What is it, Nello?"

"Chaucer," he said. "It's Chaucer."

I recognized the name. Chaucer was another habitué of the Row, like Nello an educated man who had lost part of himself sometime, somewhere, somehow; he had once taught English Literature at a high school in Kansas or Nebraska, and that was where his nickname had come from. He and Nello had been companions on the Row for a long time.

I said, "What about him?"

"He's dead," Nello said dully. "I just heard about it a little while ago. The cops found him early this morning in an alley off Hubbell Street, near the railroad yards. He was beaten to death."

"Christ. Do they know who did it?"

Nello shook his head. "But I think I might know the reason he was killed."

"Have you gone to the police?"

"No."

I didn't need to ask why not. Noninvolvement with the law was one of the codes by which the Row people lived—even when one of their own died by violence. But I said, "If you have some information that might help find Chaucer's killer, you'd better take it to them."

"What good would it do? The cops don't care about a man like Chaucer—a wino, a bum, a nobody. Why should they bother when one of us is murdered?"

"Some cops feel that way, sure. But not all of them."

"Enough," Nello said. "Too many."

"Then why did you come to me? I was a cop once, remember; in a way I'm still a cop. If you don't think the police will care, what made you think I would?"

"I don't know," he said. "You were always decent to me, and you're not on the force anymore. I thought . . . Look, maybe I just better go."

"It's up to you."

He hesitated. There was a struggle going on inside him between an almost forgotten sense of duty and the adopted attitudes of the Row. This time, duty—given strength by his friendship with Chaucer—won out; he moved forward in a ponderous way and sat in one of the clients' chairs. He put the hat on his knee, looked at the veined backs of his hands.

"I can't pay you anything, you know," he said.

"Never mind that. About the only thing I can do is take whatever you tell me to the police and see that it gets into the proper hands."

He took a breath, coughed and wiped at his mouth with the palm of one hand. When he began talking, his voice was low, almost monotonous. "Three weeks ago, Chaucer and I were sharing a bottle in a doorway on Fifth down near Folsom. It was after midnight, not much traffic on the streets. Old Jenny—you know her?"

I shook my head.

"One of us. A bag lady," Nello said. "She was standing on the corner across the street, waiting for the light to change, and when it did she stepped down and started to cross. She was right out in the middle when the car hit her. It came racing up Fifth, right through a red light; knocked her thirty feet into the wall of a building. Wasn't time for Chaucer or me to yell a warning. Wasn't time for anything. The car slowed after it hit her, but then it speeded up again and made a fast turn left on Howard. There wasn't anything we could do for Old Jenny, not the way she'd been thrown into that building, so we beat it out of there before the cops came."

Again, the code of noninvolvement. Nello

rubbed a hand over his face, as if the length of his explanation had left him momentarily drained. I waited without speaking, and pretty soon he went on.

"Last weekend, Chaucer was panhandling up by the Hilton and saw the hit-and-run car parked on O'Farrell Street. It had been repaired, had a fresh paint job. He told me about it later."

I said, "How did he know it was the same car?"

"He got the license number when the driver slowed after hitting Old Jenny. Even with two bottles of port in him, he had an eye like a camera."

"Did he tell you what the number was?"

"No," Nello said. "He didn't tell me he found out the owner's name from the registration last weekend either, but that's what I think he did. I saw him yesterday afternoon, early; he looked excited. Said he had to take care of some business, that if it worked out the way he hoped he'd look me up later and we'd go celebrate. I never saw him again."

"Uh-huh. So you figure he went to see the owner of the hit-and-run car and tried to shake him down. And got himself killed instead."

He nodded.

"Chaucer didn't mention the make and model of the car?"

"No."

"Or where the owner lived?"

"No."

"Did he say anything that might lead to either the car or the owner?"

"No," Nello said. "I told you everything he told me."

I got my cigarettes out and lit one. Nello's bloodshot eyes were hungry as he watched me. I thought: What the hell, he made the effort to come here, didn't he? and tossed him the half-full package. He swiped at it, dropped it, picked it up and put it into the pocket of his coat. His eyes thanked me, even if he couldn't make his mouth say the words.

"All right," I said, "I'll see what I can do. As soon as anything turns up, I'll let you know."

He nodded again, listlessly this time, and got to his feet. It was plain to see, as he shuffled out, that he didn't believe anything would turn up at all.

Eberhardt was in conference with some people when I got down to the Hall of Justice, so I sat in the squad room and smoked a couple of cigarettes out of a new pack and discussed the political situation with an inspector named Branislaus, whom I knew slightly. After half an hour three men in business suits, two of them carrying briefcases, came out of Eberhardt's office. They marched out of the squad room in single-file cadence, like Army recruits on a parade field.

Branislaus announced me over the intercom, but it was another five minutes before Eberhardt decided to let me see him. He was cleaning out the bowl of his pipe with a penknife when I went in, not being particularly careful about it; bits of dottle were scattered across the paper-littered surface of his desk. He said without looking up, "So what the hell do *you* want?"

"How about a kind word?"

"You see those three guys who just left?"

"I saw them, sure."

"They're with the state attorney general's office," Eberhardt said, "and they've been giving me a hard time for a week on a certain matter. I haven't seen Dana in two days, and I haven't eaten since eleven o'clock yesterday morning. On top of all that, I think I've got an abscessed tooth. So whatever it is you came for, the answer is no."

I said, "Okay, Eb. But it has to do with a homicide last night."

He frowned. "Which homicide?"

"A guy from Skid Row called Chaucer."

"What do you know about that?"

"I can tell it to whichever team of inspectors is handling the investigation—"

"You can tell it to me," he said. "Sit down."

I sat down. And got my cigarettes out and lit one.

Eberhardt said, "You smoke too damned much, you know that?"

"Sure," I said. "You remember a guy named Nello? Friend of Chaucer's on the Row?"

"I remember him."

"He came to see me this morning," I said, and outlined for him what Nello had told me.

Eberhardt put the cold pipe between his teeth, took it out again, scowled at it and set it in his ashtray. "There might be a connection, all right. Why didn't Nello come down himself with this?"

"You know the answer to that, Eb."

"Yeah, I guess I do." He sighed. "Well, I was reading the preliminary report a little while ago, before those state clowns came in. I recognized Chaucer's name. There's not much in it."

"Nello said he was beaten to death."

"That's right. Lab boys found blood on the wall of one of the buildings in the alley; way it looks, his head was batted against the wall until it cracked. There were other marks on him, too—facial and body bruises."

"What was the approximate time of death?"

"Coroner figures it at between midnight and two A.M."

"Was there anything in the alley?"

"In the way of evidence, you mean? No. And nobody saw or heard anything; that area round the Southern Pacific yards is like a mausoleum after midnight."

"Did Chaucer have anything in his pockets?"

"A pint of scotch and thirty-eight dollars, plus some change."

"That's a lot of money, and pretty fancy liquor, for a wino to be carrying around."

"Uh-huh."

"Gives credence to Nello's theory, wouldn't you say?"

"Maybe. But if this hit-and-run guy killed Chaucer, why would he give him the money first?"

"Could be that Chaucer asked for a hell of a lot more than what he had in his pockets," I said. "The guy could have given him that as a down payment, then arranged to meet him last night with the rest."

"And gave him a different kind of payoff instead," Eberhardt said. "Well, it could have happened like that."

"Look, Eb, I'd like to poke into this thing myself if you don't mind."

"I was wondering when you'd get around to that. What's your big interest in Chaucer's death?"

"I told you, Nello came to see me this morning."

"But not to hire you. I don't believe that."

"No," I admitted.

"Then who's going to pay your fee?"

"Maybe I'll do the job gratis. I'm not working on anything else right now."

"You feel sorry for Nello, is that it?"

"Some, yes. You know what he thinks? He thinks the cops don't give a damn about finding Chaucer's killer. Chaucer was a nobody, just another bum. Who cares, Nello said, if some wino gets knocked off."

Eberhardt sighed again and got wearily to his feet. "I think I can spare a couple of minutes," he said. "Come on, we'll go down to Traffic. See what Hit-and-Run has on Old Jenny."

We rode the elevator down to the Traffic Bureau on the main floor and went in to see an inspector named Aldrich, who was in charge of the Hit-and-Run Detail. He was a big, red-haired guy with a lot of freckles on his face and hands. Eberhardt told him what we wanted, and Aldrich dug around in one of his file cabinets and came up with a thin cardboard folder. He spread it open on his desk, squinted at the contents; I had the impression that he needed glasses but was too stubborn or too proud to admit it.

He said at length, "Woman named Jenny Einers, sixty-three years old, hit-and-run at Fifth and Folsom streets three weeks ago. That the one?"

"That's the one," Eberhardt said.

"We've got damned little on it," Aldrich told him. "Happened at approximately twelve-thirty A.M., and there were no witnesses."

"Yes there were," I said. "Two, in fact."

"Oh?"

I filled him in on what Nello had told me. Then I asked, "Was there any broken glass at the scene?"

"Yes. From one of the headlights, probably. No way to identify the make and model from it, though."

"What about paint scrapings?"

"Uh-huh. Forest green. General Motors color, 1966 to 1969. Same thing applies. It could have come off any one of several GM cars."

"Was there any fender or grille dirt?"

Aldrich nodded. "The lab put it through chemical analysis, of course. Common ground dirt, a little sand, some gravel chips, a few other things. But nothing unusual that we could work with."

Eberhardt asked, "You find anything else?"

"Just some sawdust," Aldrich said.

"Sawdust?"

"Several particles on the street near the point of

impact. White pine, spruce, redwood. You make anything conclusive out of that? We couldn't."

Both Eberhardt and I shook our heads.

"We sent out word to all the body shops in the Bay area right away," Aldrich said. "That's the standard procedure. There were a couple of late-model GM's with forest-green paint jobs brought in for bodywork, but one was involved in a routine fender-bender and the other had the left front door banged up. We checked the accident reports on both; they were clear. Nothing else came up." He spread his hands and shrugged. "Dead end."

We thanked Aldrich for his time and went out to the elevators. When Eberhardt pushed the UP button he said, "I can't take any more time on this right now, so you can poke around if you want. But make sure you call me if you turn up anything."

"You know I will."

"Yeah," he said. "But it doesn't hurt to remind you."

The elevator doors slid open, and I watched him get inside and press four on the panel. Then I crossed the lobby, went out to Bryant Street. Fog banks were massing to the west in puffy swirls, like carnival cotton candy. The wind was up, carrying the first streamers of mist over the city. I buttoned my coat and hurried to where I had parked my car.

For a time I sat inside with the engine running and the heater on, wondering what to do next. Nello had said he'd last seen Chaucer early yesterday afternoon, apparently just before Chaucer left

the Row; and Eberhardt had told me that the
coroner had fixed the time of death at between
midnight and two A.M. That left close to twelve
hours of Chaucer's time unaccounted for. Assuming he'd had the money found on him for some
time prior to his murder, and knowing the type of
person he'd been, it seemed logical that he would
have circulated on the Row even though Nello
hadn't come across him. If that was the case, then
one of the other habitués had to have seen him,
maybe even spent some time with him.

I drove over to Mission Street and put my car in
the lot near Seventh and Mission, opposite the
main post office. Then I walked to Sixth and
began to canvass the Row from Market to Folsom
north-south, from Sixth to Third west-east.

During the next three hours, I walked streets
littered with debris and windswept papers and
hundreds of empty wine and liquor bottles, even
though the city sanitation department works the
area every morning. I talked to stoic, hard-eyed
bartenders in cheerless saloons; to dowdy wait-
resses with faces the color of yeast in greasy
spoons that sold hash and onions for a dollar; to
tired, aging hookers with names like Hey Hattie
and Annie Orphan and Black Mariah; to liquor
store clerks who counted each nickel and each
dime with open contempt before serving their
customers; to knots of men white and black huddled together in doorways, on street corners, in
the small "Wino Park" on Sixth just south of
Mission that had, amazingly enough, been sanc-
tioned by the city in an effort to keep the Row

people from clogging the sidewalks—men called Monkeyface and Yahoo and Big Stick, who spent their days panhandling indifferent passersby and drinking from paper-bag-wrapped bottles with only the necks showing.

I learned nothing.

By the time I got to Third and Folsom, I was cold and tired and my feet had started to hurt. But I wasn't ready to give it up yet; I kept thinking about Nello and the hopeless way he had shuffled out of my office. So I wandered down past Harrison toward where South Park used to be and went into a place called Packy's.

One of the men sitting at the bar was a study in various shades of gray—dirty iron-gray hair, washed-out gray eyes, red-veined gray skin, a soiled gray pinstripe suit that had not been new when Eisenhower was President. His name was Freddy the Dreamer and he was an old-timer on the Row, like Nello and Chaucer. I went up to him, told him why I was there and asked my questions again for the hundredth time.

And he said in the dreamy voice that had given him his nickname, "Sure, I seen Chaucer yesterday. Hell of a thing, what happened to him. Hell of a thing."

"What time, Freddy?"

"Around six. He just come off a bus up at the Greyhound depot."

"Which bus?"

He shrugged. "Who knows?"

"Think, Freddy. Was it a Muni bus? Or a Greyhound?"

"Daly City," Freddy said. "Yeah. He said he come from Daly City."

Daly City was a small community tacked onto San Francisco to the southwest. I said, "Did he tell you what he was doing there?"

"Nah." Freddy grinned reminiscently. "We had us a party," he said. "Scotch whisky, can you believe? Old Freddy with his very own jug of scotch whisky."

"Chaucer paid for it?"

"He was carrying a nice little roll. He bought that scotch and we went to my flop on Natoma."

"Where did he get the roll?"

"Chaucer was a kidder, you know? Him with his fancy education, a great kidder. I asked him where he picked it up, who did he mug, and he just laughed. 'Robin Hood,' he says. 'I got it from Robin Hood.'"

"Robin Hood?"

"That's what he said."

"Is that all he said about it?"

"Yeah, that's all."

"What time did he leave your flop last night?"

"Who knows?" Freddy said. "With a jug of real scotch whisky, who knows?"

"You know where he went when he left?"

"To see Robin Hood."

"Is that what he told you?"

"He was a kidder, you know? A great kidder."

"Yeah."

"Good old Chaucer," Freddy said dreamily. "Man, I can still taste that scotch whisky . . ."

I got out of there. Robin Hood, I thought as I

walked back toward Mission. It could have meant something, or nothing at all. The same way the sawdust Aldrich had mentioned could mean something or nothing at all. The only thing definite I had found out was that Chaucer had been in Daly City yesterday—but without some idea of *where* in Daly City, that information wasn't worth much.

I picked up my car and drove over to a restaurant on Van Ness and had something to eat; the food, through no fault of the management, was tasteless. I felt a little depressed, the way I used to feel when I was working the Row as a patrolman. There didn't seem to be much else I could do for Nello, no leads I could follow that might identify Chaucer's killer.

When I got back to my building on Taylor Street I found a single piece of mail in the lobby box. I carried it upstairs, turned on the valve on the steam radiator—it was cold in there, as usual—and then sat down and opened the letter. Another bill from a magazine readership club. In a weak moment some time back I had succumbed to the sales pitch of a doe-eyed college girl; but I had never received any of the magazines I'd subscribed to. Across the bottom of the bill was typed: *Your continued refusal to pay will leave us no alternative but to turn your account over to our legal department. This could seriously damage your credit rating. Remit the above amount today!*

I crumpled the bill and the envelope, said aloud, "What credit rating?" and threw them into the wastebasket. Then I sat there and smoked a cigarette and looked at the wall and listened to the ringing knock of the radiator as it warmed up.

Robin Hood, I thought.

Sawdust.

I stood after a time and took the pot off the two-burner and looked at what was left of my morning coffee. A thin sheen of oil floated on the surface, but I put it back on the hot plate anyway and turned the thing on. And sat down again and checked with my answering service to find out if there had been any calls. There hadn't. I got out one of the issues of *Black Mask* I keep in a desk drawer to pass idle time, but I couldn't concentrate on the Frederick Nebel story I tried to read. I put the pulp away and lit another cigarette.

Sawdust, I thought.

Robin Hood.

And Daly City . . .

Damn! I thought. Well, maybe the police could make those three things connect up. Before I left the office for the day—my watch said it was quarter of five—I would call Eberhardt and tell him what I'd found out from Freddy the Dreamer. After that, like it or not, I would be out of it.

The coffee began to boil. I poured some into my cup, carried it to the window behind my desk. The city looked cold and gray through the restless patterns of fog. I glanced down at Taylor Street; rush hour had started and there were a lot of cars jammed up down there. A large flatbed truck was blocking two lanes of traffic, trying to back into a narrow alley across the way. It was carrying a load of plywood sheeting, and the driver was having difficulty jockeying the truck into the alley mouth.

I watched him for a time, listening to the angry horn blasts from the blocked cars, still thinking about sawdust and Robin Hood and Daly City— and my subconscious opened up and disgorged the memory of a place in Daly City I'd visited several months ago, on a routine skip-trace. I spilled some of the coffee getting the cup down on the desk. From the bottom drawer I dragged out the San Francisco telephone directory, which included Daly City, and opened it to the yellow pages. Half a minute later, my finger came to rest on a boxed, single-column advertisement on one of the pages under *Lumber—Retail.* Freddy the Dreamer had been right, I thought then. Chaucer, the former teacher of English literature, had been a great kidder.

I caught up the telephone, dialed the Hall of Justice. Eberhardt was in, and he came on the wire right away.

"I think I might have a line on the man who killed Chaucer," I said. "I've got a hunch he works for a lumber outfit in Daly City."

"What lumber outfit?"

"A place called Sherwood Forest Products."

"It was the owner's son—Ted Sherwood," Eberhardt said. "The car, one of those El Camino pickups—a jazzed-up '68 model—was parked in the company lot when Branislaus went there this morning to check out your hunch. Registration told him it belonged to the Sherwood kid, and he went and question him. The kid got nervous, made a couple of slips, acted guilty enough so that Branislaus brought him in."

I nodded and drank a little of my beer. We were sitting in a small tavern on Boardman Place, near the Hall of Justice. It was after five o'clock the following day, and Eberhardt had just come off duty. He'd called me forty minutes ago; I had been waiting for him for about fifteen.

I asked, "Did he confess?"

"Not right away. The old man insisted he have his lawyer present before the kid did any more talking, so that took a while. But the lawyer's one of these smart young pricks; he advised Sherwood to tell it straight. The idea being full cooperation so he can cop manslaughter pleas on both homicide charges and get the kid off with a reduced sentence. He'll probably get away with it, too."

"*Did* Sherwood tell it straight?"

"He did. The night he ran Old Jenny down, he'd been out cruising with his girl friend and had just taken the girl home up on Potrero Hill. We figure he was probably stoned on pot or booze, or both, although he won't admit it. In any case, he swears the light was green at the intersection, the bag lady was crossing against it and he didn't see her until he hit her. Then he panicked and kept on going."

"The sawdust must have been jarred out of the pickup's bed," I said. "Am I right it got there because Sherwood made small deliveries of lumber from time to time?"

Eberhardt nodded. "So he told us."

"How did he get the dents ironed out?"

"Some friend of his works in a body shop, and the two of them did the job at night; that's why Hit-and-Run didn't get a report on the repairs. With the new paint job, and the fact that nothing happened in three weeks, he figured he was home free."

"And then Chaucer showed up."

"Yeah. He wanted five hundred dollars to keep what he'd seen quiet, the damned fool. Sherwood put him off with fifty, arranged to meet him down on the Embarcadero last night with the rest. He picked Chaucer up there and took him to that alley on Hubbell Street. Sherwood swears he didn't mean to kill him; all he was going to do, he said, was rough Chaucer up a little to get him to lay off. But he's a pretty big kid, and he waded in too heavy and lost his head. When he saw Chaucer was dead, he panicked the way he had after the hit-and-run and beat it out of there."

"Which explains why Chaucer still had the rest of the fifty dollars on him when he was found."

"Uh-huh." Eberhardt watched me finish the last of my beer. "Listen," he said then, "I called Dana before I left the Hall and told her to put on some steaks. You want to come for supper?"

"Rain check," I said. "I've got something to do."

"What's that?"

"Go hunt up Nello. I promised I'd let him know if anything turned up. Maybe when I tell him about Sherwood, it'll restore some of his faith in humanity. Or at least in the minions of the law."

"After fifteen years on the Row? Fat chance."

"Well, you never know."

Eberhardt lifted his glass toward me in a kind of mock salute "So long, social worker," he said.

"So long, cop."

I went out into the cold, damp night.

One of Those Cases

It was one of those cases you take on when you're on your uppers. You want to turn it down—it's an old story, a sordid one, a sad one—but you know you can't afford to. So you look into tear-filmed eyes, and you sigh, and you say yes. . . .

Her name was Judith Paige. She was in her late twenties, attractive in a quiet, shy sort of way. She had pale blond hair, china-blue eyes, and the kind of translucent white skin that seems brittle and makes you think of opaque and finely blown glass. Until the previous year, she had lived in a small town in Idaho and had come to San Francisco "to search for some meaning in life." Which probably meant that she had come looking for a husband.

And she'd found one, a salesman named Walter Paige. They had been married six weeks now, and it was something less than the idyllic union she had expected. It wasn't that Paige abused her in any way, or was a drinker or a gambler; it was just that, in the past month, he'd taken to leaving her alone in the evenings. He told her it was business—he worked for a real estate firm out near

the Cow Palace—and when she pressed him for
details he grew short-tempered. He was working
on a couple of large prospects, he said, that would
set them up for the future.

She figured he was working on another woman.

Like I said, an old, sordid, sad story. And one of
those cases.

She wanted me to follow him for a few days,
either to confirm or deny her suspicions. That was
all. You don't need to prove adultery, or much of
anything else, to obtain a divorce in the state of
California these days, so I would not be required
to testify in any civil proceedings. It was just that
she had to know, one way or the other—the tears
starting then—and if she were right, she wanted
to dissolve the marriage and go back to Idaho. She
had a little money saved and could pay my standard rates; and she was sure I was honest and
capable, which meant that she hoped I wouldn't
take advantage of her in any way.

I sat there behind my desk feeling old and tired
and cynical. It was a nice day outside, and I had
the window open a little; the breeze off the Bay
was cool and fresh, but the air I was pulling into
my lungs tasted sour somehow. I lit a cigarette.
And then took one of the contract forms out of
the bottom drawer and slid it over for her to
examine.

When she had, without much interest, I drew it
back and filled it out and had her sign it. Then I
said, "All right, Mrs. Paige. What time does your
husband come home from work?"

"Usually about six o'clock."

"Does he use public transportation or drive?"

"He drives."

"What kind of car?"

"A dark-blue VW."

"License number?"

"It has one of those personalized plates. WALLY P."

"Uh-huh. What time does he leave again when he goes out?"

"Right after supper," Mrs. Paige said. "Seven-thirty or so."

"He comes back at what time?"

"Around midnight."

"How often does this happen?"

"Four or five times a week, lately."

"Any particular nights?"

"No, not really."

"Saturdays and Sundays?"

"Saturdays, sometimes. Not Sundays, though. He . . . he always spends that day with me."

Never on Sunday, I thought sourly. I said, "Which real estate company does he work for?"

"I'm sorry," she said, "I don't know. Walter is very closemouthed about his job."

"He's never told you where he works?"

"Well, he did once, but I can't remember it. Is it important?"

"Probably not." I put down the pencil I had been using to take notes. "I think I have everything I need for now, Mrs. Paige. I'll be on the job tonight if your husband goes out."

"You won't let him know you're following him, will you? I mean, if I'm wrong and he's, well, just working, I wouldn't want him to know what I've done."

"I'll be as careful as I can."

"Thank you," she said, and dabbed at her eyes with her handkerchief and cleared her throat. "Will you call me as soon as you find out anything?"

"Right away."

"I'll give you a check. Will fifty dollars be all right?"

"Fine."

I looked away while she made out the check, out through the window. Sunlight and bright blue sky softened the look of the ugly, crumbling buildings in the Tenderloin. Even the panhandlers and dope pushers seemed to be enjoying the weather; they were out in droves this afternoon.

A nice day for a lot of people, all right. But not for Judith Paige and not for me.

At seven o'clock I was sitting behind the wheel of my car, parked four buildings down and on the opposite side of the street from the stucco-fronted apartment house the Paiges lived in. The dark-blue VW with the WALLY P license plate was thirty feet away, facing in the same direction.

This was a fairly well-to-do neighborhood in the Parkside district; kids were out playing, husbands and wives were still arriving home from work. If you're staked out in an area like that, you run a risk by sitting around in a parked car for any length of time. People get suspicious, and the next thing you know, you've got a couple of patrol cops pulling up and asking questions. But if you don't stay more than an hour, and if you keep glancing at your watch and show signs of increasing annoyance; you can get away with it; the residents tend to think you're waiting for somebody and leave you alone. I expected to be here less than an hour, so I wasn't worried.

I went through the watch-checking-and-annoyance routine, smoked a couple of cigarettes and glanced through a 1949 issue of *FBI Detective* that I'd brought along to help pass the time. And at twenty of eight, Paige came out and walked straight to the VW. The sun had gone down by then, but there was still enough reddish twilight to let me see that he was a tall, slender guy dressed in a blue suit, with one of those toothbrush mustaches that looked from a distance like a caterpillar humped on his upper lip.

I started my car just as he swung out, and I let him have a half-block lead before I went after him. He drove without hurry, observing the speed limits. Whenever possible, I put another car between us—and on the four-lane streets like Ocean Avenue, I used the lane opposite to the one he was in. You pick up ways and means like that over the years, but if you're following a pro, or somebody alert to the possibility of a tail, there's not much you can do; the subject will spot you nine times out of ten.

Paige was not expecting a tail, though, and I had no trouble staying with him. We picked up Highway 280 near the City College, followed it to where it connects with the Bayshore Freeway southbound. Fifteen minutes later, Paige exited in South San Francisco and went up Grand Avenue and finally turned into the parking lot of a big shopping center. He parked near a large cut-rate liquor store. I put my car into a slot in the next row, watched him get out and enter the liquor store. Five minutes later, he came back out with a bottle of some kind in a small paper sack and got back into his car. But he didn't go anywhere—he just sat there.

I figured it this way: Paige was playing around, all right, and the woman he was playing with was probably married as well, which necessitated a neutral meeting ground. He was waiting for her now, and when she arrived they would go to a motel or maybe to a little love nest they had set up somewhere—and that would be it as far as I was concerned. I'd get the license number of the woman's car when she showed, then follow her and Paige to wherever it was they had their assignations. Then I would call Mrs. Paige and listen to her cry; they always cry when you tell them, even though they expect the worst. And then I would go home and try to sleep.

So we sat there in the lot, Paige and I, waiting. It got to be nine o'clock; most of the stores were closing for the night, and there were not nearly as many cars as there had been earlier. I thought that if the lot became too empty, I would have to move out to the street somewhere; I did not want Paige noticing me, questioning the presence of another guy waiting alone as he was doing.

At nine-thirty, the woman still hadn't shown

up. Everything was closed in the center except the liquor store and a bowling alley over at the far end. I had about decided it was time for me to move when Paige abruptly got out of the VW and headed toward the bowling alley.

He's going to call her, I thought. He wants to know why she stood him up tonight.

I let him get inside the building before I followed. League bowlers were occupying all twenty lanes in there; after the relative silence of the past hour, the noise was deafening. I went down by the coffee shop, where there was a phone booth, but I didn't see Paige anywhere. I came back and went into the bar. He was there, in another booth, talking animatedly on the phone.

I found a place to sit at the bar where I could see the booth in the back-bar mirror and ordered a beer. It was close to ten minutes before Paige finished his conversation. He stopped at the bar long enough to toss off a shot of bourbon neat; he did not even glance in my direction. I gave him two minutes and then moved after him.

He was just pulling out of the lot when I reached my car. I got going in plenty of time to pick him up, but it was pointless, really: he led me straight back to San Francisco and the Parkside district. From down the block, with my headlights dark, I watched him park the VW and then enter his apartment building. He didn't come out again in the next ten minutes.

I said to hell with it and went home to bed.

*   *   *

In the morning, from my office, I called Judith Paige and made my report. She tried to muffle her tears, but I could hear the sob in her voice; it grated at my nerves like fingernails across a blackboard.

"Then . . . then it's true, isn't it?" she said. "Walter has another woman."

"I'll be blunt with you, Mrs. Paige," I said, even though I did not feel blunt at all. "The chances of it are pretty good. He wasn't working last night, and he was obviously waiting for someone in that parking lot."

"But there's still a chance that he was there for some other reason, isn't there?"

"Yes, there's a chance."

"I have to be sure," she said. "You understand, don't you?"

"I understand."

"You'll be there tonight?"

"Yes, Mrs. Paige," I said. "I'll be there."

Paige did not leave that night until after eight. I was beginning to think that he wasn't going at all, and I was growing nervous about sitting there much longer, when he finally appeared. He got into the VW and led me along the same route he had last night, past the City College and onto 280. I decided he was heading for the same shopping center in South San Francisco; I dropped back a little, giving him plenty of room. And that was just where he went.

He parked in about the same place. I took a slot farther back this time and a little more to one side, in the event we were in for another long wait past the closing time of the center's shops.

It developed just that way. Nine-thirty came, and then ten, and the parking area was just about empty. But it was dark where I was, and I had slumped low in the seat with the window down and my eyes on a level with the sill. I was pretty sure Paige couldn't see me from where he was.

So we waited, and I was about ready to call it another bust. Damn it, I thought, why doesn't she come? This kind of job played on my nerves anyway; the waiting only made it worse. If she was—

There was movement at the periphery of my vision. When I turned my head, I saw a lone figure hurrying across the darkened lot from the direction of the bowling alley. It moved in a straight line toward Paige's car, glancing left and right, its gaze flicking over my car but not lingering. And when it got to the VW and opened the door and slipped inside, the flash of the dome light let me see a leather jacket, jeans—crew cut hair.

Paige's visitor was a man, not a woman.

What the hell? I thought. Paige had not struck me as the homosexual type, but then you never knew these days who might have leanings in that direction; I could not figure any other immediate explanation for this kind of meeting. I sat there a little nonplussed, thinking about Mrs. Paige, waiting for them to leave.

Only they didn't leave, not yet. The driver's door opened and Paige stepped out; he was wearing a hat now, a long overcoat that he must have put on while he'd been sitting in the darkness.

Dimly, I could see the other guy slide over under the wheel. Paige walked to the liquor store, went inside. There was no other activity at this end of the lot—and no one else had entered the liquor store in the past five minutes.

I began to get it then, but by the time I put it all together it was too late for me to do anything about it. The new guy started the VW and took it slowly toward the lot's entrance a few doors down from the liquor store, keeping it clear of the bright outspill from the store's fluorescent lighting. I couldn't see what was happening inside the store, because of the angle.

Three minutes after he'd gone inside, Paige came running out with one hand jammed up under his coat and the other gripping a small sack of some kind. He ran down to where the other guy had the VW rolling forward, jerked open the door and jumped in. The car pitched ahead, burning a little rubber, and when it turned east out of the lot its headlights came on for the first time. There was no movement over at the liquor store, no one in the lot to see or wonder what had happened except me.

I'd had the engine of my car going before Paige appeared, but I stayed where I was until the VW was a half-block away. Then I went after it, running dark, hanging back as far as I could without losing sight of its taillights.

The other car was moving fast but not recklessly; they must have figured they'd pull it off clean, and they didn't want to call attention to themselves. The streets were dark here, except for

intermittent house lights and the yellow puddles
cast by street lamps. Clouds had begun to pile up,
blotting out the moon: that made it all the darker
and easier for me to follow without being seen. I
was able to stay within a block of them.

They were heading for Hillside Boulevard; I
could tell that before we'd gone a dozen blocks.
That road runs along the western foot of the San
Bruno Mountains, connecting to the southeast
with the Bayshore Freeway and to the northeast
with Daly City. It was a toss-up as to which way
they would turn when they got there.

I wasn't at all sure now that I was doing the
right thing. Maybe I should have gone into the
liquor store to check on the clerk, make sure he
was all right; then I could have telephoned the
local police and given them Paige's name and that
WALLY P license plate of his. But my instinctive
reaction had been to give chase, to be able to
pinpoint them when I finally did make the call.
Wise or not, I had made my choice and I would
have to stand by it.

When the VW neared Hillside Boulevard, I
dropped back to see how it would go. They turned
left. Daly City, then, and on into San Francisco
that way. Or maybe they had another destination
along the line.

I could still see the red glow of their taillights
when I got to the intersection, but they were
diminishing rapidly: the driver had opened it up
now. It would have been dangerous for me to try
driving that dark road without lights; I switched
on my headlamps before I made the turn. And

then bore down on the accelerator to match their speed.

As I drove, I thought about how wrong Mrs. Paige and I had been about her husband. He didn't have another woman, or if he did she had nothing to do with these nocturnal outings of his. They were all explainable in the same way. There had been a string of liquor store holdups the past month, in a different Bay area city each time— two men, one to pull the job and the other to drive the car. I hadn't thought of Paige in connection with the holdups; there was no reason I should have. I had been hired to investigate infidelity, not armed robbery.

So Paige and this other guy were the heisters; and that put an altogether different explanation on last night's events. Paige hadn't been waiting at the shopping center for anyone; he'd been casing the liquor store—the same thing he had probably done the past few nights, and on some or all of the other jobs they'd pulled. He would have been checking on how much traffic went in and out of the lot around this time of night, how many clerks and customers there were in the store, things like that. When he'd gone to the bowling alley, it had been to call his partner and make a report. It had looked good to them, and they were ready, and so they'd set it up for tonight.

The only things that weren't clear were why the other guy had showed up at the parking lot on foot instead of meeting Paige and driving there with him, and why they were using Paige's VW, with that easy-to-remember WALLY P license plate, as the getaway car. But I could find out the answers to those questions later on. They didn't matter much at this point.

What mattered was staying with those two, seeing to it they were arrested and put away. What mattered was how Judith Paige would feel when she found out her husband was something much worse than unfaithful . . .

The VW was in Colma now, a small community that had the dubious distinction of being the primary burial grounds for the San Francisco area. There were a dozen different cemeteries along here, and one golf course—Cypress Hills—sitting there incongruously in the middle of it all. This stretch of Hillside Boulevard was very dark; no other cars moved on it in either direction.

Another tenth of a mile clicked off on my odometer. And then the VW's brake lights came on ahead, and the car made a sharp right-hand turn into Cynthia Street—a narrow lane that marked the boundary between the golf course on the right and Mount Olivert Cemetery on the left. At its upper end, there were a couple of short dead-end streets and the looming black shapes of the San Bruno Mountains. Maybe the one guy lived there, I thought, and they were going to his place. Or maybe they were planning to stop for a few minutes and split the take from the liquor store.

I slowed, waiting until the VW passed behind a screen of eucalyptus lining the lane, then switched off my lights and swung up after them. The other car was better than a hundred yards ahead by then. We traveled a fifth of a mile with that much distance between us—and suddenly the taillights winked out, their headlights did the same and heavy darkness folded in on the road.

I punched the brake pedal, thinking they'd pull off onto the shoulder, getting ready to do the same thing. Only then the VW's backup lights flared, and when I heard the sharp whine of its engine in reverse I realized what a damned fool I'd been. They knew I was there, they had known it all along; somehow they'd spotted me tailing them. So they'd maneuvered me up here, where it was isolated, with the idea of ramming me, forcing me off the road.

I said a short, vicious word and managed to do three things at once: jammed the gearshift lever into reverse with my right hand, found the headlight switch and flicked it on with my left hand, and brought my left foot down on the high-beam button on the floor. The car leaped backward, yawing a little. The VW was almost on top of me by then, a hurtling black-and-red shape; its rear end missed my front bumper by a foot or less, then veered off toward the fence bordering the cemetery on the left. The guy behind the wheel had to fight it around, straighten out again, and that gave me a couple of extra seconds.

Hunched around on the seat now, I leaned over the back to look through the rear window and pushed the accelerator all the way down. The high white glare of my headlights, the crimson wash from my backup lights, bleached the darkness enough so that I could see the road behind me. It was pretty straight, and I had a white-fisted grip on the wheel. I kept my eyes on the road, not looking to see where the VW was; the metallic taste of fear was sharp in my mouth. I wasn't armed—I had not carried a gun since I'd been on the cops years ago—and these characters had at least one and probably two weapons. I had nowhere to go if I lost control of the car or they managed to get me off the road.

The intersection with Hillside Boulevard came up quickly, less than a hundred yards away now. Sweat half-blinded me, but when I dropped below the screen of trees I could see there were headlights approaching from the direction of South San Francisco—two sets of them. Relief dulled the edge of my fear. The nearest set of lights was maybe five hundred yards off: enough time, just enough time.

There was a sudden, glancing impact: the VW had rammed me, but not hard enough to do the job for them. I managed to keep the rear end straight as the intersection rushed up, held off using the brakes as long as I could; then I touched them lightly and laid my other hand on the horn ring and swung the wheel hard to the right. The tires screamed as I slid sideways, rocking, out onto Hillside Boulevard.

Another horn blared; there was more shrieking of rubber. The first of the oncoming cars swerved to the left, nosing off the road, to avoid a collision with me; the second braked hard and skidded around to the side of the first one—and in the next second a red light began revolving on its roof, sweeping the darkness with an eerie pulsing glow. It was a county police cruiser, a traffic unit that patrols Hillside for speeders at night.

I turned my head to see where the VW was, saw it right in front of me. They had swung out in the same direction I had, but the red light on the cruiser had made them quit worrying about me. The little car rocked as the transmission was thrown into a forward gear; rubber howled again. They had been half turned around on the road, as I had been, and they tried to come out of it too fast, with too much power. The rear end fishtailed and they started to slide one way, then the other. And then the VW spun around twice in the middle of the road, like a toy car in the hands of a playful kid; tilted and went over, rolling; finally settled on its top in the culvert between the road and the cemetery fence.

The county patrol car slid around mine and cut diagonally in front, blocking me off. One of the two cops who came out of it ran to where the VW lay in the culvert like a huge beetle on its back, wheels spinning lazily in the light-spattered darkness; the other cop came over to me with his service revolver drawn. He looked in through the open window. "What the hell's going on here?" he demanded.

I told him—as much as he needed to know right away. It took him a couple of minutes to believe me, but when I showed him the photostat of my investigator's license and told him what he would find in the wreckage, he was convinced. He left me to use his car radio, because the other cop was still at the wrecked VW and yelling for an ambulance and a tow truck; Paige and his partner were wedged inside, and he couldn't tell if they were dead or alive.

I was pretty shaky for a while, but by the time the ambulance and the tow truck arrived I was all right. A couple of guys went to work on the WV with blowtorches. When they got Paige and the other one out, they were still alive but cut up and unconscious; Paige had a broken leg, too. The ambulance took them away to the nearest emergency hospital.

The county officers escorted me to the police station in South San Francisco, where I made a formal statement. None of the cops was too pleased that I had given chase after the robbery, instead of notifying the law like a good citizen was supposed to do, but they didn't make an issue of it. They let me go on home after a couple of hours.

I had bad dreams that night. But they could not have been any worse than the dreams Judith Paige would be having. . . .

In the morning I learned, through my friend Eberhardt at the Hall of Justice, that Paige was an ex-con—four years at San Quentin for armed robbery—who'd figured that his job as a real estate salesman wasn't paying off and wasn't likely to. Two months ago, he'd reestablished contact with another armed robber he'd met in prison, and they had worked out the liquor store heists. The other guy's name was Stryker.

The rest was about as I'd figured it. Stryker, alert and strung out after the holdup, had spotted me coming out of the lot after them. They'd figured me for a heroic-citizen type, and at first they'd thought of trying to outrun me; but the VW didn't have all that much power, they had no idea how good a driver I was and they didn't want to risk alerting a cop by exceeding the speed limits. So they'd hit on Cynthia Street—and although they refused to admit it to the police, they would have killed me if they'd succeeded in forcing me off the road.

As for why Stryker had been on foot that night—and why they'd used Paige's VW, with its distinctive WALLY P license plate, instead of Stryker's car—the reason was so simple and ironic that it made me laugh sardonically when I heard it. Stryker lived down the Peninsula, near South San Francisco, and he was married, and his wife had insisted on using their car to attend an audition: she was a singer, and there was a job she badly wanted in the city. So he'd given in, notified Paige and then had her drop him off at the shopping center on her way into San Francisco.

Crooks, I thought. Christ!

There was irony, too, in the fact that Paige had apparently been faithful to Judith all along. He had married her because he loved her, or had some kind of feeling for her. If she hadn't suspected him of playing around, and come to me, he and Stryker might have carried on their string of liquor store heists for quite a while before they screwed up and got themselves caught.

The police had been the ones to break the news to Judith Paige last night; better them than me. But I knew I had to see her again anyway: it was one of those things you have to do. So I drove out to the Parkside district late that afternoon and spent twenty minutes with her—twenty long minutes that were not easy for either of us.

She told me she was going to file for divorce and then go home to Idaho, which struck me as the wisest decision she could have made. She would meet another guy there someday, and she'd get remarried, and maybe then she would be happy. I hoped so.

I would never see her again in any case, but the future would still bring another Judith Paige. There is always another Judith Paige for somebody in my business. One of these days she would walk into my office, and I would hear the old story again—the old, sad, sordid story.

Only that next time it would probably be true.

Sin Island

When the Iberian Airlines jet came in sight of the Balearic island of Majorca, ninety miles off the southern coast of Spain, I took my nose out of the pulp I'd been trying bleary-eyed to read and put it over next to the window glass. Far below, the island sat basking in the cobalt blue of the Mediterranean like a huge amulet reflecting the early-morning October sun. I could see a jagged, pine-covered mountain range running along the western peninsula; deep green valleys and terraced hills and sheer cliffs falling away to small inlets and strips of white beach; an almost symmetrical patchwork of green and brown fields running through the interior.

I yawned and stretched and rubbed at my gritty eyes. It had been a long trip, close to twenty-four hours all told—San Francisco to London, London to Madrid, Madrid to Majorca's capital city of Palma—and I had never been able to sleep much on airplanes. But now that it was almost at an end, I began to perk up a little. It wasn't every day

66

that I got to go someplace halfway around the world.

The buildings of Palma came into view as we banked low over the water and began our landing approach: old-fashioned, dun-colored architecture, both Moorish and Spanish, interlaced with modern, steel-and-glass office and apartment buildings and dozens of high-rise luxury hotels ringing the wide sweep of the harbor. Pretty soon the dusty tan of the Son San Juan Airport appeared ahead of us. I watched the runway rush up to meet us, felt the jar as the wheels touched down.

Well, I thought, here you are, guy. Sin Island, the playland of Europe, home of the Jet Set and the Idle Rich. Wine, women and a year-round mean temperature of sixty-five degrees. Are the stories they tell true? Is it really all that easy to get laid here?

As we rolled to a stop near the terminal, I wondered if my bank account was sturdy enough to stand three or four days at one of those luxury hotels I'd seen from the air. If everything went well in Palma Nova, the job that had brought me here would be finished in a few hours and I would be on my own; and the return-trip ticket in my coat pocket was paid for and good anytime. A couple of days of lying in the sun, of finding out whether or not a middle-aged, bearish guy with a beer belly could attract some female companionship, was not too much of a vacation to give myself. After all, the chances were I'd never have another opportunity like this one.

I was still a little disbelieving of my good fortune. Thirty-six hours ago I had been sitting in my office in San Francisco, staring out the window at a threatening sky and wondering where the Indian summer we'd been promised was, when an attorney named Bathsgate called; he wanted to know if I had a valid passport, and if so, would I be available for a job which entailed an immediate trip to Europe. I told him I had a passport—I had applied for it a few years ago for an abortive trip to Central America and used it once to go to West Germany on a job—and said I was available, all right, depending on what it was I was supposed to do in Europe. He gave me an address up on Russian Hill and told me I would be expected within the hour.

The address turned out to be one of those imposing, turn-of-the-century mansions clinging majestically to the fog-shrouded hill; in clear weather it would command an impressive view of the Bay. A butler who must have been seventy and who had skin like fine old parchment let me in, conducted me up a marble staircase and into a darkened bedroom.

The man lying propped up in the bed was about the same age as the butler, with haggard gray features and sunken cheeks and eyes that had known a lot of pain. A wheelchair, faintly grim in its emptiness, sat beside the bed. The butler announced me, and when he was gone the man in the bed said, "I am Millard Frost."

It surprised me a little. Millard Frost was a multimillionaire and a dominant figure in West Coast shipping for more than forty years, founder of Frost Lines, Inc. He had once been strong, forceful, outspoken, but this sick old man was just a shadow of that dynamic individual. As I took the chair he indicated near the foot of his bed, I remembered that he had been stricken with some kind of spinal disease about two years before, leaving him bedridden.

He had, he said, what he hoped to be a simple reason for wanting the services of a private detective; you could hear in his voice the echoes of the strength and force of will he'd once had. I sat with my hat on my knees and listened attentively. Frost went on to say that I had been chosen by Bathsgate, his attorney, on the basis of my record of integrity and discretion, and because I was fully bonded. Men who operated major corporations, who were in the public eye, could ill afford the wrong kind of publicity and would not tolerate dishonesty. Did I understand?

I said I did.

From the night table at his elbow, he took a small sheet of flimsy paper that he identified as an overseas cable. He had received it from his son, Dale, an hour before I was summoned. He handed it to me with thin, gnarled fingers and told me to read it.

It said:

DAD NEED TEN THOUSAND DOLLARS CASH URGENT. NO TIME TO WAIT FOR BANK TRANSFER CAN SOMEBODY BRING SOONEST PLANE. WILL EXPLAIN LATER. DALE.

Frost began talking again as soon as I lifted my eyes from the cable. He explained that Dale was twenty-two and had graduated that June from one of the Ivy League colleges back East; but before accepting an executive position with Frost Lines, Inc., he had wanted to spend a year traveling around Europe—a sort of youthful last fling before settling down to the sobriety of the business world.

Dale had entered Spain toward the end of July, after a period in France and England. Majorca was an attractive lure, and he'd fallen in love with the island; he had written to his father that he would be staying on there for an indefinite period, that he had rented a villa in Palma Nova, one of the sun-and-fun areas on the southern coast. Since then he had corresponded faithfully, once a week, if only a line or two; the last letter had arrived three days ago. It had given no indication that the youth was in any financial difficulties. His regular monthly allotment, which I assumed to be substantial enough although Frost did not mention the sum, had seemed to be taking care of his needs more than adequately.

One part of my job was to deliver the ten thousand dollars Dale had asked for; even without explanation, the fact that his only son needed the money was enough for Millard Frost. But Frost did want to know what was behind the sudden request, and that was the second part of my job: to find out, directly or indirectly, and to let him know immediately by telephone. For these two things, Frost would buy my round-trip plane tickets, incur any necessary expenses and pay me five hundred dollars besides.

I took the job without even having to think about it.

Frost had already authorized one of his banks to have the ten thousand delivered to him, and a messenger showed up with it a few minutes later. The old man counted the money, returned it to the chain-lock briefcase it had come in and handed it over to me; I was not to let it out of my sight until it was delivered. Then he got on the phone and ordered somebody to make the ticket bookings with the airlines, to send a wire to Dale letting him know someone was coming. And then he gave me the address of Dale's villa and two hundred dollars in cash for expenses.

He did not say anything else to me, or offer to shake my hand. I left him staring out the bedroom window at the overcast sky, hiding his feelings behind his mask of suffering. . . .

I'd had to clear Spanish Customs in Madrid when I came off the London flight, and I'd been a little worried about it at the time; if they opened the briefcase and saw the ten thousand dollars, there were liable to be questions and delays, even though I had an explanatory letter prepared by Millard Frost for just that reason. But all the Customs officers had checked had been my passport. Here on Majorca, nobody bothered to do even that much, since the Iberia flight was from Madrid and Majorca was a Spanish possession.

I went straight from the plane to the baggage-claim area and picked up the one suitcase I'd had time to pack. At an exchange booth, I traded a fifty-dollar bill for close to 3,500 pesetas. Then I walked out to where a line of taxis waited in front of the terminal. I poked my head through the open passenger window of the first one in line and asked the driver if he spoke English. He said, "A little bit, *señor*," and I said, "Good enough," and got into the back seat and told him where I wanted to go.

It was pretty hot for October; we rode with the windows rolled down—automobile air conditioning was probably a luxury few people could afford over here—and I took in the sights like any other tourist. Palma Nova was some twenty-five kilometers from the airport, on the western end of the Bahia de Palma. Traffic was heavy, but the Spaniards seemed to drive with a certain amount of disregard for life and limb, and my driver was no exception. We made it out there in about twenty minutes.

It was an attractive if touristy village: streets and galleries lined with expensive souvenir and curio shops, a couple of discos, a profusion of sidewalk bars and cafés, and a dozen or so hotels similar to the ones in Palma. On the left was the beach, long and narrow and jammed with near-naked humanity ranging in skin tones from pure white to an almost gold-black.

Near the cutout circle that served as the village center, we turned off to the right and climbed up into low brown hills overlooking the sea. The driver made a couple more turns, then swung onto a short, graveled dead-end street. At its end, a small tile-roofed villa, its facade covered with purple bougainvillea, sat partially hidden behind a high stone wall. There was a gate in the wall off to one side, and a silver MG roadster sitting on the drive inside, pointed toward the street; Millard Frost had told me Dale had bought the MG in England and brought it to Spain on the Southampton-Bilbao car ferry.

I paid the taxi driver a couple of hundred pesetas, added another fifty for a tip and went in through the gate. On the porch, I rang the bell. The door opened right away, and I was looking at a tall, thin youth wearing a mod-design shirt and a pair of flared slacks with a wide and ornate leather belt. His black hair was long and a little unkempt. Eyes like a pair of Spanish olives flicked over me, over the briefcase in my left hand.

I said, "Dale Frost?"

"Yes. You're from my father?"

"That's right." I introduced myself, set down my suitcase and gave him my hand. He took it, released it almost immediately and stepped back a little.

"Did you bring the money?"

"I brought it. Do you mind if I come in?"

"Why?"

"I'd like to talk to you for a minute."

"I've got things to do," he said. "I don't have time to talk."

"Come on, Dale, I won't take up much of your time. And I'll need you to sign a release for the money, to prove that I delivered it."

He hesitated. Then he said, "All right, come in, then," without any enthusiasm for the idea.

Inside, it was dark and a little cooler. The furnishings were sparse; a long refectory table took up most of one-half of the room lengthwise. Through an archway I could see a terrace, and beyond it in the distance the sparkling blue of the Mediterranean.

I said, "You wouldn't happen to have a beer, would you? I could sure use one."

"Sorry, no."

"Well, I'll take anything you've got that's tall and cold."

"I don't have a thing, I'm sorry." He wiped the palms of his hands on his slacks. "Look, mister, I don't mean to be rude or anything, but I really have got things to do. Can we get this over with? You can get a beer or something in one of the cafés down on the strip."

I studied him for several seconds without speaking, watching his eyes; he kept avoiding my gaze. He's not only nervous, I thought, he's scared. "Your father's worried about you, Dale," I said. "He thinks you might be in some kind of trouble."

"I'm not in any trouble."

"Why do you need ten thousand dollars so badly?"

"That's none of your business."

"No," I said, "but it is your father's business."

"I'll discuss it with *him* when the time comes."

"I think he'd like you to discuss it with me."

"Is that what he said?"

"He wants to be sure everything is all right."

"I told you, everything is fine."

"Then you shouldn't mind telling me why you need so much cash."

"I don't have to tell you anything," he said angrily. "Why don't you just give me my money and leave me alone?"

"My instructions from your father," I said, stretching the truth a little, "were to find out why you need it first."

"I don't believe you. I know my father better than that." He took a step toward me. "Give me my money."

"Look, son—"

He took another step and punched me quick and hard just under the left eye. With his other hand, he plucked at the briefcase and pulled it out of my fingers as I staggered backward. My calves hit the low, hammered-copper top of a coffee table, and I lost my balance and went over it and down. The back of my head cracked into the linoleum flooring; pain erupted behind my eyes, blurred my vision. I rolled over and pushed up onto my hands and knees, shaking my head, hearing the front door slam.

I got unsteadily to my feet, put a hand up to where he'd hit me; the fingers came away bloody. By the time I got to the front door and threw it open, the silver roadster was just shooting out of the drive with its tires making banshee noises on the pavement. It skidded to the right and was gone behind the high front wall.

I stood there for some time, holding onto the door, until I could no longer hear the MG's engine.

Then I went back inside and hunted up the bathroom and inspected my cheek in the mirror. There was a gash in it a half-inch long, trickling blood. I found some antiseptic and a gauze bandage in the medicine cabinet and fixed the cut up so that the bleeding stopped. The place where my head had struck the floor was sore to the touch, and I had a hell of a headache, but there was nothing I could do about that. There weren't any aspirins in the cabinet or anywhere else on the premises.

The villa had five rooms—two bedrooms, the front room, the bathroom and a kitchen. From an old rolltop desk in the front room, I dredged up a monthly statement from a Palma Nova café called Señor Pepe's; it was for a substantial sum, and I gathered from the itemization that Dale spent a good deal of his time there. I made a mental note of the address.

One of the bedrooms contained nothing at all. In the other one, on the nightstand beside the big double bed, was a small color photograph in a cardboard frame. It was of a girl about twenty, very blond, with bronzed skin and bright blue eyes; I thought she was probably Scandinavian. Across the lower left-hand corner, written in a neat feminine hand, were the words: *For my Dale from his Brita*. I slipped the photo out of its frame and put it into the pocket of my slacks.

Back in the front room, I stood looking around one last time without seeing anything I had overlooked. My head throbbed dully. Well, all right. I didn't have much to go on, but I had started with less before. I picked up my bag, moved out into the thick heat that was Majorca in the early afternoon and went to find out what kind of trouble Dale Frost was in.

Señor Pepe's had a rust-colored tile roof, whitewashed stucco walls and a lot of vine-draped arches inside and out. I threaded my way through a cluster of bamboo tables on the promenade in front, all of which were occupied by noisy tourists drinking gin-and-tonics and cuba libres, and went inside.

Behind an L-shaped bar, a short, sandy-haired guy in his late twenties was filling a cooler with bottles of San Miguel beer. He had a clipped, sandy goatee and an air. of sober industriousness. I stepped up to the bar and put my bag down and sat on one of the stools. When the sandy guy looked up at me, I said, "I'll take one of those cold, if you've got it."

"I do," he said. He was British, or maybe Scottish; I couldn't tell which. He pulled another of the bottles from beneath the ice and popped the cap and poured a glass for me. I drank a third of it, took a breath and drank another third. It had been a long walk from the villa, and my throat was parched and my head felt as if it were full of drums. ·

I asked the sandy guy, "Are you on here regularly?"

"Aye. I'm the owner."

"Then you probably know a young fellow

named Dale Frost. An American, rents a villa up on Calle Lluch."

"Sure, I know Dale. He used to come in most every night. One of my best customers."

"Used to come in?"

"Well, I haven't seen much of him lately."

"Why is that?"

He shrugged. "I couldn't tell you. They come and they go."

"How long ago did Dale stop being a regular?"

"About three weeks ago." He gave me a quizzical look. "Why would you be asking?"

"I represent his father," I said. "There's been a small misunderstanding—or maybe I should say a lack of communication."

"Oh, I see."

He didn't see at all, but I was not going to enlighten him. I said, "Do you have any idea where Dale has been keeping himself these past few weeks?"

"Sorry, no, I don't."

"Do you know any of his friends?"

"Dale has a lot of friends, mister," the sandy guy said. "Popular chap, good-looking, plenty of money."

"Anyone in particular?"

"Male or female?"

"Anyone who might be close to him."

He smiled and winked at me. "Dale has been close to several ladies, if you know what I mean."

I took the snapshot of the young, tanned blond girl out of my pocket and let him see it. "Is she one of them?"

"Aye," he said. "That's Brita. Quite a bird, that one. Dale brought her in here a couple of times."

"Where can I find her?"

"She works in a Swedish bar in Magalluf. The Little John."

"Where would Magalluf be?"

"Just up the road. Half a kilometer."

"How do I find the Little John?"

"It's on the main street. You can't miss it."

I paid him for my beer, got him to give me a few other names of people Dale knew and went out into the heat again. I had noticed a line of taxis in the village center; I walked back there and got into the nearest one and had the driver take me to Magalluf, which looked to be an extension of Palma Nova. He let me off before a small restaurant-bar set into a line of shops on an esplanade well back from the street.

A young, dark-haired guy with a thick mustache that formed three sides of a frame for thin lips was behind the bar inside. I asked him if Brita was there.

"Yes, she's here," he said in Swedish-accented English.

"Could I talk to her?"

He shrugged and went away through a door. I walked over to a row of booths against the right-hand wall, sat down in one of them. I lit a cigarette and rubbed sweat from my forehead with a napkin and wished it wasn't so damned hot. I was not used to this kind of heat in October.

After a couple of minutes the door behind the bar opened and the dark-haired guy came out and held it for the girl just behind him. She was taller than I expected from the photograph, a little fuller in the hips; she wore a miniskirt and a frilly blouse and gold-loop Gypsy earrings. I tried not to stare at her legs as she came from behind the bar and slipped into the booth opposite, but they were very good legs. And a man never stops looking.

"I am Brita," she said. She brushed a heat-dampened wisp of blond hair away from her eyes. "Lars said you wish to talk to me?"

"Yes. About Dale Frost."

Her smile turned sad. "Dale?"

"Do you mind?"

"No, I guess I don't."

I told her my name and where I was from and that I represented Dale's father. Then I said, "I understand you know Dale pretty well, Brita."

"Well," she said, "I was going to bed with him."

It was such a matter-of-fact statement that it made me think about generation gaps and wonder how I would feel about today's sexual freedom if I had ever gotten married and raised a daughter. I lit another cigarette to have something to do with my hands.

"You're not . . . seeing Dale anymore?" I asked her.

"No."

"How long has it been since you've talked to him?"

"About two weeks, I think."

"Why did the two of you break up?"

"It was because of this boy he became friends with."

"What boy is that?"

"An American boy like Dale. Peter York."

Peter York was one of the names the sandy guy at Señor Pepe's had given me. "You don't like this York, Brita?"

"No. Not his girl friend either, always talking silly. They make a fine couple, I think, with their green eyes like jungle cats. I hated to look at them; they made me cold."

"Did you and Dale have an argument about York?"

She nodded emphatically. "I told him if he kept Peter as a friend, I didn't want him to be my friend anymore. I told him he was going to get in a lot of trouble because of Peter, but he wouldn't listen. He just got mad and went away."

"What kind of trouble did you mean?"

She studied me for a couple of seconds. "I guess I better tell you," she said. "I should have told somebody before this, but I didn't know who. I don't want Dale to be hurt; he's a nice boy, except for that Peter."

"What about Peter?"

"I think he takes drugs," Brita said.

"You think so—but you're not sure?"

"No. I heard some things."

"What sort of things?"

"About drug parties."

"Do you know what kind of drugs?"

"Marijuana. And maybe that LSD."

"Did Dale ever use them?"

"Not with me. Not until he met Peter, maybe."

"You're afraid Peter talked him into it?"

"Yes. He wouldn't listen to me, but he listened to Peter, I think."

Yeah, I thought. And maybe that was why Dale had needed that ten thousand dollars so urgently. You can buy a hell of a lot of pot or speed or LSD with that kind of money—and the people who sell it are always in a hurry for their payoff.

I asked Brita, "Where does Peter live?"

"In a chalet near Cala Ratjada."

"Where's that?"

"On the other side of the island."

"How do I get there?"

She told me. "Dale is a nice boy," she said then. "Really, he is. I hope you can make him understand about Peter, about those drugs."

"So do I," I said.

The harbor at Cala Ratjada was studded with better than a hundred small fishing smacks and trollers, bobbing at anchor on the still blue water. They supplied most of the island's fresh seafood—prawns, squid, *raya*, denton, a dozen other varieties. That information had been provided, along with a small Spanish Seat sedan and a topographical map of Majorca, by an English-speaking guy in the rental agency I'd located in Palma Nova.

The cross-island drive had taken an hour and a half; the road was pretty good, but only two lanes, and there had been a lot of traffic. I circled through the fishing village-cum-resort, followed the road along the rim of rocky promontories on the northern side of the harbor. It was late afternoon now, and the setting sun was laying a path

of golden fire across the open sea as I swung out
onto the Pta. des Farayos.

There wasn't much out there. The road was
unpaved, little more than a rutted lane; barren
rock and dry grass and a few stunted cypress trees
dominated the terrain. Brita had said that York's
chalet was the middle one of three balanced on
the cliffs there.

When the first rust-colored tile roof came into
sight, I pulled the Seat off onto the verge and
stepped out. A gentle sea breeze had come up, and
there was a crisp brackish smell in the air; it was
not nearly as hot as it had been in Palma and
Palma Nova.

I walked up the trail until I got to where I could
see the three chalets. They were built of rough
stone blocks, with glass-bead curtains serving as
doors on two of them and green louvered shutters
over the facing windows. I stood in the shade of a
cypress tree and studied the one in the middle. It
seemed deserted. There was no sign of a car, of
people; nothing stirred at the other two cottages.

I lit a cigarette and waited there for a couple of
minutes while I smoked it. Then I went across to
the center chalet, stopped in front of the curtained
doorway. Evidently nobody worried much about
burglary out here. But then, with the political
situation in Spain being what it was, lawbreakers
would be dealt with harshly by *La Guardia Civil*.
Very harshly. Which was one more reason why I
needed to find and talk to Dale Frost as soon as
possible.

"Hello inside!"

The beads made a faint tinkling sound in the sea breeze; that was all there was to hear. I hesitated for a moment, and then I said to hell with it and pushed aside the bead strings and stepped inside.

It was dim in there with the shutters closed. I could make out a table, four chairs, a blackened hearth with a lot of bottles and pottery on a board shelf above it. Through an archway on my right was a bedroom with a couple of unmade cots and not much else. Straight ahead were two more archways, with what looked to be a small kitchen set between them; beyond the second one I could see a balcony jutting out toward the Mediterranean.

I moved slowly across the main room and stepped out onto the balcony. But only by two paces; then I stopped and backed up into the arch. I have a problem with vertigo, and there seemed to be nothing underneath the balcony except five hundred feet of empty space and then the rocky shore. There wasn't much to see out there anyway—just a couple of towels spread out for sunbathing and a woman's floppy straw hat. Off to my right, the sun-fire was almost blinding in its reflection off the ocean.

A quick search of the bedroom netted me nothing either. But while I was conducting it, something jarred in my memory. I was standing there thinking hard on it when the glass-bead curtains clicked suddenly in the other room.

When I went out there, he was standing just inside the doorway, staring in my direction. On his right and a little behind him was a girl with braided hair, dressed in shorts and a sleeveless blouse and wearing an Indian headband. I hadn't heard the roadster drive up; I thought that they must have parked it back where I'd left the rented Seat.

The kid wore the same outfit he'd had on earlier in the day, and his long black hair was wind tangled. In his right hand was the briefcase containing Millard Frost's ten thousand dollars.

"Hello, Peter," I said.

Peter York didn't move; his gaze was steady, his expression dispassionate. The girl clung to his arm, looking nervous and frightened.

He said finally, "So you know."

"Yeah. I know."

"How?"

"Something a girl named Brita told me today," I said. "About Peter York, and about how she didn't care for green eyes. You've got green eyes, sonny—like Spanish olives—but I'd be willing to bet Dale Frost doesn't."

York said nothing. His hand tightened around the handle of the briefcase; he moved his feet apart a little.

I said, "It was a clever little idea you had. Get Dale to tell you what you need to know about his father, put him out of commission, then send that overseas cable and sit back at his villa and wait for somebody to bring you the money. You must have wanted that ten thousand pretty bad not to wait four or five days for a bank transfer and then force Dale to pick it up for you."

He watched me—sullen, silent.

"You might have gotten away with it," I said, "If you hadn't panicked this morning. That was pretty stupid, you know, hitting me and grabbing the money. If you'd hung onto your nerve and made up some explanation for needing the cash, and forged Dale's signature on the release, I'd probably have been satisfied."

The girl took a step forward. "Listen—"

"Shut up, Nina," York told her.

I said, "Where's Dale Frost?"

"How should we know?"

"Where is he?"

"Blow it out your ass, fatso."

"You little bastard, where is he!"

I started to move as I spoke, and York dropped the briefcase and shoved the girl away. His right hand dropped to the pocket of his flared slacks. I sensed what he was going for, but he was quick and I only had time for two more steps before he came out with the knife. He held it extended in front of him—a long, thin switch knife that gleamed darkly in the shadowed room.

I stopped moving. "What do you think that's going to get you, York?"

"Freedom, that's what. Nina and me, we're making a good buy tonight in Palma—ten kilos of good Algerian hash—and nobody's going to stop us. With the customers I've got lined up, that ten thousand is worth five times as much on the streets. Fifty thousand is big money, man."

"Big enough to kill for?"

"Yeah—that big."

"How about Dale Frost? You use that knife on him, too?"

York was silent. But the girl, Nina, pushed frightened words into the stillness. "Dale's not dead; we didn't kill him. We tried to get him to go in on the hash deal with us. He said he'd think it over, and we had it all arranged, and then he wouldn't go through with it. We *had* to have the money, you see? There wasn't any other way to get it."

"Where is he?"

"The chalet next door. It's vacant, and we put him in there and doped him to keep him out of the way. But we're not going to kill him. . . .

"No?" I said. "Ask your boyfriend about that now."

"Peter?" she said to York. "Peter, please, I don't want anything to do with murder!"

"You'd better listen to her, York. Put the knife up."

"Suppose you take it away from me." His face was white and tense. The girl kept on pleading, but for him she wasn't even there.

He came toward me holding the knife out in front of him, palm turned up, moving the blade in slow little circles. I did not look at his face; you can't defend yourself against a knife by looking anywhere except at the knife. The muscles in my stomach were knotted, and I could feel the fear flowing through me like hot wax. A knife is the most terrifying of weapons.

But I had anger, too—the dark, dangerous kind—and I stood my ground and let him come. I wanted him to think I was paralyzed by terror. His fingers were loose around the knife's handle; I watched them, waiting. When he made his move, the fingers would tighten in reflex an instant early.

The sound of our breathing was harsh and unnaturally loud in the small room. Sweat rolled down from under my arms. I could feel a tic trying to start up below my left eye, but I didn't dare blink. Just that much time would give him—

The fingers tightened; York made a noise in his throat and lunged forward with the knife.

I twisted to one side, sucking in my belly, arching my back. The underhand slash cut through the thin material of my shirt, hung up there without breaking skin. I got his wrist in my left hand and his elbow in my right and brought my knee up and his arm down at the same time. There was a cracking sound; York screamed and the knife slid free of my shirt, dropped clattering to the floor. He went down to one knee beside it, but there was no more fight left in him. He didn't move as I kicked the knife to one side, then picked it up and closed it and put it away in my pocket.

The girl came away from the wall where she'd been huddled, knelt beside York and tried to put her arm around him. He shoved her aside roughly, moaning; his eyes were dull and wet with pain. I went away from them, outside. Delayed reaction set in then, the way it always does after something like this: shaking, nausea, cold sweat. But it did not last long, and when it was over it purged the fear and the dark anger, and I was all right again.

I went looking for the silver MG, found it not far from the Seat. I opened the engine compartment and jerked off the rotor and put that in my pocket, too. York and Nina wouldn't get far on foot before I reported to the Spanish authorities.

Dale Frost was where the girl had said he would be, unconscious but breathing more or less normally. I spent a couple of minutes trying to bring him around, but whatever they'd doped him with, it was potent: his eyelids didn't flutter and he didn't make a sound. He was tied up with some heavy twine; I cut it loose with York's knife, then carried him down to the rented sedan and laid him on the back seat.

I did not see York or the girl as I got into the seat and drove away from there.

Standing on the balcony of my hotel room in Palma the following night, I smoked a cigarette and looked out at the cars rushing along the brightly lighted Paseo Maritimo, at the harbor of Palma beyond. Far out, near the breakwater, I could see several night-fishing boats that were probably in search of anchovies; each of them had a single yellow lantern attached to a center mast, and from this distance they looked like sluggish fireflies on the black water.

It was some nice view, and some nice night. Peaceful, which was just what I needed, and plenty of it, after the past twenty-four hours or so. After I'd left the Pta. des Farayos I'd found a guy in Cala Ratjada who spoke English, and he'd gone with me to the local *Guardia Civil* station. Red tape and the language barrier hung me up there most of the night. But Dale had been treated immediately by a local doctor and then taken to a hospital in Palma. And York and Nina had been found and detained in custody, pending a full investigation.

Today, there had been more questions, a visit with the American consul, papers to fill out, a trip to the hospital, accommodations to find, a call to Brita at the Little John Bar in Magalluf and an overseas call to Millard Frost in San Francisco. Dale was going to be fine; the doctors said he would suffer no permanent damage from the drugs he'd been given—amphetamines, mostly—and that he would be back on his feet again in a few days. I had told that to Brita, and I had told it to Millard Frost along with the rest of the story. Both of them were relieved and both of them were grateful—Frost to the sweet offer of a week's paid vacation for my trouble.

So here I was. I'd had a nap and a late supper in the hotel's lavish dining room, and as I stood on the balcony I could hear the sultry beat of Spanish guitars drifting up from the patio garden below. It got into your blood, that music. I wondered if I ought to go down there and join the festivities. Well, why not? I could have a beer or two and watch the people dancing—and maybe, just maybe, I could find a lonely, English-speaking lady to keep me company.

Even for an old fart like me, there might still be a little magic in a warm Mediterranean night. . . .

Private Eye Blues

Sunday Morning Coming Down . . .

That's the title of a sad popular song by Kris Kristofferson, about a man with no wife and no children and nowhere to go and very little to look forward to on a quiet Sunday morning. On this quiet Sunday morning I was that man. Nowhere to go and very little to look forward to.

I carried a cup of coffee into the living room of my flat in San Francisco's Pacific Heights. It was a pretty nice day out, cloudless, a little windy. The part of the Bay I could see from my front windows was a rippled green and dotted with sailboats, like a bas-relief map with a lot of small white flags pinned to it.

I moved over the tier of bookshelves that covered one wall, where most of my six-thousand-odd detective and mystery pulp magazines were arranged. I ran my fingers over some of the spines: *Black Mask, Dime Detective, Clues, Detective Fiction Weekly, Detective Story.* I had started collecting them in 1947, and that meant almost three decades of my life were on those shelves—nearly three-fifths of the time I had been on this earth—and next Friday, I would be fifty years old.

I took one of the Black Masks down and looked at the cover: Chandler, Whitfield, Nebel, Babcock—old friends whom once I could have passed a quiet Sunday with, who would have lifted me out of most any depressed mood I might happen to be in. But not this Sunday. . . .

The telephone rang.

I keep the thing in the bedroom, and I went in there and caught up the receiver. It was Eberhardt, a sobersided lieutenant of detectives and probably my closest friend for about the same number of years as I had been collecting the pulps.

"Hello, hot stuff," he said. "Get you out of bed?"

"No. I've been up for hours."

"You're getting to be an early bird in your old age."

"Yeah."

"Listen, how's for a little cribbage and a lot of beer this afternoon? Dana's off to Sausalito for the day."

"I don't think so, Eb," I said. "I'm not in the beer-and-cribbage mood."

"You sound like you're in a mood, period."

"I guess I am, a little."

"Private eye blues, huh?"

"Yeah—private eye blues."

He made chuckling sounds. "Wouldn't happen to have anything to do with your fiftieth coming

up, would it? Hell, fifty's the prime of life. I ought
to know, tiger, I been there almost a year now."

"Sure."

"Well, you change your mind about the beer, at
least, come on over. I'll save you a can."

We rang off, and I went back to the living room
and finished my coffee and tried not to think
about anything. I might as well have tried not to
breathe. I got up and paced around for a while,
aimlessly.

Sunday morning coming down . . .

Abruptly, the old consumptive cough started
up. So I sat down again, handkerchief to my
mouth, and listened to the dry, brittle sounds
echo through the empty flat. Cigarettes—damned
cigarettes! An average of two packs a day for
thirty-five years, thirty-five out of fifty. More than
a half-million cigarettes. More than ten million
lungfuls of tobacco smoke . . .

Knock it off, I told myself. What's the use in
that kind of thinking? Once more I got to my
feet—all I seemed to be doing this morning was
standing up and sitting down. Well, I had to get
out of there, that was all, before I became claustro-
phobic. Go somewhere, do something. A long
solitary drive, maybe; I just did not want to see
Eberhardt or anybody else.

I put on an old corduroy jacket, left the flat and
picked up my car. The closest direction out of the
city was north, and so I drove across the Golden
Gate Bridge and straight up Highway 101. Some

two hours later, in redwood country a few miles north of Cloverdale, I swung off toward the coast—and eventually, past two o'clock, I reached Highway One and turned south again.

There, the sun was invisible above a high-riding bank of fog, and you could smell the sharp, clean odor of the sea; traffic was only sporadic. The breakers hammering endlessly against the shoreline began to have a magnetic attraction, and near Anchor Bay I pulled off onto a bluff. I left my car in the deserted parking area, found a path leading down to an equally deserted beach.

I walked along the beach, watching the waves unfold, listening to their rhythmic roar and to the sound of gulls wheeling unseen somewhere in the mist. It was a lonely place, but the loneliness was part of its appeal. A good spot for me on this Sunday.

The cold began to get to me after half an hour or so, and the cough started again. I came back up the path, and when I reached the bluff I saw that another vehicle had pulled into the parking area— a dusty, green pickup truck with a small, dusty camper attached to the bed. It listed a little to the left in back and the reason for that was evident enough: the tire there was flat. Nearby, motionless except for wind-tossed hair and clothing, two men and a girl stood looking at the tire, like figures in some sort of alfresco exhibit.

I started in their direction, the direction of my car. The crunching sound of my steps carried above the whisper of the surf, and the three of them glanced up. They did some shifting of position that I didn't pay much attention to, exchanged a few words; then they stepped away from the pickup and approached me, walking in long, matching strides like marchers in a parade. We all stopped, a few feet apart, along the driver's side of my car.

"Hi," one of the men said. He was in his early twenties, the same approximate age as the other two, and he had longish red hair and a droopy mustache; wore a poplin windbreaker, blue jeans and chukka boots. He looked nervous, his smile nothing more than a forced stretching of his lips.

Both the other guy and the girl seemed to be just as nervous. His hair was dark, cut much shorter than the redhead's, and he had a dark, squarish face; his outfit consisted of slacks, a plaid lumberman's jacket and brown loafers. She was plain, thin-lipped, pale, wearing a long heavy car coat and a green bandanna tied forward around her head like a monk's cowl. Chestnut-colored hair fell across her shoulders. All three of them had their hands buried in their pockets.

I nodded and said, "Hi."

"We've had a flat," the redhead said.

"So I see."

"We haven't got a jack."

"Oh. Well, I've got one. You're welcome to use it."

"Thanks."

I hesitated, frowning a little. You get feelings sometimes, when you've been a cop in one form or another most of your life, and you learn to trust them. I had one of those feelings now, and it said something was wrong here—very wrong. Their nervousness was part of it, but there was also a heavy, palpable tension among the three of them: people caught up in some sort of volatile and perhaps dangerous drama. Maybe it was none of my business, but the cop's instinct, the cop's innate curiosity, would not allow me to ignore the feeling of wrongness.

I said, "It's a good thing I happened to be here. There doesn't seem to be much traffic in these parts today."

The redhead took his left hand out of his pocket and pressed diffident fingers against his mustache. "Yeah," he said, "a good thing."

The girl snuffled a little from the cold, produced a handkerchief, snapped it open and blew her nose. Her eyes were focused straight ahead.

The dark-haired guy shifted his feet, and his gaze was furtive. He drew the flaps of his jacket in across his stomach. "Pretty cold out here," he said pointedly.

I glanced over at the pickup; it had Oregon license plates. "Going far?"

"Uh . . . Bodega Bay."

"You on vacation?"

"More or less."

"Must be a little cramped, the three of you in that camper."

"We like it cramped," the redhead said. His voice had gone up an octave or two. "How about your jack, okay?"

I got my keys out and stepped back around the car and opened the trunk. The three of them stayed where they were, watching me. They don't belong together, I thought, not those three—and that, too, was part of the feeling of wrongness. The redhead was the mod type, with his long hair and mustache, and the dark one had a more conservative look. Did that mean anything? One *could* be an interloper, the unwanted third wheel—though in a situation that may have had a lot more meaning than the average kind of two's-company-three's-a-crowd thing. If that was it, which one? The girl had not looked at one guy more than the other; her eyes, crinkled against the wind, were still focused straight ahead.

I unhooked the jack and took it out and closed the trunk again. When I returned to them I said, "Maybe I'd better set this up for you. It's trickier to operate than most."

"We can manage," the dark guy said.

"Just the same . . ."

I took the jack over to the rear of the pickup; the spare tire was propped against the bumper. There were little windows in each of the camper doors, one of them draped in rough cloth and the other one clear. I glanced inside through the clear window. There were storage cupboards, a small table with bunk-type benches on two sides, a ladder that led up to sleeping facilities above the cab; all of it neat and clean, with everything put away or tied down that might roll around when they were in motion.

The three of them came over and formed another half-circle, the girl in the middle this time. I got down in a crouch and slid the jack under the axle and fiddled with it, getting it in place. As soon as I began to work the handle, both the redhead and the dark-haired one pitched in to help. Nothing passed between any of them that I could see.

It took us fifteen minutes to change the tire. I tried several times to make conversation, small talk that might give me a clue as to what was going on among them, which of them didn't belong, but they weren't having any. The boys gave me occasional monosyllables, and the girl, snuffling, did not say anything at all.

When I had worked the handle to lower the truck onto all four tires again and pulled the jack out from underneath, I said, "Well, there you go. You'd better get that flat repaired at the first station you come to. You don't want to be driving around without a spare."

"We'll do that," the dark guy said.

I gave them a let's-bridge-the-generation-gap smile. "You wouldn't happen to have a beer or a soft drink or something inside, would you? Manual labor always makes me thirsty."

The redhead looked at the girl, then at the dark-haired one, and began to fidget "Sorry—nothing at all."

"We'd better get moving," the dark guy said, and he picked up the flat and slid it into the metal holder attached to the undercarriage, locked it down. Then the three of them went immediately to the driver's door.

I did not want to let them go, but there was no way I could think of to keep them there. Following, I watched the redhead open the door and climb in. That gave me a good look inside the cab, but there wasn't much to see; nothing there that shouldn't be there, nothing at all on the seat or on the little shelf behind the seat, or on the dashboard or on the passenger-side floorboards. The girl got in second, and that made the dark one the driver. He swung the door shut, started the engine.

"Take it easy," I said, and lifted my hand. None of them looked at me. The pickup jerked forward, a little too fast, tires spraying gravel, and pulled out onto Highway One. It went away to the south, gathering speed.

I stood watching until they were out of sight. Then I went back to my car and got inside and started her up and put the heater on high. So now what? Drive back to San Francisco, forget about this little incident? That was the simplest thing to do. But I could not get it out of my head. One of those kids, or maybe even more than one, did not belong. The more I thought about it, the more I felt I ought to know which of them it was. More importantly, there was that aura of tension and anxiety all three had projected.

I had no real cause to play detective, but I did have a duty to my conscience and to the vested interests of others, and I did have a strong disinclination to return to my empty, quiet flat. So all right. So I would do some of what I had been doing in one form or another, for bread and butter, the past thirty-one years.

I put the car in gear and drove out and south on

the highway. It took me four miles to catch sight of them. They were moving along at a good clip, maybe ten over the speed limit but within the boundaries of safety. I adjusted my speed to match theirs, with several hundred yards between us. It was not the best time of day for a shagging operation—coming on toward dusk—and the thick, drifting fog cut visibility to a minimum; but the pickup's lights were on and I could track it well enough by the diffused red flickers of the tail lamps.

We went straight down the coast, through Stewart's Point and past Fort Ross. There was still not much traffic, but enough so that we weren't the only two vehicles on the road. The fog got progressively heavier, took on the consistency of a misty drizzle and forced me to switch on the windshield wipers. Daylight faded into the long, cold shadows of night. When we reached Jenner, at the mouth of the Russian River, it was full dark.

A few miles farther on, the pickup came into Bodega Bay and went right on through without slowing. So that made the dark-haired one a liar about their destination. I wondered just where it was they were really headed, and asked myself how far I was prepared to follow them. I decided all the way, until they stopped somewhere, until I satisfied myself one way or another about the nature of their relationship with each other. If that meant following them into tomorrow, even into another state—okay. I had no cases pending, nothing on my hands and too much on my mind;

and work, purposeful or purposeless, was the only real antidote I knew for self-pity and depression.

Valley Ford, Tomales, Point Reyes . . . the pickup did not alter its speed. We were maybe thirty miles from the Golden Gate Bridge then, and I was running low on gas; I had enough to get me into San Francisco, but not much farther than that.

The problem of stopping to refuel turned out to be academic. Just south of Olema Village the pickup slowed and I saw its brake lights flash. Then it swung off onto a secondary road to the west, toward the Point Reyes National Seashore.

When I got to the intersection a couple of minutes later, my headlamps picked up a sign with a black-painted arrow and the words *Public Campground, 3 Miles.* So maybe they were going to stop here for the night, or for supper anyway. I debated the wisdom of running dark. The fog was thinner along here, curling tendrils moving rapidly in a sharp, gusty wind, and you could see jagged patches of sky, like pieces in an astronomical jigsaw puzzle. Visibility was fairly good, and there did not figure to be much traffic on the secondary road, and I did not want to alert them. I switched off the lights, turned onto the road and drove along at less than twenty.

The terrain had a rumpled look because this area was a major San Andreas Fault zone. I passed a little "sag pond" where runoff water had collected in depressions creted by past earthquakes. Exactly three miles in, close to the ocean—I could hear again the whisper of combers—the campground appeared on the left. Backed in against

high sand dunes westward, and ringed by pine and
fir to the east and south, it was a small, state-
maintained facility with wooden outhouses and
stone barbecues and trash receptacles placed in
reminder every few yards.

The pickup was there, lights still on, pulled
back near the trees on the far edge of the grounds.

I saw it on a long diagonal, partially screened by
the evergreens. Instead of driving abreast of the
entrance and beyond, where they might see or
hear me, I took my car onto the berm and cut off
the engine. Ten seconds later, the pickup's lights
went out.

I sat motionless behind the wheel, trying to
decide what to do next, but the mind is a funny
thing: all the way here I had been unable to clarify
the reasons why I felt one or more of those three
didn't belong, and now that I was thinking about
something else, memory cells went click, click,
click, and all at once I knew just what had been
bothering me—three little things that, put together, told me which of them was the interloper.
I felt myself frowning. I still had no idea what the
situation itself was, but what I had just figured
out made the whole thing all the more strange
and compelling.

I reached up, took the plastic dome off the
interior light and unscrewed the bulb; then I got
out of the car, went across the road. The wind,
blowing hard and cold, had sharp little teeth in it
that bit at the exposed skin on my face and hands.
Overhead, wisps of fog fled through the darkness
like chilled fingers seeking warmth.

Moving slowly, cautiously, I entered the trees and made my way to the south, parallel to where the pickup was parked. Beyond the second of two deadfalls I had a glimpse of it through the wind-bent boughs, maybe forty yards away. The cab was dark and seemed to be empty; faint light shone at the rear of the camper, faint enough to tell me that both door windows were now draped.

I crossed toward the pickup, stopped to listen when I was less than ten yards from it and hidden in shadow along the bole of a bishop pine. There was nothing to hear except the cry of the wind and the faint murmuring of surf in the distance. I stared in at the cab. Empty, all right. Then I studied the ground along the near side of the pickup: no gravel, just earth and needles that would muffle approaching footsteps.

One careful pace at a time, I went from the pine to the side of the pickup. Near the end of the camper I stopped and leaned in close and pressed my ear against the cold metal, put my right index finger in the other ear to shut out the wind. At first, for a full thirty seconds, there were faint sounds of movement inside but no conversation. Then, muffled but distinguishable, one of them spoke—the one who didn't belong.

"Hurry up with those sandwiches."

"I'm almost finished," another voice said nervously.

"And I'm damned hungry—but I don't want to sit around here any longer than we have to. You understand?"

"It's a public campground. The state park people won't bother us, if that's what—"

"Shut up! I told both of you before, no comments and no trouble if you don't want a bullet in the head. Do I have to tell you again?"

"No."

"Then keep your mouth closed and get those sandwiches ready. We got a lot of driving left to do before we get to Mexico."

That exchange told me as much as I needed to know about the situation, and it was worse than I had expected. Kidnapping, probably, and God knew what other felonies. It was time to take myself out of it, to file a report with the closest Highway Patrol office—Olema or Point Reyes. You can take private detection just so far, and then you're a fool unless you turn things over to a public law-enforcement agency. I pulled back, half-turned and started to retreat into the trees.

In that moment, the way things happen sometimes—unexpectedly, coincidentally—the wind gusted and blew a limb from one of the deadfalls nearby, sent it banging against the metal side of the camper.

From inside, in immediate response, there was a scraping and a crashing of something upended. I was still backing away, but it was too late then for running. The camper's doors rattled open and one of them came lurching out and into my vision, saw me and shouted, "Hold it, you! Hold it!" In one extended hand was something long and black, something that could only be a gun. I held it.

The figure was the one who didn't belong, of

course—and the one who didn't belong was the girl.

Only he wasn't a girl.

He stood there with his feet spread, crouching slightly, holding the gun in both hands; nervous, scared, dangerous. He was not wearing the wig or the bandanna now; his hair was clipped close to his scalp, and it was light-colored, almost white in the darkness. Except for his pale, girlish face, his hairless hands—physical quirks of nature— there was nothing at all effeminate about him.

"Move up this way," he said.

I hesitated, and then I did what he told me. He backed away quickly, into position to cover both me and the rear of the camper. When I was three long strides from him I stopped, and I could see the other two standing between the open doors, silhouetted in the light from inside. They were motionless, eyes flicking between me and the one holding the gun.

"What the hell?" the guy with the gun said. He had recognized me. "You followed us."

I did not say anything.

"Why? Who are you, man?"

I watched him for a moment; then, stretching the truth a little because I wanted to see his reaction, I said, "I'm a cop."

He didn't like that. A tic started up on the left side of his mouth and he made a swaying motion with the gun, as if he could not quite keep his hands steady. He wasn't at all chary about using the weapon, I was pretty sure of that—on me or on the two scared kids by the camper. You get so

you can gauge the depths of a man, how far he'll
go, what he's capable of; this one was capable of
murder, all right, and in his agitated state it would
not take much to push him into it.

He said finally, "That's your problem," and
made a sound that might have been a grunt or a
skittish laugh. "You don't seem surprised that I'm
not a female."

"No."

"What put you onto me?"

"Three things," I said. "One was the way you
blew your nose back there in the parking area.
You took your handkerchief out and snapped it
open in front of you; that's a man's gesture, not a
woman's. Second thing was the way you walked.
Long, hard strides—masculine movements, same
as the other two kids. Third thing, you weren't
carrying a purse or a handbag, and there wasn't
one inside the camper or cab. I never knew a girl
yet who didn't have some kind of handbag within
easy reach at all times."

He rubbed the back of his free hand across his
nose. "I'll have to watch those things from now
on," he said. "You're pretty sharp, old man."

Old man, I thought. I said, "Yeah, pretty sharp."

The redheaded kid said, "What are you going to
do?" in a shaky voice.

The guy with the gun did not answer immediately; he was staring at me, mouth still twitching.
I watched him think it over, making up his mind.
Then he said to the other two, "You got rope or
anything inside there?"

"Some clothesline," the dark one answered.

"Get it. We'll tie the cop up and take him with us."

Anger started up inside me. You let him tie you up, I told myself, you stand a good chance of dying that way, helpless; you and those two kids, dead by the side of the road somewhere. I said, "Why not shoot me right here and be done with it? Here or someplace else, what difference does it make?"

His face darkened. "Shut up, you!"

I took a measured step toward him.

"Stand still!" He made a convulsive stabbing motion with the gun. "I'm warning you, old man. I'll shoot if you don't stop."

"Sure you will," I said, and jumped him.

The gun went off a foot in front of my face. Flame and powder seared my skin, half-blinded me, and I felt the heat of the bullet past my right cheek. The roar of the shot was deafening, but I got my left hand on his wrist, coming in close to him, and twisted the arm away before he could fire again. I hit him twice with my right—short, hard blows to the stomach and chest. Breath spilled out of his mouth; he staggered, off balance. I kicked his legs out from under him, wrenched the gun free as he fell and then went down on top of him. When I hit him again, on the lower jaw, I felt him go limp. He was out of it.

I pulled back on one knee, stood up holding the gun laxly at my side. My cheek was sore and inflamed, and my eyes stung, watered, but that was all the damage I'd suffered. Except for a liquidy feeling in my legs, I did not seem to have any delayed reaction to what I had just done.

The redhead and the dark guy moved forward jerkily, the way people will after a release of tension; their faces, stark and white, were animated with a kind of deliverance.

"Okay," I said to them, "you'd better get that clothesline now."

We used my car to deliver the one who didn't belong, whose name turned out to be Cullen, to the Highway Patrol office in Point Reyes. On the way, the other two—Tony Piper and Ed Holmberg—gave me an account of what had been for them a twelve-hour ordeal.

They were students at Linfield College in McMinnville, Oregon, and they had set out from there early this morning for a two-day camping trip along the Rogue River. Near Coos Bay they had made the mistake of stopping to offer a ride to what they thought was a girl hitchhiker. Cullen pulled the gun and forced them to drive down the coast into California. He wanted to go to Mexico, he'd told them, and because he did not know how to drive himself, they were elected to be his chauffeurs all the way.

He had also told them that he'd escaped from the local county jail, where he had been held on one count of armed robbery and two of attempted murder after an abortive savings-and-loan holdup. Following his escape, with a statewide alert out on him, he had broken into an empty house looking for clothing and money. The house apparently belonged to a spinster, since there hadn't been any male clothing around, but there had been a couple of wigs and plenty of female apparel of Cullen's size. That was when he had gotten the idea to disguise himself as a woman.

When we arrived at the Highway Patrol office, Cullen was still unconscious. Piper and Holmberg told their story again to an officer named Maxfield, the man in charge. I gave a terse account of my part in it, but they insisted on embellishing that, making me out, in their gratitude, to be some sort of hero.

Maxfield and I were alone in his private office when I showed him the photostat of my license. He gave me a cynically amused smile. "A private eye, huh? Well, the way you disarmed Cullen was private eye stuff, all right. Just like on TV."

"Sure," I said. "Just like on TV."

"You've got a lot of guts, that's all I can say."

"No, I don't have a lot of guts. I've never done anything like that before in my life. I just couldn't let those kids be hurt, if I could help it. Cullen might have killed them, sooner or later, and they've got plenty of living left to do."

"He almost killed *you*, my friend," Maxfield said.

"I didn't much care about that. Just the kids."

"The selfless op, right?"

"Wrong."

"Then why didn't you care what happened to you?"

I did not say anything for a time. Then, because I had kept it inside me long enough: "All right, I'll tell you. In fact, you'll be the first person I've been able to tell. My best friend doesn't even know."

"Know what?"

I went over to the window and looked out so I would not have to face Maxfield's reaction. "I've got a lesion on one of my lungs," I said, "and my doctor thinks it might be malignant. If it is, I've got maybe eighteen months to live."

Afterword

When this story was first published in 1975, the last two sentences were not as they appear above. In the original version, they read: " 'Unless something of a minor miracle takes place, the doctors give me maybe eighteen months to live,' I said, 'I've got terminal lung cancer.' "

"Private Eye Blues," you see, was intended at the time to be the last entry in the 'Nameless' series. Some bad advice, not a little of it self-inflicted, and delusions of grandeur had convinced me that I ought to concentrate on writing "big commercial novels" instead of detective stories. So, because I dislike series which end without some sort of resolution, I determined to kill poor "Nameless" off in this rather unpleasant, but appropriate fashion.

Several months after the story was published, however, I began to have second thoughts. Big commercial novels are all well and good, but if they were that easy to write and sell, everybody in the business would be rich and famous; and besides which, detective stories in general, and

"Nameless" stories in particular, had been fun to write. Once I realized what a mistake I had made, I set out to rectify it by doing a novel, Blowback, in which "Nameless" faces the threat of lung cancer and comes to terms with his own mortality. And, of course, it turns out later that the lesion on his lung is not malignant after all.

As a result of his ordeal, I not only wanted "Nameless" to give up smoking (which he does) but to change his outlook and to develop in a somewhat different direction. You'll find in the remaining five stories that he's mellower, more cheerful (usually) and shows more of his sense of humor. And you'll also find that the types of cases he becomes involved in are somewhat different, too; that they're a bit more, um, puzzling than his straightforward investigations during the pre-lesion period.

I think I made the right decision in keeping "Nameless" around. You're the final judge as to whether or not I made the right decision in his character development and in his new casefile.

The Pulp Connection

The address Eberhardt had given me on the phone was a corner lot in St. Frances Wood, half-way up the western slope of Mt. Davidson. The house there looked like a baronial Spanish villa—a massive two-story stucco affair with black iron trimming, flanked on two sides by evergreens and eucalyptus. It sat on a notch in the slope forty feet above street level, and it commanded an impressive view of Lake Merced and the Pacific Ocean beyond. Even by St. Francis Wood standards—the area is one of San Francisco's moneyed residential sections—it was some place, probably worth half a million dollars or more.

At four o'clock on an overcast weekday afternoon this kind of neighborhood is usually quiet and semideserted; today it was teeming with people and traffic. Cars were parked bumper to bumper on both fronting streets, among them half a dozen police cruisers and unmarked sedans and a television camera truck. Thirty or forty citizens were grouped along the sidewalks, gawking, and I saw four uniformed cops standing watch in front of the gate and on the stairs that led up to the house.

I didn't know what to make of all this as I drove past and tried to find a place to park. Eberhardt had not said much on the phone, just that he wanted to see me immediately on a police matter at this address. The way it looked, a crime of no small consequence had taken place here today— but why summon me to the scene? I had no idea who lived in the house; I had no rich clients or any clients at all except for an appliance outfit that had hired me to do a skip-trace on one of its deadbeat customers.

Frowning, I wedged my car between two others a block away and walked back down to the corner. The uniformed cop on the gate gave me a sharp look as I came up to him, but when I told him my name his manner changed and he said, "Oh, right, Lieutenant Eberhardt's expecting you. Go on up."

So I climbed the stairs under a stone arch and past a terraced rock garden to the porch. Another patrolman stationed there took my name and then led me through an archway and inside.

The interior of the house was dark, and quiet except for the muted sound of voices coming from somewhere in the rear. The foyer and the living room and the hallway we went down were each ordinary enough, furnished in a baroque Spanish style, but the large room the cop ushered me into was anything but ordinary for a place like this. It contained an overstuffed leather chair, a reading lamp, an antique trestle desk-and-chair and no other furniture except for floor-to-ceiling bookshelves that covered every available inch of wall space; there were even library-type stacks along one side. And all the shelves were jammed with paperbacks, some new and some which seemed to date back to the 1940s. As far as I could tell, every one of them was genre—mysteries, Westerns and science fiction.

Standing in the middle of the room were two men—Eberhardt and an inspector I recognized named Jordan. Eberhardt was puffing away on one of his battered black briars; the air in the room was blue with smoke. Eighteen months ago, when I owned a two-pack-a-day cigarette habit, the smoke would have started me coughing but also made me hungry for a weed. But I'd gone to a doctor about the cough around that time, and he had found what he was afraid might be a malignant lesion on one lung. I'd had a bad scare for a while; if the lesion *had* turned out to be malignant, which it hadn't, I would probably be dead or dying by now. There's nothing like a cancer scare and facing your own imminent mortality to make you give up cigarettes for good. I hadn't had one in all those eighteen months, and I would never have one again.

Both Eberhardt and Jordan turned when I came in. Eb said something to the inspector, who nodded and started out. He gave me a nod on his way past that conveyed uncertainty about whether or not I ought to be there. Which made two of us.

Eberhardt was wearing a rumpled blue suit and his usual sour look; but the look seemed tempered a little today with something that might have been embarrassment. And that was odd, too, because I had never known him to be embarrassed by anything while he was on the job.

"You took your time getting here, hotshot," he said.

"Come on, Eb, it's only been half an hour since you called. You can't drive out here from downtown in much less than that." I glanced around at the bookshelves again. "What's all this?"

"The Paperback Room," he said.

"How's that?"

"You hear me. The Paperback Room. There's also a Hardcover Room, a Radio and Television Room, a Movie Room, A Pulp Room, a Comic Art Room and two or three others I can't remember."

I just looked at him.

"This place belongs to Thomas Murray," he said. "Name mean anything to you?"

"Not offhand."

"Media's done features on him in the past—the King of the Popular Culture Collectors."

The name clicked then in my memory; I had read an article on Murray in one of the Sunday supplements about a year ago. He was a retired manufacturer of electronic components, worth a couple of million dollars, who spent all his time accumulating popular culture—genre books and magazines, prints of television and theatrical films, old radio shows on tape, comic books and strips, original artwork, Sherlockiana and other such items. He was reputed to be one of the foremost experts in the country on these subjects, and regularly provided material and copies of material to other collectors, students and historians for nominal fees.

I said, "Okay, I know who he is. But I—"

"Was," Eberhardt said.

"What?"

"Who he *was*. He's dead—murdered."

"So that's it."

"Yeah, that's it." His mouth turned down at the corners in a sardonic scowl. "He was found here by his niece shortly before one o'clock. In a locked room."

"Locked room?"

"Something the matter with your hearing today?" Eberhardt said irritably. "Yes, a damned locked room. We had to break down the door because it was locked from the inside, and we found Murray lying in his own blood on the carpet. Stabbed under the breastbone with a razor-sharp piece of thin steel, like a splinter." He paused, watching me. I kept my expression stoic and attentive. "We also found what looks like a kind of dying message, if you want to call it that."

"What sort of message?"

"You'll see for yourself pretty soon."

"Me? Look, Eb, just why did you get me out here?"

"Because I want your help, damn it. And if you say anything cute about this being a big switch, the cops calling in a private eye for help on a murder case, I won't like it much."

So that was the reason he seemed a little embarrassed. I said, "I wasn't going to make any wisecracks; you know me better than that. If I can help you I'll do it gladly—but I don't know how."

"You collect pulp magazines yourself, don't you?"

"Sure. But what does that have to do with—"

"The homicide took place in the Pulp Room," he said. "And the dying message involves pulp magazines. Okay?"

I was surprised, and twice as curious now, but I said only, "Okay." Eberhardt is not a man you can prod.

He said, "Before we go in there, you'd better know a little of the background. Murray lived here alone except for the niece, Paula Thurman, and a housekeeper named Edith Keeler. His wife died a few years ago, and they didn't have any children. Two other people have keys to the house—a cousin, Walter Cox, and Murray's brother David. We managed to round up all four of those people, and we've got them in a room at the rear of the house.

"None of them claims to know anything about the murder. The housekeeper was out all day; this is the day she does her shopping. The niece is a would-be artist, and she was taking a class at San Francisco State. The cousin was having a long lunch with a girl friend downtown, and the brother was at Tanforan with another horseplayer. In other words, three of them have got alibis for the probable time of Murray's death, but none of the alibis is what you could call unshakable.

"And all of them, with the exception of the housekeeper, have strong motives. Murray was worth around three million, and he wasn't exactly generous with his money where his relatives are concerned; he doled out allowances to each of them, but he spent most of his ready cash on his popular-culture collection. They're all in his will—they freely admit that—and each of them stands to inherit a potful now that he's dead.

"They also freely admit, all of them, that they could use the inheritance. Paula Thurman is a nice-looking blonde, around twenty-five, and she wants to go to Europe and pursue an art career. David Murray is about the same age as his brother, late fifties; if the broken veins in his nose are any indication he's a boozer as well as a horseplayer— a literal loser and going downhill fast. Walter Cox is a mousy little guy who wears glasses about six inches thick; he fancies himself an investments expert but doesn't have the cash to make himself rich—he says—in the stock market. Edith Keeler is around sixty, not too bright, and stands to inherit a token five thousand dollars in Murray's will; that's why she's what your pulp detectives call 'the least likely suspect.' "

He paused again. "Lot of details there, but I figured you'd better know as much as possible. You with me so far?"

I nodded.

"Okay. Now, Murray was one of these regimented types—did everything the same way day after day. Or at least he did when he wasn't off on buying trips or attending popular-culture conventions. He spent two hours every day in each of his Rooms, starting with the Paperback Room at eight

A.M. His time in the Pulp Room was from noon until two P.M. While he was in each of these Rooms he would read or watch films or listen to tapes, and he would also answer correspondence pertaining to whatever that Room contained— pulps, paperbacks, TV and radio shows, and so on. Did all his own secretarial work—and kept all his correspondence segregated by Rooms."

I remembered these eccentricities of Murray's being mentioned in the article I had read about him. It had seemed to me then, judging from his quoted comments, that they were calculated in order to enhance his image as King of the Popular Culture Collectors. But if so, it no longer mattered; all that mattered now was that he was dead.

Eberhardt went on, "Three days ago Murray started acting a little strange. He seemed worried about something, but he wouldn't discuss it with anybody; he did tell the housekeeper that he was trying to work out 'a problem.' According to both the niece and the housekeeper, he refused to see either his cousin or his brother during that time; and he also took to locking himself into each of his Rooms during the day and in his bedroom at night, something he had never done before.

"You can figure that as well as I can: he suspected that somebody wanted him dead, and he didn't know how to cope with it. He was probably trying to buy time until he could figure out a way to deal with the situation."

"Only time ran out on him," I said.

"Yeah. What happened as far as we know it is this: the niece came home at twelve forty-five,

went to talk to Murray about getting an advance
on her allowance and didn't get any answer when
she knocked on the door to the Pulp Room. She
got worried, she says, went outside and around
back, looked in through the window and saw him
lying on the floor. She called us right away.

"When we got here and broke down the door,
we found Murray lying right where she told us.
Like I said before, he'd been stabbed with a splinterlike piece of steel several inches long; the outer
two inches had been wrapped with adhesive
tape—a kind of handle grip, possibly. The weapon
was still in the wound, buried around three inches
deep."

I said, "That's not much penetration for a fatal
wound."

"No, but it was enough in Murray's case. He was
a scrawny man with a concave chest; there wasn't
any fat to help protect his vital organs. The
weapon penetrated at an upward angle, and the
point of it pierced his heart."

I nodded and waited for him to go on.

"We didn't find anything useful when we
searched the room," Eberhardt said. "There are
two windows, but both of them are nailed shut
because Murray was afraid somebody would open
one of them and the damp air off the ocean would
damage the magazines; the windows hadn't been
tampered with. The door hadn't been tampered
with either. And there aren't any secret panels or
fireplaces with big chimneys or crap like that. Just
a dead man alone in a locked room."

"I'm beginning to see what you're up against."

"You've got a lot more to see yet," he said. "Come on."

He led me out into the hallway and down to the rear. I could still hear the sound of muted voices; otherwise the house was unnaturally still—or maybe my imagination made it seem that way.

"The coroner's people have already taken the body," Eberhardt said. "And the lab crew finished up half an hour ago. We'll have the room to ourselves."

We turned a corner into another corridor, and I saw a uniformed patrolman standing in front of a door that was a foot or so ajar; he moved aside silently as we approached. The door was a heavy oak job with a large, old-fashioned keyhole lock; the wood on the jamb where the bolt slides into a locking plate was splintered as a result of the forced entry. I let Eberhardt push the door inward and then followed him inside.

The room was large, rectangular—and virtually overflowing with plastic-bagged pulp and digest-sized magazines. Brightly colored spines filled four walls of floor-to-ceiling bookshelves and two rows of library stacks. I had over 6,000 issues of detective and mystery pulps in my Pacific Heights flat, but the collection in this room made mine seem meager in comparison. There must have been at least 15,000 issues here, of every conceivable type of pulp digest, arranged by category but in no other particular order: detective, mystery, horror, weird menace, adventure, Western, science fiction, air-war, hero, love. Then and later I saw what appeared to be complete runs of *Black Mask*,

Dime Detective, Weird Tales, The Shadow and *Western Story;* of *Ellery Queen's Mystery Magazine* and *Alfred Hitchcock's Mystery Magazine* and *Manhunt;* and of titles I had never even heard of.

It was an awesome collection, and for a moment it captured all my attention. A collector like me doesn't often see anything this overwhelming; in spite of the circumstances it presented a certain immediate distraction. Or it did until I focused on the wide stain of dried blood on the carpet near the back-wall shelves, and the chalk outline of a body which enclosed it.

An odd, queasy feeling came into my stomach; rooms where people have died violently have that effect on me. I looked away from the blood and tried to concentrate on the rest of the room. Like the Paperback Room we had been in previously, it contained nothing more in the way of furniture than an overstuffed chair, a reading lamp, a brass-trimmed rolltop desk set beneath one of the two windows and a desk chair that had been overturned. Between the chalk outline and the back-wall shelves there was a scattering of magazines which had evidently been pulled or knocked loose from three of the shelves; others were askew in place, tilted forward or backward, as if someone had stumbled or fallen against them.

And on the opposite side of the chalk outline, in a loosely arranged row, were two pulps and a digest, the digest sandwiched between the larger issues.

Eberhardt said, "Take a look at that row of three magazines over there."

I crossed the room, noticing as I did so that all the scattered and shelved periodicals at the back wall were detective and mystery; the pulps were on the upper shelves and the digests on the lower ones. I stopped to one side of the three laid-out magazines and bent over to peer at them.

The first pulp was a 1930s and 1940s crime monthly called *Clues.* The digest was a short-lived title from the 1960s, *Keyhole Mystery Magazine.* And the second pulp was an issue of one of my particular favorites, *Private Detective.*

"Is this what you meant by a dying message?"

"That's it," he said. "And that's why you're here."

I looked around again at the scattered magazines, the disarrayed shelves, the overturned chair. "How do you figure this part of it, Eb?"

"The same way you're figuring it. Murray was stabbed somewhere on this side of the room. He reeled into that desk chair, knocked it over, then staggered away to those shelves. He must have known he was dying, that he didn't have enough time or strength to get to the phone or to find paper and pencil to write out a message. But he had enough presence of mind to want to point *some* kind of finger at his killer. So while he was falling or after he fell he was able to drag those three magazines off their shelves; and before he died he managed to lay them out the way you see them. The question is, why those three particular magazines?"

"It seems obvious why the copy of *Clues*," I said.

"Sure. But what clues was he trying to leave us with *Keyhole Mystery Magazine* and *Private Detective?* Was he trying to tell us how he was killed or who killed him? Or both? Or something else altogether?"

I sat on my heels, putting my back to the chalk outline and the dried blood, and peered more closely at the magazines. The issue of *Clues* was dated November 1937, featured a Violet McDade story by Cleve F. Adams and had three other, unfamiliar authors' names on the cover. The illustration depicted four people shooting each other.

I looked at *Keyhole Mystery Magazine.* It carried a June 1960 date and headlined stories by Norman Daniels and John Collier; there were several other writers' names in a bottom strip, a couple of which I recognized. Its cover drawing showed a frightened girl in the foreground, fleeing a dark, menacing figure in the background.

The issue of *Private Detective* was dated March, no year, and below the title were the words, "Intimate Revelations of Private Investigators." Yeah, sure. The illustration showed a private eye dragging a half-naked girl into a building. Yeah, sure. Down in the lower right-hand corner in big red letters was the issue's feature story: "Dead Man's Knock," by Roger Torrey.

I thought about it, searching for connections between what I had seen in here and what Eberhardt had told me. Was there anything in any of the illustrations, some sort of parallel situation?

No. Did any of the primary suspects have names which matched those of writers listed on any of the three magazine covers? No. Was there any well-known fictional private eye named Murray or Cox or Thurman or Keeler? No.

I decided I was trying too hard, looking for too specific a connection where none existed. The plain fact was, Murray had been dying when he thought to leave these magazine clues; he would not have had time to hunt through dozens of magazines to find particular issues with particular authors or illustrations on the cover. All he had been able to do was to reach for specific copies close at hand; it was the titles of the magazines that carried whatever message he meant to leave.

So assuming *Clues* meant just that, clues, *Keyhole* and *Private Detective* were the sum total of those clues. I tried putting them together. Well, there was the obvious association: the stereotype of a private investigator is that of a snooper, a keyhole peeper. But I could not see how that would have anything to do with Murray's death. If there had been a private detective involved, Eberhardt would have figured the connection immediately and I wouldn't be here.

Take them separately then. *Keyhole Mystery Magazine.* Keyhole. That big old-fashioned keyhole in the door?

Eberhardt said, "Well?" You got any ideas?" He had been standing near me, watching me think, but patience had never been his long suit.

I straightened up, explained to him what I had been ruminating about and watched him nod: he had come to the same conclusions long before I got here. Then I said, "Eb, what about the door keyhole? Could there be some connection there, something to explain the locked-room angle?"

"I already thought of that," he said. "But go ahead, have a look for yourself."

I walked over to the door, and when I got there I saw for the first time that there was a key in the latch on the inside. Eberhardt had said the lab crew had come and gone; I caught hold of the key and tugged at it, but it had been turned in the lock and it was firmly in place.

"Was this key in the latch when you broke the door down?" I asked him.

"It was. What were you thinking? That the killer stood out in the hallway and stabbed Murray through the keyhole?"

"Well, it was an idea."

"Not a very good one. It's too fancy, even if it was possible."

"I guess you're right."

"I don't think we're dealing with a mastermind here," he said. "I've talked to the suspects and there's not one of them with an IQ over a hundred and twenty."

I turned away from the door. "Is it all right if I prowl around in here, look things over for myself?"

"I don't care what you do," he said, "if you end up giving me something useful."

I wandered over and looked at one of the two windows. It had been nailed shut, all right, and the nails had been painted over some time ago.

The window looked out on an overgrown rear
yard—eucalyptus trees, undergrowth and scrub
brush. Wisps of fog had begun to blow in off the
ocean; the day had turned dark and misty. And
my mood was beginning to match it. I had no
particular stake in this case, and yet because Eberhardt had called me into it I felt a certain commit-
ment. For that reason, and because puzzles of any
kind prey on my mind until I know the solution,
I was feeling a little frustrated.

I went to the desk beneath the second of the
windows, glanced through the cubbyholes; correspondence, writing paper, envelopes, a packet of
blank checks. The center drawer contained pens
and pencils, various-sized paper clips and rubber
bands, a tube of glue, a booklet of stamps. The
three side drawers were full of letter carbons and
folders jammed with facts and figures about pulp
magazines and pulp writers.

From there I crossed to the overstuffed chair
and the reading lamp and peered at each of them
in turn. Then I looked at some of the bookshelves
and went down the aisles between the library
stacks. And finally I came back to the chalk
outline and stood staring down again at the issues
of *Clues*, *Keyhole Mystery Magazine* and *Private
Detective*.

Eberhardt said impatiently, "Are you getting
anywhere or just stalling?"

"I'm trying to think," I said. "Look, Eb, you told
me Murray was stabbed with a splinterlike piece
of steel. How thick was it?"

"About the thickness of a pipe cleaner. Most of

the 'blade' part had been honed to a fine edge and the point was needle-sharp."

"And the other end was wrapped with adhesive tape?"

"That's right. A grip, maybe."

"Seems an odd sort of weapon, don't you think? I mean, why not just use a knife?"

"People have stabbed other people with weapons a hell of a lot stranger," he said. "You know that."

"Sure. But I'm wondering if the choice of weapon here has anything to do with the locked-room angle."

"If it does I don't see how."

"Could it have been *thrown* into Murray's stomach from a distance, instead of driven there at close range?"

"I suppose it could have been. But from where? Not outside this room, not with that door locked on the inside and the windows nailed down."

Musingly I said, "What if the killer wasn't in this room when Murray died?"

Eberhardt's expression turned even more sour. "I know what you're leading up to with that," he said. "The murderer rigged some kind of fancy crossbow arrangement, operated by a tripwire or by remote control. Well, you can forget it. The lab boys searched every inch of this room. Desk, chairs, bookshelves, reading lamp, ceiling fixtures—everything. There's nothing like that here; you've been over the room, you can tell that for yourself. There's nothing at all out of the ordinary or out of place except those magazines."

Sharpening frustration made me get down on

one knee and stare once more at the copies of
Keyhole and *Private Detective*. They had to mean
something, separately or in conjunction. But
what? What?

"Lieutenant?"

The voice belonged to Inspector Jordan; when I
looked up he was standing in the doorway, gestur-
ing to Eberhardt. I watched Eb go over to him and
the two of them hold a brief, soft-voiced conference. At length Eberhardt turned to look at me
again.

"I'll be back in a minute," he said. "I've got to
go talk to the family. Keep working on it."

"Sure. What else?"

He and Jordan went away and left me alone. I
kept staring at the magazines, and I kept coming
up empty.

Keyhole Mystery Magazine.

Private Detective.

Nothing.

I stood up and prowled around some more,
looking here and there. That went on for a couple
of minutes—until all of a sudden I became aware
of something Eberhardt and I should have noticed
before, should have considered before. Something
that was at once obvious and completely unobtru-
sive, like the purloined letter in the Poe story.

I came to a standstill, frowning, and my mind
began to crank out an idea. I did some careful
checking then, and the idea took on more weight,
and at the end of another couple of minutes I had
convinced myself I was right.

I knew how Thomas Murray had been murdered in locked room.

Once I had that, the rest of it came together pretty quick. My mind works that way; when I have something solid to build on, a kind of chain reaction takes place. I put together things Eberhardt had told me and things I knew about Murray, and there it was in a nice ironic package: the significance of *Private Detective* and the name of Murray's killer.

When Eberhardt came back into the room I was going over it all for the third time, making sure of my logic. He still had the black briar clamped between his teeth and there were more scowl wrinkles in his forehead. He said, "My suspects are getting restless; if we don't come up with an answer pretty soon, I've got to let them go on their way. And you, too."

"I may have the answer for you right now," I said.

That brought him up short. He gave me a penetrating look, then said, "Give."

"All right. What Murray was trying to tell us, as best he could with the magazines close at hand, was how he was stabbed and who his murderer is. I think *Keyhole Mystery Magazine* indicates how and *Private Detective* indicates who. It's hardly conclusive proof in either case, but it might be enough for you to pry loose an admission of guilt."

"You just leave that part of it to me. Get on with your explanation."

"Well, let's take the 'how' first," I said. "The

locked-room angle. I doubt if the murderer set out to create that kind of situation; his method was clever enough, but as you pointed out we're not dealing with a mastermind here. He probably didn't even know that Murray had taken to locking himself inside this room every day. I think he must have been as surprised as everyone else when the murder turned into a locked-room thing.

"So it was supposed to be a simple stabbing done by person or persons unknown while Murray was alone in the house. But it wasn't a stabbing at all, in the strict sense of the word; the killer wasn't anywhere near here when Murray died."

"He wasn't, huh?"

"No. That's why the adhesive tape on the murder weapon—misdirection, to make it look like Murray was stabbed with a homemade knife in a close confrontation. I'd say he worked it the way he did for two reasons: one, he didn't have enough courage to kill Murray face to face; and two, he wanted to establish an alibi for himself."

Eberhardt puffed up another great cloud of acrid smoke from his pipe. "So tell me how the hell you put a steel splinter into a man's stomach when you're miles away from the scene."

"You rig up a death trap," I said, "using a keyhole."

"Now, look, we went over all that before. The key was inside the keyhole when we broke in, I told you that, and I won't believe the killer used some kind of tricky gimmick that the lab crew overlooked."

"That's not what happened at all. What hung

both of us up is a natural inclination to associate the word 'keyhole' with a keyhole in a door. But the fact is, there are *five other keyholes* in this room."

"What?"

"The desk, Eb. The rolltop desk over there."

He swung his head around and looked at the desk beneath the window. It contained five keyholes, all right—one in the rolltop, one in the center drawer and one each in the three side drawers. Like those on most antique rolltop desks, they were meant to take large, old-fashioned keys and therefore had good-sized openings. But they were also half-hidden in scrolled brass frames with decorative handle pulls; and no one really notices them anyway, any more than you notice individual cubbyholes or the design of the brass trimming. When you look at a desk you see it as an empty: you see a *desk*.

Eberhardt put his eyes on me again. "Okay," he said, "I see what you mean. But I searched that desk myself, and so did the lab boys. There's nothing on it or in it that could be used to stab a man through a keyhole."

"Yes, there is." I led him over to the desk. "Only one of these keyholes could have been used, Eb. It isn't the one in the rolltop because the top is pushed all the way up; it isn't any of the ones in the side drawers because of where Murray was stabbed—he would have had to lean over at an awkward angle, on his own initiative, in order to catch that steel splinter in the stomach. It has to be the center drawer then, because when a man sits down at a desk like this, that drawer—and that keyhole—are about on a level with the area under his breastbone."

He didn't argue with the logic of that. Instead, he reached out, jerked open the center drawer by its handle pull and stared inside at the pens and pencils, paper clips, rubber bands and other writing paraphernalia.

Then, after a moment, I saw his eyes change and understanding come into them.

"Rubber band," he said.

"Right." I picked up the largest one; it was about a quarter-inch wide, thick and strong—not unlike the kind kids use to make slingshots. "This one, no doubt."

"Keep talking."

"Take a look at the keyhole frame on the inside of the center drawer. The top doesn't quite fit snug with the wood; there's enough room to slip the edge of this band into the crack. All you'd have to do then is stretch the band out around the steel splinter, ease the point of the weapon through the keyhole and anchor it against the metal on the inside rim of the hole. It would take time to get the balance right and close the drawer without releasing the band, but it could be done by someone with patience and a steady hand. And what you'd have then is a death trap—a cocked and powerful slingshot."

Eberhardt nodded slowly."

"When Murray sat down at the desk," I said, "all it took was for him to pull open the drawer with the jerking motion people always use. The point of the weapon slipped free, the rubber band released like a spring, and the splinter shot through and sliced into Murray's stomach. The shock and impact drove him and the chair backward, and he must have stood up convulsively at the same time, knocking over the chair. That's when he staggered into those bookshelves. And meanwhile the rubber band flopped loose from around the keyhole frame, so that everything looked completely ordinary inside the drawer."

"I'll buy it," Eberhardt said. "It's just simple enough and logical enough to be the answer." He gave me a sidewise look. "You're pretty good at this kind of thing, once you get going."

"It's just that the pulp connection got my juices flowing."

"Yeah, the pulp connection. Now, what about *Private Detective* and the name of the killer?"

"The clue Murray left us there is a little more roundabout," I said. "But you've got to remember that he was dying and that he only had time to grab those magazines that were handy. He couldn't tell us more directly who he believed was responsible."

"Go on," he said, "I'm listening."

"Murray collected pulp magazines, and he obviously also read them. So he knew that private detectives as a group are known by all sorts of names—shamus, op, eye, snooper." I allowed myself a small, wry smile. "And one more, just as common."

"Which is?"

"Peeper," I said.

He considered that. "So?"

"Eb, Murray also collected every other kind of popular culture. One of those kinds is prints of old television shows. And one of your suspects is a small, mousy guy who wears thick glasses; you told me that yourself. I'd be willing to bet that some time ago Murray made a certain obvious comparison between this relative of his and an old TV show character from back in the fifties, and that he referred to the relative by that character's name."

"*What* character?"

"Mr. Peepers," I said. "And you remember who played Mr. Peepers, don't you?"

"Well, I'll be damned," he said. "Wally Cox."

"Sure. Mr. Peepers—the cousin, Walter Cox."

At eight o'clock that night, while I was working on a beer and reading a 1935 issue of *Dime Detective*, Eberhardt rang up my apartment. "Just thought you'd like to know," he said. "We got a full confession out of Walter Cox about an hour ago. I hate to admit it—I don't want you to get a swelled head—but you were right all the way down to the Mr. Peepers angle. I checked with the housekeeper and the niece before I talked to Cox, and they both told me Murray called him by that name all the time."

"What was Cox's motive?" I asked.

"Greed, what else? He had a chance to get in on a big investment deal in South America, and Murray wouldn't give him the cash. They argued about it in private for some time, and three days ago Cox threatened to kill him. Murray took the threat

seriously, which is why he started locking himself
in his Rooms while he tried to figure out what to
do about it.

"Where did Cox get the piece of steel?"

"Friend of his has a basement workshop, builds
things out of wood and metal. Cox borrowed the
workshop on a pretext and used a grinder to hone
the weapon. He rigged up the slingshot this morning—let himself into the house with his key while
the others were out and Murray was locked in one
of the Rooms."

"Well, I'm glad you got it wrapped up and glad I
could help."

"You're to be even gladder when the niece talks
to you tomorrow. She says she wants to give you
some kind of reward."

"Hell, that's not necessary."

"Don't look a gift horse in the mouth—to coin
a phrase. Listen, I owe you something myself. You
want to come over tomorrow night for a home-
cooked dinner and some beer?"

"As long as it's Dana who does the home cook-
ing," I said.

After we rang off I thought about the reward
from Murray's niece. Well, if she wanted to give
me money I was hardly in a financial position to
turn it down. But if she left it up to me to name
my own reward, I decided I would not ask for
money at all; I would ask for something a little
more fitting instead.

What I really wanted was Thomas Murray's run
of *Private Detective*.

Where Have You Gone,
Sam Spade?

I.

The Brinkman Company, Specialty Imports, was located just off the Embarcadero, across from Pier Twenty-six in the shadow of the San Francisco-Oakland Bay Bridge. It was a good-sized building, made out of wood with a brick facade; it didn't look like much from the outside. I had no idea what was on the inside, because Arthur Brinkman, the owner, hadn't told me on the phone what sort of "specialty imports" he dealt in. He hadn't told me why he wanted to hire a private detective either. All he'd said was that the job would take a full week, my fee for which he would guarantee, and would I come over and talk to him? I would. I charged two hundred dollars a day, and when you multiplied that by seven it made for a nice piece of change.

It was a little after ten A.M. when I got there. The day was misty and cold, whipped by a stiff wind that had the sharp smell of salt in it—typical early-March weather in San Francisco. Drawn up at the rear of the building were three big trucks from a waterfront drayage company, and several men were busily engaged in unloading crates and boxes and wheeling them inside the warehouse on dollies and hand trucks. I parked my car up toward the front, next to a new Plymouth station wagon, and went across to the office entrance.

Inside, there was a small anteroom with a desk along the left-hand wall and two closed doors along the right-hand wall. A glass-fronted cabinet stood between the doors, displaying the kinds of things you see on knick-knack shelves in some people's houses. Opposite the entrance, in the rear wall, was another closed door, that one led to the warehouse, because I could hear the sounds the workmen made filtering in through it. And behind the desk was a buxom redhead rattling away on an electric typewriter.

She gave me a bright professional smile, finished what she was typing and said, "Yes, may I help you?" in a bright professional voice as she rolled the sheet out.

Along with a professional smile of my own, I gave her my name.

"Oh, yes," she said, "Mr. Brinkman is expecting you." She stood and came around from behind the desk. She had nice hips and pretty good legs; chubby calves, though. "My name is Fran Robbins, by the way. I'm the receptionist, secretary and about six other things here. A Jill-of-all-trades, I guess you could say."

The last sentence was one she'd used before,

probably to just about everyone who came in; you could tell that by the way she said it, the faint expectancy in her voice. She wanted me to appreciate both the line and her cleverness, so I said obligingly, "That's pretty good—Jill-of-all-trades. I like that."

She smiled again, much less impersonally this time; I'd made points with her, at least. "I'll tell Mr. Brinkman you're here," she said, and went over and knocked on one of the doors in the right-hand wall and then disappeared through it.

The anteroom was not all that warm, despite the fact that a wall heater glowed near Miss Robbins' desk. Instead of sitting in the one visitor's chair, I took a couple of turns around the room to keep my circulation going. I was just starting a third turn when the left-hand door opened and Miss Robbins came back out.

With her was a wiry little man in his mid-forties, with colorless hair and features so bland they would have, I thought, the odd reverse effect of making you remember him. He looked as if a good wind would blow him apart and away, like the fluff of a dandelion. But he had quick, canny eyes and restless hands that kept plucking at the air, as if he were creating invisible things with them.

He used one of the hands to pat Miss Robbins on the shoulder; the smile she gave him in return was anything but professional—doe-eyed and warm enough to melt butter. I wondered if maybe the two of them had something going and decided it was a pretty good bet that they had. My old private eyes were still good at detecting things like that, if not much else.

Brinkman came over to me, gave me his name and one of his nervous hands, and then ushered me into his office. It wasn't much of an office— desk, a couple of low metal file cabinets, some boxes stacked along one wall and an old wooden visitor's chair that looked as if it would collapse if you sat in it. That chair was what I got invited to occupy, and it didn't collapse when I lowered myself into it; but I was afraid to move around much, just the same.

Sitting in his own chair, Brinkman lit a cigarette and left it hanging from one corner of his mouth. "You saw the trucks outside when you got here?" he asked.

I nodded. "You must be busy these days."

"Very busy. They're bringing in a shipment of goods that arrived by freighter from Europe a few days ago. Murano glass from Italy, Hummel figurines from West Germany, items like that."

"Are they the sort of things you generally import?"

"Among a number of other items, yes. This particular shipment is the largest I've ever bought; I just couldn't pass it up at the bulk price that was offered to me. Deals like that only come along once in ten years."

"The shipment is valuable, then?"

"Extremely valuable," Brinkman said. "When those trucks deliver the last of it later today, I'll have more than three hundred thousand dollars' worth of goods in my warehouse."

"That's a lot of money, all right," I agreed.

He bobbed his head in a jerky way, crushed out his cigarette and promptly lit another one. Chain-smoker, I thought. Poor bastard. I'd been a heavy smoker myself up until a couple of years ago, when a lesion on one lung made me quit cold turkey. The lesion had been benign, but it could just as easily have gone the other way. For Brinkman's sake, I hoped he had the sense to quit one of these days, before it was too late.

"The goods will be in here about a week," he said. "It will take that long to inventory them and arrange for the bulk of the items to be shipped out to my customers."

"I see."

"That's where you come in. I want you to guard them for me during that time. At night, when no one else is around."

So that was it. He was afraid somebody might come skulking around after dark to steal or vandalize his merchandise, and what he wanted was a nightwatchman. Not that I minded; nobody had wanted me to do any private skulking of my own in recent days, and there was that guarantee of wages for a full week.

I said, "I'm your man, Mr. Brinkman."

"Good. You'll start right away tonight."

I nodded. "When should I be here?"

"Six o'clock. That's our closing time."

"What time do you open in the morning?"

"Eight-thirty. But I'm usually here by seven."

"So you want me on the job about thirteen hours."

"That's right," Brinkman said. "I realize that's a much longer day than you normally work; I'm willing to compensate you for the extra time. Would two hundred and fifty a day be all right?"

It was just fine, and I said so.

He put out his second cigarette. "I'll show you around now," he said, "get you familiarized with the building and where everything is. When you come back tonight I'll show you what I want you to do on your rounds—"

There was a knock on the door. Brinkman was half out of his chair already; he stood all the way up as the door opened and a heavyset guy around my age, early fifties, with a drinker's nose and the thick, gnarled hands of a longshoreman poked his head inside.

"See you a minute, Art?" the guy said.

"Sure. Come in, Orin; I want you to meet the man I've hired to guard the new shipment."

The heavyset guy came in, and we shook hands as Brinkman introduced us. His name was Orin McIntyre, and he was the firm's bookkeeper. Which was something of a small surprise; even though he was wearing a white shirt open at the throat and a pair of slacks, I had taken him, foolishly enough, for a warehouseman or a truck driver because of his physical appearance. He could have gone on the old "What's My Line?" television show and nobody would have guessed his occupation. So much for stereotypes.

"If you don't mind my saying so," McIntyre said to me, "I think Art is wasting his money hiring a nightwatchman. This place is built like a fortress; when it's locked up tight nobody can get in."

Brinkman gave him an irritated look. "You don't know that for certain, Orin. Neither do I."

"Well, the place has never been broken into, has it?"

"Not yet. But there's a first time for everything."

McIntyre said to me, "This building used to belong to an import-export outfit that dealt in high-priced artwork. They installed a number of safeguards: steel shutters over the windows on the outside, iron gates that you can padlock across the doors and windows on the inside. How can anybody get in through all of that?"

"It doesn't sound as if anybody can," I said. "But then, it didn't seem anybody could get into the Bank of England, either, and yet somebody did."

"Exactly," Brinkman agreed. He lit another cigarette; his hands plucked and fidgeted in the air, like a magician doing conjuring tricks behind a screen of smoke. He was one of the most nervous people I had ever encountered; he made *me* nervous just watching him. "I don't want to take any chances, that's all. This shipment is important to us all—"

"I know that as well as you do," McIntyre said. "Probably better, in fact."

Brinkman gave him another irritated look. There was some sort of friction between these two; I wondered what it was. And why Brinkman, the boss, put up with it.

I said, "I've been a cop of one kind or another

for thirty years; if there's one thing I've learned in all that time, it's that there's no such thing as too much precaution against crime. The more prepared you are, the less likely you'll get taken by surprise."

"That sounds like a self-serving statement," McIntyre said.

"No, sir, it's not. It's a statement of fact, that's all."

"Uh-huh. Well, if you ask me—"

"That's enough, Orin," Brinkman said. "You've got better things to do than stand around here questioning my judgment or this man's integrity. So have I. Now, what did you want to see me about?"

"One of the bills of lading on the shipment is screwed up." McIntyre sounded faintly miffed, as if he didn't like having been put in his place. It was what he'd tried to do to me, but the "Do unto others" rule was one some men never learned; he knew how to dish it out, but he couldn't take it worth a damn. "You want to talk here, in front of him"—he gestured in my direction—"or in my office?"

"Your office." Brinkman looked at me. "This won't take long. Then I'll show you around."

"Fine," I said.

The three of us went out into the anteroom, and Brinkman and McIntyre disappeared into McIntyre's office. Miss Robbins was busy at her desk, so I went over and stood quietly in front of the wall heater. From there I noticed that, as McIntyre had said, there was an iron-barred folding gate drawn back beside the front door. When it was extended and bolted into a locking plate on the other side of the door, it would provide an extra seal against intruders.

Brinkman was back in five minutes, alone. He fired another cigarette, hung it on his lower lip, did the conjuring trick with his hands and then led me off on the guided tour.

II.

The warehouse door off the anteroom led into a short corridor, beyond which was a section partitioned off with wall board: bathroom on the right, L-shaped shipping counter on the left. And beyond there was the warehouse itself, a wide, spacious area with rafters crisscrossing under a high roof, a concrete floor and white-painted walls. A cleared aisleway ran straight down its geometrical center to the open rear doors where the warehousemen were unloading the drayage trucks. Built into the joining of the right-side rear walls, ten feet above the floor, was a thirty-foot-square loft; a set of stairs led up to it and its jumble of boxes and storage items.

To the right of the aisle, down to the loft stairs, were perpendicular rows of platform shelving, with narrow little aisles between them; some of the shelves were filled with merchandise both packed and unpacked, the unpacked boxes showing gouts of either straw packing or excelsior. To the left of the aisle was open floor space jammed with stacked crates, pallets, dollies, bins full of more straw packing and carts with metal wheels—all arranged in such a mazelike way that you could, if you were careful, move among them without knocking or falling over something.

Brinkman led me through the clutter to the nearest window. An iron-barred gate was drawn across it, firmly padlocked to an iron hasp, and through the windowpane I could see that the outside shutter was in place. When I'd had my look at the window, he took me to the rear doors and showed me that they had double locks and their own set of iron-barred gates. He also mentioned the fact that the walls and roof were reinforced with steel rods.

The place was a minifortress, all right. About the only way anybody was going to break in there was with blasting caps or chain saws.

After we finished examining the security, Brinkman showed me some of the items in the big shipment from Europe and explained what the rest were. In addition to the Hummel figurines and the Murano glass, there were special flamenco dolls from Spain, crystal from Sweden and Denmark, pewter from Norway, Delft porcelain miniatures from Holland, intricate dollhouse accessories from France.

Looking at all of that, I thought that this was going to be a pretty easy job. I could understand how Brinkman felt, why he was so nervous about the possibility of theft, but the plain fact was, he had very little cause for alarm. In the first place, there was the fortresslike makeup of the building. And in the second place, his merchandise may have been valuable, but it was not the kind that would tempt thieves, professional or otherwise. There are people around who will steal anything, of course, but not very many who were likely to get hot and bothered over Italian glass candy dishes or Delft miniatures. And where would you fence stolen flamenco dolls or French dollhouse accessories?

I mentioned those facts to Brinkman, just for the record, but it didn't make him think twice about hiring me; he was bound and determined to have a nightwatchman on the premises for the coming week, as an added precaution, and nothing and nobody were going to make him change his mind. Nor did what I said reassure him much. He was a worrier, and there's never anything you can say that will reassure one of that breed. The more you tell them everything is going to be all right, the more fretful they get.

Through all of the tour, the warehousemen continued to unload the trucks and wheel crates inside and stack them here and there. There were four of them, three part-timers and Brinkman's full-time "warehouse supervisor," a guy named Frank Judkins. Brinkman intercepted Judkins on his way in with a hand truck loaded with boxes and introduced him to me.

He was a brawny guy in his forties, tough-looking—the kind you used to see, and probably still could, in longshoremen's bars along the waterfront. He had lank black hair that grew as thickly on his arms, and no doubt on the rest of him, as it did on his head; he also had vacuous eyes and a wart the size of a dime on his chin.

He said, "How's it going, pal?" as he caught hold of my hand and made an effort to crush the bones in it, either by accident or to show me how strong he was.

I've got a pretty good grip myself; I tightened it to match his and looked him square in the eye. "Pretty good, pal," I said. "How about yourself?"

Judkins liked that; he laughed noisily. Some of his teeth were missing, and what remained were either yellow or black with cavities. He let go of my hand and stood there grinning at me like a Neanderthal.

Brinkman said to him, "Everything going all right out here, Frank?"

"Yeah. Almost done with the first load."

"They'll bring the rest of the merchandise after lunch?"

"Yeah."

"Good." Brinkman told him I would be coming in at six to assume my nightwatchman's duties. "You'll have everything off-loaded and inside by then, won't you?"

"Yeah."

"See to it that you do. I don't want this place open after dark."

"Yeah," Judkins said. It seemed to be his favorite word, probably because it had only one syllable and required no mental effort to utter.

Judkins grinned at me again and looked at my hand as if he wanted to shake it some more, to see if my grip was really as strong as it seemed.

But I didn't have to put up with any more attempts at bone crushing; Brinkman told him to
get back to work and steered me away through the
shipping area and into the office anteroom.

Fran Robbins was on the phone when we came
in. She said, "One moment please," into the receiver, took it away from her ear and put her hand
over the mouthpiece, and tilted her head toward
Brinkman. "It's the Consolidated chain," she said.
"I think you'd better talk to them. Arth—uh, Mr.
Brinkman. There's some problem about their order."

"Damn," Brinkman said. "Okay, tell them just
a second and put 'em on hold."

She gave him her butter-melting smile. They
had something going, all right; I could see it in
her eyes. I wondered what those eyes saw in him.
But then, *de gustibus non est disputandam.*
Which was a Latin phrase I'd read somewhere that
meant there was no accounting for taste. In this
world, there was somebody for everyone; and
Brinkman was obviously Miss Robbins' somebody.

He turned to me as she spoke again into the
telephone. "I think we've covered just about everything for now," he said. "Unless you have any
more questions?"

"No, I can't think of any."

"I'll see you at six, then."

"Right. Six sharp."

"Your cheque will be ready when you get here,"
he said, and hurried into his office to take his call.

I said good-bye to the Jill-of-all-trades, went out

to my car and drove downtown to my office on Taylor Street. I checked my new answering machine first; there hadn't been any calls. Then I prepared one of my standard contract forms for Brinkman to sign, stipulating the payment we had agreed upon. And then, because I had no other work to attend to, and because I was going to be up all night, I went home to my flat in Pacific Heights and took myself a nap.

At five o'clock I was up and dressed and ready to go, and at ten minutes to six I was back at the Brinkman Company, Specialty Imports. The drayage trucks were gone and the warehouse was closed. Miss Robbins and Orin McIntyrc and the warehousemen were gone, too; Brinkman was there alone. I gave him the contract form to sign, exchanged a countersigned copy for my retainer check. After we got that taken care of, he took me out into the warehouse again and showed me what he wanted me to do "on my rounds." Which amounted to checking the doors and windows periodically, and making sure none of the straw packing and excelsior caught fire, because they were highly combustible materials. He also warned me not to let anyone in, under any circumstances; there was no reason for anyone to come around, he said, and if anyone did come around, it had to mean they were there to steal something.

I assured him, with more patience than I felt, that I would do what he'd asked of me and that I was competent at my job. He said, "Yes, I'm sure you are," and fluttered his hands at me. "It's just that I worry. I'll call you later, before I go to bed, to check in. So it's all right for you to answer the phone when it rings." He paused. "You don't mind if I call, do you?"

"No," I said, "I don't mind."

"Good. It's just that I worry, you know?"

He went away pretty soon and left me alone with his $300,000 worth of knick-knacks.

It was some night.

The warehouse was unheated, and Brinkman's office, where I spent most of my time, tended to be chilly even with the wall heater turned on. Time crawled, as it always does on a job like this; there was nothing to do except to read the handful of pulp magazines I'd brought with me, eat a late supper and drink coffee from the thermos I'd also brought, and listen to foghorns moaning out on the Bay. Nobody tried to break in. Nobody called except Brinkman at a little before midnight. And the only real nightwatching I did was of the clock on the wall.

Ah, the exciting life of a private eye. Danger, intrigue, adventure, beautiful women, feats of derring-do.

Thirteen hours of boredom and a half-frozen rear end.

Where have you gone, Sam Spade?

III.

I got home at seven-thirty, gritty-eyed and grumpy, and slept until two o'clock. When I got up I packed another cold supper, made fresh coffee for the thermos and put everything into a paper sack with some issues of *Detective Tales* and *Dime Mystery* from my collection of pulp magazines. Then I drove down to my office to find out if anybody else was interested in hiring me.

Nobody was. The only message on my answering machine was from somebody who wanted to convert me to his religion; he was reading from some sort of Biblical tract, in a persuasively ministerial voice, when the message tape ran out and ended his pitch. I did a little paperwork and then sat around until five-thirty, in case a prospective client decided to walk in. It was a decision nobody made. And the phone didn't ring either.

I pulled into the Brinkman Company lot and parked my car next to Brinkman's station wagon at two minutes to six. The weather was colder and foggier than it had been yesterday; the wind off the Bay made wailing noises and slashed at me as I hurried to the office entrance with my paper sack.

The door was locked, as it had been last night; I rapped on the glass, and Brinkman came out and opened up for me. "I'm glad you're on time," he said. "I have an engagement at seven-thirty and I've got to rush."

"Everything locked up, Mr. Brinkman?"

"Yes, I think so. But you'd better double-check, make sure the windows and doors are secure."

"Right."

The door to Orin McIntyre's office opened and McIntyre came out, carrying a briefcase in each hand. He seemed upset; he was scowling and his face was heavy and dark, like a sky full of thunderclouds.

I said automatically, "How are you tonight, Mr. McIntyre?"

"Lousy," he said.

"Something wrong?"

He looked past me at Brinkman—a look that almost crackled with animosity. "Ask him."

"Don't make a scene, Orin," Brinkman said.

"Why the hell shouldn't I make a scene?"

"It won't do you any good."

"Is that a fact?"

Brinkman sighed, made one of his nervous gestures. "I'm sorry, Orin; I told you that. I wish you'd understand that my decision is nothing personal; it's just a simple matter of economics—"

"Oh, I understand, all right," McIntyre said angrily. "I understand that you're a fourteen-carat bastard, that's what I understand."

"Orin—"

"The hell with you." McIntyre glared at him and then switched the glare to me. "And the hell with *you*," he said, and went to the door and slammed out into the windy dusk.

Through the glass I watched him walk across the lot to his car. When I turned back Brinkman said, "I suppose I can't blame him for being angry."

"What happened?"

"I had to let him go. His work wasn't all it should be, and I really can't afford his salary.

Besides, I've been thinking of promoting Miss
Robbins, turning the bookkeeping job over to her.
She's had accountant's training, and she can han-
dle it along with her other duties."

Uh-huh, I thought. The firing of McIntyre may
have been for economic reasons, but I doubted
there was nothing personal involved; I had a feeling Brinkman's relationship with Fran Robbins
had had more than a little to do with it. But then,
Brinkman's private life was really none of my
concern. Nor, for that matter, were his business
decisions, except as they pertained to me.

So I just nodded, let a couple of seconds pass
and then asked him, "Everyone else gone, Mr.
Brinkman?"

"Yes." He shot the cuff of his gray sports jacket
and looked at his watch. "And I've got to be gone,
too, or I'll be late for my appointment. I'll call you
later, as usual. Around midnight."

"Whatever you say."

I followed him to the door and we exchanged
good nights. When he'd gone out I closed and
locked the door, using the latchkey he had given
me. I made it a double seal by swinging the barred
gate shut across the door and padlocking it. And
there I was, sealed in all nice and cozy until seven
A.M. tomorrow.

The next order of business was to shut off the
ceiling lights, which I did and which left the
anteroom dark except for the desk lamp glowing
beyond the half-open door to Brinkman's office. I
went in there and put my paper sack down on the

desk, came out again and crossed to the door that led back into the warehouse.

A dull, yellowish bulb burned above the shipping counter, casting just enough light to bleach the shadows past the partitions. None of the overheads was on in the warehouse proper; it was like a wall of black velvet back there with all the windows shuttered against the fading daylight. I located the bank of electrical switches and flipped each in turn. The rafter bulbs were not much brighter than the one over the counter, but there were enough of them to herd most of the shadows into corners or behind the stacks of shelving and crates.

I made my way through the clutter on the right side of the aisleway, to the nearest of the windows. The barred gate was as firmly padlocked as it had been last night. There was a second window several feet beyond, to the rear; I had a look at that one next. Secure. Then I moved over to the shelving, down one of the cross aisles past several hundred unpacked crystal candleholders that caught and reflected the light like so many prisms. The single window on that side, too, was both shuttered and barred up tight.

That left the rear doors. I went down there and rattled the gate and padlock, as I'd done at the windows, and peered through the bars at the double locks on the doors themselves. Secure. A team of commandos, I thought, would be hard-pressed to breach this place.

To pass some time, I prowled around for fifteen minutes or so, shining my flashlight into dark corners, examining glass vases and tiny pieces of dollhouse furniture, poking through what few purchase orders there were on the shipping counter. Lethargy was already starting to set in; I caught myself yawning twice. But it was as much a lack of sleep as it was boredom. I had never been able to sleep very well in the daytime, and I hadn't had enough rest during the past two days; by the end of the week I would probably be ready for about fifteen hours of uninterrupted sack time. I could have curled up in a nest of straw right here and taken a nap, of course, but my conscience wouldn't allow it. I had never cheated a client in any fashion and I was not about to start now by sleeping on the job.

So I shut off the overheads and went back to Brinkman's office, leaving the warehouse door open. It was almost as cold in there as it was in the warehouse, which was probably just as well; the chill would help keep me awake. I got my thermos bottle out of the paper sack and poured myself a cup of hot coffee. Sat back with it and one of the pulps I'd brought, bundled up in my coat, feet propped on a low metal file cabinet to one side of the desk.

And I was ready to begin another long night in my brief career as nightwatchman.

IV.

The minute hand dragged itself around the clock on the office wall. In the pulp—the December 1936 issue of *Detective Tales*—I read "Satan

Covers the Waterfront" by Tom Roan and "The Case of the Whispering Terror" by George Bruce. Outside, the velocity of the wind increased; I could hear it rattling a loose drain gutter on the roof as I read "Malachi Gunn and the Vanishing Heiress" by Franklin H. Martin.

Eight-forty.

I poured another cup of coffee. None of the other stories in the issue of *Detective Tales* looked interesting; I put it down and picked up the May 1935 *Dime Mystery*, and read "House of the Restless Dead" by Hugh B. Cave and "Mistress of Terror" by Wyatt Blassingame. The wind slackened again, and the only background noises I had to listen to then were creaking joints and the distant moan of foghorns on the bay.

Ten-oh-five.

I read "The Man Who Was Dead" by John Dixon Carr, which was a nice little ghost story set in England. The "Dixon" was no doubt a misspelling and the author was John Dickson Carr, the master of the locked-room mystery; I'd read somewhere that Carr had published a few stories in mid-1930s pulps, one other of which I'd read in the third or fourth issue of *Detective Tales*.

My eyes were beginning to feel heavy-lidded and sore from all the reading; I rubbed at them with my knuckles, closed the magazine, yawned noisily, and looked at the thermos and the three salami-and-cheese sandwiches and two apples inside the sack. But I wasn't hungry just yet, and the coffee had to last me the rest of the night. I got to my feet, stretching; glanced at the clock again in spite of myself.

Ten thirty-three.

And something made a noise out in the warehouse—a dull thud like a heavy weight falling against another object.

The hair poked up on my neck; I stood frozen, listening, for three or four seconds. The silence seemed suddenly eerie. Sounds in the night seldom bothered me, but this was different. This was a building in which I was alone and sealed up, and yet I was sure the thudding noise had come from *inside* the warehouse.

I grabbed my flashlight off the desk, switched it on and ran into the anteroom. Just as I reached the open warehouse door, I had an almost subliminal glimpse of a streak of light winking out beyond the night-lit shipping counter. Somebody else with a flash? I threw my own beam down the corridor, went through the doorway after it.

In the clotted darkness ahead, there was a faint thumping sound.

Without slowing I veered past the shipping counter and over to the bank of light switches. The flash beam illuminated the near third of the main aisleway, but its diffused glare showed me nothing except inanimate objects.

Another thump. And then a kind of clicking or popping. Both noises seemed to come from somewhere diagonally to my left.

I threw all the switches at once, slapping upward with the palm of my free hand. When I hurried ahead into the aisle, the pale rafter lights

let me see the same tableau as earlier—nothing
altered, nothing subtracted, nothing added. Except for one thing.

There was a dead man lying a few feet to the
left of the aisle, half-draped across one of the
wooden crates.

I saw him when I was no more than twenty feet
into the warehouse, and I knew right away he was
dead. He was facing toward me, twisted onto his
side, features half-hidden behind an upflung arm;
there was blood all over the leather jacket and
blue turtleneck sweater he wore, and the one eye
I could see was wide open. Hesitantly, gawping a
little, I moved to where he was and bent over him.

Sam Judkins, the warehouseman.

He'd been shot once in the left side, under the
breastbone, at point-blank range with a small-
caliber gun: scorch and powder marks were visible
around the hole, and there was no exit wound.

His jacket and trousers were wet in front. And
they smelled of . . . wood alcohol?

Ripples of cold flowed over my back. The eerie
silence, the dead man, the bullet wound, the
wood-alcohol smell all combined to give me a
feeling of surreality, as though I were asleep and
dreaming all of this. I backed away from the body,
shaking my head. He couldn't have got in here,
but here he was. He couldn't have been murdered
in here, but here he was. It was murder, all right;
there was no gun near him, which had to mean
that whoever had shot him still had it. And what
had happened to *him*? Where did *he* go?

Still in here somewhere, hiding?

I stopped moving and made myself stand still for thirty seconds. No movement anywhere. No sounds anywhere. Over to my left, lying on a metal-wheeled cart, was one of those curved iron bars used for prying lids off wooden crates; I caught it up and held it cocked against my shoulder, wishing that I hadn't decided I would not need a handgun for this job.

But nothing happened as I paced back into the aisle, along it through the shipping area. Nor was there anything more to see or hear.

In Brinkman's office, I dialed the number of the Hall of Justice. Eberhardt, my sober-sided cop friend, was on night duty this week, and I got through to him with no problem. He grumbled and did some swearing, told me to stay where I was and not to do anything stupid, and hung up while I was reminding him I used to be a police officer myself.

I went back into the anteroom and took another look through the door leading to the warehouse. But if whoever had killed Judkins was still here, why hadn't he come after me by now? It didn't make sense that he would let me call the cops and then hang around to wait for them.

The front door seemed to be as secure as before; that was the first thing I checked. Nobody could possibly have come in through there when I was in Brinkman's office earlier, or gone out through there after I heard those noises. I walked back into the warehouse again, taking the pry bar with me just in case. Not touching anything, I checked the gates and padlocks on all the windows and the rear doors. And each of them was also as secure as before.

So how had Judkins and whoever killed him got in?

And how had the killer got out?

V.

When the banging started at the front entrance I was back in Brinkman's office, just hanging up the telephone for the third time. I hurried out and unlocked the gate and swung it aside; unlocked the door and opened it.

"What the hell are you guarding in there?" Eberhardt asked sourly. "Gold bullion?"

There were a half-dozen other cops with him: an inspector I knew named Klein, two guys from the police lab outfitted with field kits, a photographer and a brace of patrolmen. I moved aside without saying anything and let all of them crowd past me into the anteroom. Then I shut the door again to cut off the icy blasts of wind.

Eberhardt made a gnawing sound on the stem of his pipe and glowered at me. The glower didn't mean anything; like the pipe—one of twenty or thirty battered old briars he owned—it was a permanent fixture, part of his professional persona. The only times he smiled or relaxed were when he was off duty.

He asked me, "Where's the victim?"

"Warehouse area, in back."

I led him and the others out there. The two lab guys and the photographer headed straight for the body; Eberhardt told Klein and one of the patrolmen—the other had stayed in the anteroom—to have a look around, and then made it a foursome around the dead man. The alcohol smell coming off Judkins' clothes was strong on the cold air; I retreated from it, across the center aisle, and stood waiting against one of the platform shelves.

Nine or ten minutes passed. I watched Klein and the patrolman poking around, peering at the windows and doors, checking for possible hiding places. The patrolman climbed up into the loft and shone his flashlight among the boxes and things. More light flashed over near the body as the photographer began taking his Polaroid shots.

Klein came back from the rear doors just as an assistant coroner bustled in from the anteroom; the two of them joined Eberhardt for a brief consultation, after which Klein disappeared up front, the coroner's man moved to the corpse and Eb came over to where I was.

"You got anything to add to what you told me on the phone?" he asked.

"Not much," I said. "There's nothing missing from among the merchandise in here, at least as far as I can tell, and the place is still sealed up tight. I tried calling Brinkman after I talked to you, but there was no answer."

"Any idea where he might be?"

"He said he had an engagement at seven-thirty. I figured it might be with the receptionist, Fran Robbins, because it looks like they've got a thing going. But there's nobody home at her place either; I found her number in Brinkman's address book and tried it."

"Dead man worked here, too, that right?"

I nodded. "He was the warehouseman."

"Was he around when you got here tonight?"

"No."

"How many other employees?"

"Just one. Bookkeeper named Orin McIntyre. But he's an ex-employee as of today."

"Oh? Quit or fired?"

"Fired," I said. "Brinkman told me his work wasn't up to par and that he couldn't afford McIntyre's salary. McIntyre left just after I got here; he didn't look any too happy."

"You think there might be a connection between that and the murder?"

"I don't know. I tried McIntyre's number, too, just before you came. Third straight no-answer."

"All right. Let's go over your story again, in detail this time. Don't leave anything out."

I gave him a complete rundown of the night's events as I knew them. And the more I talked, the more he glowered. What we had here was a mystery, and mysteries annoyed the hell out of him.

Klein returned just as I finished. He said to Eberhardt, "I looked around outside. Nothing in the parking lot or anywhere else in the vicinity."

"You check the doors and windows?"

"Yep. All secured with inside-locking shutters."

"You're certain they're locked?"

"Positive."

"Same thing in here, too, huh? With the gates?"

"Afraid so, Eb."

Eberhardt muttered something under his breath—and up front, in the anteroom, the telephone began to ring. I glanced at my watch. Almost midnight.

"That'll be Brinkman," I said. "He said he'd call about this time to check in."

"You get it," Eberhardt said to Klein. "Wherever he is, tell him to come here right away."

"Right."

When Klein had gone again Eb said to me, "What is it with you? Every time I turn around you're mixed up in some kind of screwball case."

I said wryly, "Where have you gone, Sam Spade?"

"How's that?"

"Just something I was thinking earlier today."

"Yeah, well, from now on try to keep it simple, will you? No more homicides. Do skip-traces or find somebody's missing cousin like other private eyes."

"At least I don't go around getting hit on the head."

"It wouldn't hurt you much if you did," he said.

The assistant coroner called to him before I could say anything else, and he went over for another short conference. Just after they broke it up, Klein reappeared from the anteroom. He and Eberhardt converged on me again.

Eb said, "Was that Brinkman?"

"Uh-huh. He'll be right down."

"Where was he calling from?"

"The apartment of one of his employees," Klein said, "a woman named Fran Robbins. He says he's

just given her a promotion and they've been celebrating all evening—at her place for dinner, then
out for a couple of drinks around ten. They just
got back. He sounded pretty upset when I told
him what'd happened here."

"Wouldn't you be?" Eberhardt got a leather
pouch out of his coat pocket and began thumbing
shag-cut tobacco into the bowl of his pipe, scowling all the while.

Klein asked him, "Coroner's man have anything
to say yet?"

"Confirmed the obvious, that's all. Shot once at
close range, death instantaneous or close to it.
Small-caliber weapon, looks like; we'll know what
size and make when the coroner digs out the
bullet and Ballistics gets hold of it."

I said speculatively, "Maybe a twenty-two with
a silencer."

"Why a silencer?"

"Because I didn't hear the shot."

"The gun could have been muffled with something else. Heavy cloth, cushion of some kind—
anything along those lines."

"Sure. But it was pitch-dark in here except for
the killer's flashlight; it'd be kind of awkward to
hold a flash on somebody and muffle and fire a
gun all at the same time."

"Well, a silencer seems just as doubtful," Eberhardt said. "They don't leave powder and scorch
marks like the ones on Judkins."

"Then why didn't I hear the shot?"

None of us had a ready answer for that. Klein
said, "What about the alcohol smell?"

"Wood alcohol, evidently," Eberhardt told him. "Judkins had a bottle of it zipped inside his jacket pocket; the bullet shattered the bottle on its way into him."

"Was he drinking it, you suppose?"

"He was crazy if he was; that stuff will destroy your insides. No way to be sure yet, though. There's a strong alcohol odor around the mouth, but it could be gin."

I said, "Was there anything else on the body?"

"Usual stuff people carry in their pockets."

"How much money in his wallet?"

"Fifty-eight dollars. You thinking robbery?"

"It's a possibility."

"Yeah, but not of Judkins so much as by him and somebody else. Of what's in this warehouse, I mean. That would explain what he and whoever killed him were doing here tonight."

"It would," I said, "except that it doesn't add up. Nothing seems to be missing; so if two guys come to a place to rob it, why would one of them shoot the other *before* the robbery?"

"And how did they get in and out in the first place?" Klein added.

Eberhardt jabbed his pipe in my direction. "Listen, are you sure you were alone when you locked up after Brinkman left?"

"Pretty sure," I said. "I came out here first thing and checked the windows and doors. Then I wandered around for a while, looking things over. I didn't see or hear anything."

"But somebody—Judkins, say—*could* have been hiding in here, just the same."

"It's possible, I guess. Up in the loft, maybe; I didn't go up there. But Brinkman told me Judkins had gone for the day, and it just isn't reasonable that he could've slipped back in without somebody seeing him. And I still think I'd have felt something. You know when you're alone and when you're not alone, at least most of the time. You get what the kids nowadays call vibes."

"Yeah," Eberhardt said. "Vibes."

Klein said, "Even if Judkins was hiding in here, what was the point in it? To steal something? Hell, he worked here; he could have committed theft during business hours. And it doesn't explain how the killer got in and out either."

"There's one explanation that'll cover all of that," I said. "But I don't like it much; it's pretty farfetched."

"Go ahead."

"Nobody got in and out of here because there's no killer. Judkins committed suicide."

Everhardt made a growling noise. "Suicide," he said, as if it were a dirty word. "If he shot himself, where the hell is the gun?"

"He could've dropped it somewhere and staggered down here and fallen where he is now. A thorough search would turn it up."

"Why would he pick a place like this to knock himself off in?"

"He wasn't too bright, Eb. Suppose he hated Brinkman for some reason and figured the publicity would damage the business. Suppose he wanted familiar surroundings when he pulled the trigger . . ." I spread my hands because Eberhardt was shaking his head in a disgusted way. "Well, I told you it was pretty farfetched," I said.

"The other possibilities are just as improbable," Klein said. "One person, or even two, could have been hiding in here tonight without you realizing it, but there's nobody hiding in here now. Which means Judkins' killer had to get out, if not in—and how could he do that when all the doors and windows are double- or triple-sealed?"

"Maybe he's a magician or a ghost," Eberhardt said with heavy sarcasm. "Maybe he walked through the damned wall."

The patrolman who had been searching the warehouse came up and reported that he hadn't found anything of significance, unless you wanted to count an empty gin bottle tucked under some rags in the loft. Then a couple of white-coated interns entered with a stretcher and a body bag, and Eberhardt moved over to talk to the assistant coroner again before he gave them permission to remove the body. Klein, at Eb's instructions, returned to the anteroom to try again to get in touch with Orin McIntyre.

And I went into Brinkman's office, where it was quiet, to drink another cup of coffee from my thermos and do some thinking.

VI.

It was twelve thirty-five when Brinkman showed up. He came sailing in with Fran Robbins on one arm, looking more agitated than ever; his hands fluttered here and there, creating more of those invisible things out of the air. Robbins looked bewildered, nervous and a little frightened. She kept brushing a lock of her red hair out of one eye and casting glances around the anteroom as though she'd never seen it before.

Brinkman veered over to where I was standing in the doorway to his office. He gave me an accusing glare, as if he thought I had betrayed him somehow, and breathed stale tobacco and whiskey fumes at me; the heavy sweetness of enough cologne for a regiment was almost as unpleasant.

"What's been going on here tonight?" he demanded. "The officer on the phone told me Frank Judkins is dead, murdered."

"I'm afraid so, Mr. Brinkman."

"But how? By whom?"

"He was shot," I said. "The police don't know who did it yet. They think maybe you can help them."

"How can I help them? I don't even know what's going on." He fumbled a package of cigarettes from the pocket of his brown suit coat, got one into his mouth and fired it. "Is anything missing, stolen? Could it have been robbery?"

"Nothing stolen as far as I could tell," I said. "You'll be able to judge that a lot better yourself after you've talked to Lieutenant Eberhardt."

"Is he the man in charge?"

"Yes. He's out in the warehouse."

Brinkman nodded, started to turn away and then faced me again. "Orin McIntyre," he said, as if he were making some sort of revelation. Maybe *he* had something to do with this. You heard what he said to me tonight. He's always struck me as the vindictive sort."

"The police got him on the phone a little while ago," I said. "McIntyre claims he spent the evening barhopping alone, drowning his anger at being fired, and didn't get home until just before midnight."

Brinkman's cigarette bobbed and weaved in his restless fingers. "Do the police believe that?"

"They're reserving judgment until they check out his story. Lieutenant Eberhardt sent a patrol car for him; he'll be here pretty soon."

Brinkman hung his cigarette on his lower lip, said, "I'll go talk to the lieutenant," and headed through the warehouse doorway trailing smoke. Fran Robbins hesitated, glancing at me and biting her lip, and then went after him; the patrolman by the door watched the movement of her hips with the intensity and admiration of a confirmed ladies' man.

I shut the office door and returned to Brinkman's desk and poured the last of the coffee into my cup. It was quiet in the room—but not at all quiet inside my head. Things had begun to go clickety-click in there, like a sturdy old engine warming up and about to run smoothly.

I sat on a corner of the desk, sipping coffee and concentrating. Vague ideas sharpened and took on weight and shape; bits and pieces of information slotted themselves neatly into place. And finally—

"Sure," I said aloud. "Hell, yes."

I went into the anteroom, through the warehouse door and past the shipping counter. Ahead, near where Judkins' body had lain, Eberhardt and Klein were talking to Brinkman and Fran Robbins. And to Orin McIntyre. It surprised me that McIntyre was there; I hadn't heard him being brought in. But when I looked at my watch I saw that it was one o'clock. A good twenty minutes had passed since the arrival of Brinkman and Robbins; I had been so deep in thought that I had lost track of both the time and my surroundings.

McIntyre, I saw as I came up, looked rumpled and bleary-eyed and upset. He was talking to Eberhardt but glaring at Brinkman as he spoke. "I didn't have a damned thing to do with what happened to Judkins. I told you, I was out drinking all evening."

"You haven't told us where," Eberhardt said.

"I don't remember where." McIntyre's voice was still a little slurred; he rubbed at his slack mouth." A bunch of bars out in the Noe Valley. Listen—"

"You never did get along with Judkins," Brinkman interrupted. "You were always arguing with him."

"That was because he was a half-wit. And you're a bastard, Brinkman—a lousy bastard."

"I don't have to take that from you," Brinkman said indignantly. "For all I know, you *did* murder poor Judkins—"

I said, "No, McIntyre didn't do it."

All eyes flicked toward me. Eberhardt took the pipe out of his mouth and waved it in my direction. "How do you know that?"

"Because," I said, "Brinkman did it."

VII.

Fran Robbins made a little gasping sound. Surprise opened up Brinkman's face for an instant: guilt flickered there like a film clip on a screen. Then it was gone and his stare was full of shocked indignation.

"You're crazy," he said. He turned and appealed to Eberhardt. "He's crazy."

Eb said, "Maybe," and narrowed his eyes at me. "Well?"

"He did it, all right."

"You got proof to back that up?"

"Enough," I said, which was not quite the truth. All I had were solid deductions based on circumstantial evidence and plain logic. But I knew I was right. There was only one person who could have killed Judkins and only one way the whole thing made sense; it was a simple matter of eliminating the impossible, so that whatever you had left had to be the answer. So I was pretty sure I could prove, at least to Eberhardt's satisfaction, that Brinkman *had* to be the murderer. After that it would be up to Eberhardt to make a homicide charge stick.

McIntyre said, "I might have known it," in a satisfied voice. His eyes were still on Brinkman, and they were wolfish now.

Brinkman drew himself up, all bluff and bluster, and ripped at the air with his hands. "This accusation is ridiculous," he said to Eberhardt. "I had nothing to do with what happened here tonight. I spent the entire evening with Fran; I've already told you that."

"So you have. Is that your story, too, miss?"

Robbins looked at Brinkman, wet her lips and said, "Yes." But the word came out almost as a question. She sounded anxious and uncertain.

I said, "You're sure about that, Miss Robbins? Being an accessory to insurance fraud is a minor offense; being an accessory to murder gets you a lot of years in prison."

That sharpened the anxiety and confusion in her eyes. She put a hand on Brinkman's arm. "Arthur?"

"It's all right, Fran. He doesn't know what the hell he's talking about."

Eberhardt asked me, "What's this about insurance fraud?"

"That was the idea from the beginning," I told him. "This outfit isn't as profitable as Brinkman wants people to believe; I think he's been operating in the red and doesn't have enough capital to pay off on the merchandise that just came in from Europe, or enough buyers to take it all off his hands." I looked at McIntyre. "Am I right, Mr. McIntyre?"

"Damn right," he said. "I warned Brinkman about making the deal; I told him it was liable to put the company under. He told me to mind my own business and went ahead with it anyway. But how did you know?"

"Some inferences you made yesterday, for one thing. He also let it slip tonight that one of the reasons he fired you was that he couldn't afford your salary. And there are only a small number of purchase orders on the shipping counter, not enough to account for more than a third of the total shipment."

"So what are you suggesting?" Eberhardt said.

"That the same bright idea occurred to Brinkman that's occurred to too many small businessmen these days," I said. "Burn the place down and collect the insurance."

I watched Brinkman as I spoke. Still all bluff and bluster, still plucking away at the air; the shrewd eyes weren't admitting anything.

"Only he was smart enough to realize arson would be suspected and there'd be a thorough investigation," I went on. "So he decided to set up a neat bit of camouflage. Hire a private detective with a good reputation to act as nightwatchman, arrange an alibi for himself and then have a fire started right under the detective's nose. I wasn't supposed to get hurt; I was supposed to testify later that I was alone in a completely impenetrable building when the fire broke out. Nobody could have set it except me, and I'd be exonerated because of my record. The cause would go down as spontaneous combustion, which wouldn't be hard to believe with all the straw packing and excelsior lying around in here; he'd already planted the seed by warning me to watch out for fire during my rounds. The insurance company would have no recourse except to pay off on the claim."

"You're making sense so far," Eberhardt said. "Now where does Judkins come into it? The hired torch?"

I nodded. "He had to be. It explains the wood

alcohol he had in his pocket. That stuff is inflammable as hell; you can use it to start a dandy fire."

"But then why would Brinkman kill Judkins before he could torch the building?"

"It doesn't figure to be a premeditated homicide; murder was never part of the original plan. Judkins died because of something that happened between him and Brinkman tonight, something that made Brinkman come down here around ten o'clock—"

"I don't have to listen to any more of this," Brinkman said. His expression still showed defiance, but a muscle had begun to jump under his left eye so that he seemed to be winking spasmodically. He lit another cigarette. "I wasn't anywhere near here at ten o'clock, I tell you. I was with Fran—"

I said, "You went straight to her apartment when you left here at six?"

"That's right."

"And had dinner and then went out for a few drinks afterward?"

"Yes."

"Then why did you change clothes?"

"What?"

"You were wearing a gray sports jacket when you left here; now you're wearing a brown suit. Why the change? And when and where? Unless maybe you got the gray jacket wet and bloody when you shot Judkins, and went home to change before you went *back* to Miss Robbins' apartment. And why splash yourself with so much cologne? You weren't wearing any earlier tonight, and now you reek of it. Unless it was to cover up the smell of wood alcohol; it was all over Judkins' body, and if it got all over you, too, you wouldn't be able to get rid of the odor just by taking a shower."

The muscle kept on jumping under Brinkman's eye. He looked over at Fran Robbins; she had long since let go of his arm and backed off a couple of steps. She would not look at him now; there was a dark flush on both cheeks. She was just starting to admit to herself that he really was a murderer, and once she accepted the truth she would turn on him. That would be all Eberhardt needed.

"Keep talking," Eb said to me. "Something happened between Brinkman and Judkins tonight?"

"Right. An argument of some kind, probably over how much Judkins was to be paid. Maybe he tried to shake Brinkman down for a bigger payoff before he did the job. In any case, they met here, and one of them brought a gun, and Judkins ended up getting shot dead."

"Are you saying the shooting took place outside or inside?"

"Outside. That's why I didn't hear the shot; the wind muffled it."

"Then why put the body in here?"

"Because it probably seemed like the best alternative at the time. If Brinkman left it outside for somebody to find, the arson scheme would be spoiled and the police investigation might implicate him. And taking the body away somewhere was too risky. Both he and Judkins had to have come here on foot, because they wouldn't have wanted to alert me by driving into the lot; he couldn't carry the dead man all the way to wherever he'd left his car, and he couldn't bring the car onto the grounds for that same fear of alerting me.

"But if he took the body inside and started the fire himself, there was a chance the corpse would be burned badly enough to conceal the fact that Judkins had died from a gunshot wound. Which wouldn't have happened, forensic medicine being what it is today; but he had to have been rattled and desperate, and it looked to him like his only way out. And afterward he could claim that Judkins had set the fire on his own, for his own reasons, and been caught in it and died as a result. The insurance company, at least as he saw it, would still have to pay off.

"Only that plan backfired, too. He's a small guy and Judkins was a big guy; he got the body in here all right, but he lost control of it as he was setting it down. It landed on top of a crate and made that loud thudding noise I heard. Brinkman knew I'd come to investigate, and he was afraid I'd see him and recognize him; he panicked, shut off the flashlight he'd been using and got out."

Brinkman was standing ramrod stiff, both hands bunched together at his waist, his head wreathed in cigarette smoke. The only change in the way he looked was in the color of his face; it had gone paper-white.

"Now we come to the sixty-four-dollar question," Eberhardt said. "This place was sealed inside and out, like a damned tomb; it still is. How was Judkins supposed to get inside in the first place, and how did Brinkman get inside with the body?"

I said, "You told me the answer to that yourself a little while ago, Eb."

"*I* told you?"

"You said something sarcastic about the killer maybe walking through a wall. But you were right; that's just what Brinkman did."

"Don't give me double-talk, damn it. Say what you mean."

"He came in through the window," I said.

"Window? What window?"

I pointed to the nearest of the two in the left-hand wall, the one closest to where I had found Judkins' body. "That window."

"Nuts," Eberhardt said. "The gate is padlocked, I can see that from here. And the outside shutter is locked down—"

"Now it is," I said.

"What?"

"Eb, the beauty of Brinkman's little plan is that it's simple and it's obvious—so obvious that everybody overlooked it." I went to the window and demonstrated as I talked. "Like this: I come in here on my rounds and I test the padlock on the gate; it's firmly in place. I glance through the bars, and what do I see in this dim light? The window is closed and the shutter is lowered outside. So I automatically assume, just as anybody would, that both the window catch and the shutter catch are locked, because I *expect* them to be and because I *know* the gate is locked. For that same reason I don't bother to reach through and check either one.

"But the fact is, neither the window nor the shutter was locked at that time; just closed far enough to make me think they were. And the only person who could have rigged them that way is Brinkman. He was the one who locked up tonight. He even asked me to double-check him; he figured his little trick was foolproof, and he wanted my testimony that the building was sealed when the fire broke out.

"What he did after he shot Judkins was to lift the shutter from outside, then the window sash—slow and quiet so I wouldn't hear anything—and then reach through the bars, open the gate padlock with his key and swing the gate to one side. On his way out after he dropped the body, he closed the gate and relocked the padlock. Then he lowered the window—a little too hard in his haste, which explains the thumping sound I heard. But he couldn't have secured the window latch from the outside . . ."

I reached through the bars, caught hold of the sash and tugged. It glided upward a few inches in well-oiled shots. "And he didn't. The clicking noise I heard just before putting on the lights was him closing the shutter hard enough to make its latch catch at the bottom—something he *could* do from the outside."

"And with all the inside gates and outside shutters in place," Klein said, "who'd think to try one of the windows sandwiched between them? Or attach the right significance to it if they did." He shook his head. "I see what you mean by simple and obvious."

Brinkman saw, too. He saw the expression on Fran Robbins' face: anger and fear and a congealing hatred. He saw the expression on McIntyre's face, and on the faces of the law. All the bluff went out of him at once, and along with it whatever inner force had been holding him together; the cigarette fell out of his mouth and he sat down hard on one of the crates, like a doll with sand-stuffed legs, and covered up his own face with both hands.

They never learn, I thought. The clever ones especially—they just never learn. . . .

VIII.

"The way it happened with Judkins," Eberhardt said, "was pretty much as you called it. He telephoned Brinkman at Fran Robbins' apartment and told him he'd been thinking things over and didn't want to go ahead with the torch job for the five hundred dollars Brinkman was paying him; he wanted another five hundred, and he wanted it right away. Brinkman tried to tell him he didn't have that much cash available, but Judkins wouldn't listen. Either Brinkman delivered the money immediately or not only wouldn't he set the fire, he'd blow the whistle to the insurance company."

"I told you Judkins wasn't very smart," I said.

"Yeah." Eberhardt fired up the tobacco in his pipe. It was the following afternoon and we were sitting in a tavern on Union Street, having a companionable beer—his treat—before he headed down to the Hall of Justice for his evening tour of duty. "Anyhow, Brinkman didn't have any choice; he agreed to meet Judkins and did, just outside the company grounds. All he had on him was fifty bucks, but he promised Judkins the rest as soon as he could get it."

"Only Judkins wasn't having any of that, right?"

"Right. He was half-drunk on gin, Brinkman says, and in a belligerent mood; and he'd brought a gun with him. He started waving it around, making threats, and Brinkman got scared and ran into the lot toward the building. He says he was going to call to you for help. But Judkins caught up with him; there was a struggle, and the gun went off. End of Judkins. Brinkman threw the gun—a twenty-five-caliber Browning—away later, into a trash bin a couple of blocks from there. He led us right to it. Cooperating to beat the band, which probably means he'll cop a plea later on."

"Uh-huh. What did he tell Robbins when he got back to her place?"

"Fed her a line about some hardcases being the ones who wanted to burn down his company for the insurance; said he had to go along with them or they'd muscle him around—that kind of thing. So would she say he was with her all evening? She went along with it; she's not too bright either. After he called the company and talked to Klein, he told her it must have been the hardcases who'd killed Judkins. She went along with that, too, until you laid everything out in the warehouse. Now she can't wait to testify against him."

"Good for her."

"One other thing, in case you're wondering: Brinkman giving McIntyre the sack doesn't fit into it, except as a ploy to throw off the insurance investigators even more. Would a businessman about to burn down his own company fire one employee on the day of the blaze, and promote another? Like that."

"Cute. And when things got tough, he tried to steer the blame for Judkins' death onto McIntyre—the old vendetta motive."

"Some smart guy, that Brinkman."

"Some *dumb* guy," I said. "Judkins may not have been very bright, and Fran Robbins may not be either. But Brinkman's the dumbest of the three."

"Yeah. I wish they were all like that—all the damned criminals." Eberhardt picked up his beer. "Here's to crime," he said.

"I'll drink to that," I said, and we did.

Late that afternoon I drove across the Golden Gate Bridge for an early dinner in Sausalito. I got a window table in one of the restaurants built out into the Bay; the weather had cleared, and it was near sunset, and from there I had a fine view of the San Francisco skyline across the water.

It was a beautiful city when you saw it like this—all the buildings shining gold in the dying sunlight, the bridges and the islands and the dazzling water and the East Bay and Marin hills surrounding it. It was only when you got down into its bowels, when you came in contact with the people—the few bad ones spoiling things for the rest—that it became something else. A jungle. A breeding ground for evil, a place of tragedy and unhappiness.

I loved that city; I had been born there and I had spent half a century there and you couldn't have paid me enough to make me move anywhere else. But sometimes, my job being what it was, it made me angry and sad. Sometimes, in a lot of ways, it made me afraid.

The waitress had brought me a beer and I lifted my glass. Here's to crime, I thought, but I didn't drink to it this time.

I drank to the city instead.

And I drank to the victims.

Dead Man's Slough

I was halfway through one of the bends in Dead Man's Slough, on my way back to the Whiskey Island marina with three big Delta catfish in the skiff beside me, when the red-haired man rose up out of the water at an islet fifty yards ahead.

It was the last thing I expected to see and I leaned forward, squinting through the boat's Plexiglas windscreen. The weather was full of early-November bluster—high overcast and a raw wind—and the water was too cold and too choppy for pleasure swimming. Besides which, the red-haired guy was fully dressed in khaki trousers and a short-sleeved bush jacket.

He came all the way out of the slough, one hand clapped across the back of his head, and plowed upward through the mud and grass of a tiny natural beach. When he got to its upper edge where the tule grass grew thick and waist-high, he stopped and held a listening pose. Then he whirled around, stood swaying unsteadily as if he were caught in a crosscurrent of the chill wind. He stared out toward me for two or three seconds;

the pale oval of his face might have been pulled
into a painful grimace, but I couldn't tell for sure
at the distance. And then he whirled again in a
dazed, frightened way, stumbled in among the
rushes and disappeared.

I looked upstream past the islet, where Dead
Man's Slough widened into a long reach; the wa-
terway was empty, and so were the willow-lined
levees that flanked it. Nor was there any sign of
another boat or another human being in the wide
channel that bounded the islet on the south. That
was not surprising, at least it wouldn't have been
five minutes ago.

The California Delta, fifty miles inland from
San Francisco where the Sacramento and San Joa-
quin rivers merge on a course to San Francisco
Bay, has a thousand miles of waterways and a
network of islands both large and small, inhabited
and uninhabited, linked by seventy bridges and a
few hundred miles of levee roads. During the
summer months the area is jammed with vaca-
tioners, water skiers, fishermen and houseboaters,
but in late fall, when the cold winds start to blow,
about the only people you'll find are local mer-
chants and farmers and a few late-vacationing
anglers like me. I had seen no more than four
other people and two other boats in the five hours
since I'd left Whiskey Island, and none of those in
the half-mile I had just traveled on Dead Man's
Slough.

So where had the red-haired man come from?

On impulse I twisted the wheel and took the
skiff over toward the islet, cutting back on the

throttle as I approached. Wind gusts rustled and bent the carpet of tule grass, but there was no other movement that I could see. Ten yards off the beach, I shut the throttle all the way down to idle; the quick movement of the water carried the skiff the rest of the way in. When the bow scraped up over the soft mud I shut off the engine, pocketed the ignition key and moved aft to tilt the outboard engine out of the water so its propeller blades wouldn't become fouled in the offshore grass. Then I climbed out and dragged half the boat's length onto the beach as a precaution against it backsliding and drifting off without me.

From the upper rim of the beach I could look all across the flat width of the islet—maybe fifty yards in all—and for seventy yards or so of its length, to where the terrain humped up in the middle and a pair of willow trees and several wild blackberry bushes blocked off my view. But I couldn't see anything of the red-haired man, or hear anything of him either; there were no sounds except for the low whistling cry of the wind.

An eerie feeling came over me. It was as if I were alone on the islet, alone on all of Dead Man's Slough, and the red-haired guy had been some sort of hallucination. Or some sort of ghostly manifestation. I thought of the old-timer who had rented me the skiff on Whiskey Island—a sort of local historian well versed on Delta lore and legends dating back to the Gold Rush, when steamboats from San Francisco and Sacramento plied these waters with goods and passengers. And I thought of the story he had told me about how the slough got its name.

Back in 1860 an Irish miner named O'Farrell, on his way to San Francisco from the diggings near Sutter's Mill, had disappeared from a sidewheeler at Poker Bend; also missing was a fortune in gold dust and specie he had been carrying with him. Three days later O'Farrell's body was found floating in these waters with his head bashed in and his pockets empty. The murder was never solved. And old-time rivermen swore they had seen the miner's ghost abroad on certain foggy nights, swearing vengeance on the man who had murdered him.

But that wasn't quite all. According to the details of the story, O'Farrell had had red hair—and his ghost was always seen clutching the back of his bloody head with one hand.

Sure, I thought, and nuts to that. Pure coincidence, nothing else. Old-time rivermen were forever seeing ghosts, not only of men but of packets like the *Sagamore* and the *R.K. Page* whose steam boilers had exploded during foolish races in the mid-1800s, killing hundreds of passengers and crewmen. But I did not believe in spooks worth a damn. Nor was I prone to hallucinations or flights of imagination, not at my age and not with my temperament. The red-haired guy was real, all right. Maybe hurt and in trouble, too, judging from his wobbly condition and his actions.

So where had he gone? If he was hiding somewhere in the rushes I couldn't tell the location by looking from here, or even where he had gone into them; tule grass is pretty resilient and tends to spring back up even after a man plows through it. He could also have gone to the eastern end, beyond the high ground in the middle. The one thing I was sure of was that he was still on the islet: I could see out into the wide channels on the north and south sides, and if he had gone swimming again he would have been visible.

I pulled up the collar on my pea jacket and headed into the rushes on a zigzag course, calling out as I went, offering help if he needed it. Nobody answered me. And there was no sign of any red hair as I worked my way along. After a time I stopped, and when I scanned upward toward the higher ground I saw that I was within thirty yards of the line of blackberry bushes.

I also saw a man come hurrying up onto the hump from the opposite side, between the two willow trees.

He saw me, too, and halted abruptly, and we stood staring at each other across the windswept terrain. But he wasn't the red-haired guy. He was dark-looking, heavier, and he wore Levi's, a plaid mackinaw and a gray fisherman's hat decorated with bright-colored flies. In one hand, held in a vertical position, was a thick-butted fishing rod.

"Hello up there!" I called to him, but he didn't give me any response. Just stood poised, peering down at me like a wary animal scenting for danger. Which left the first move up to me. I took my hands out of my coat pockets and slow-walked toward him over the marshy earth. He stayed where he was, not moving except to slant the fishing rod across the front of his body, weapon-like. When I got past the blackberry bushes I was ten feet from him, on the firmer ground of the hump; I decided that was far enough and stopped there.

We did some more looking at each other. He was about my age, early fifties, with a craggy outdoorsman's face and eyes the color of butter-scotch. There was no anxiety in his expression, nor any hostility either; it was just the set, waiting look of a man on his guard.

Past him I could see the rest of the islet—another sixty yards or so of flattish terrain dominated by shrubs and tules, with a mistletoe-festooned pepper tree off to the left and a narrow rock shelf at the far end. Tied up alongside the shelf was what looked to be a fourteen-foot outboard similar to my rented skiff, except that it sported a gleaming green-and-white paint job. There was nothing else to see along there, or in the choppy expanses of water surrounding us.

Pretty soon the craggy guy said, "Who are you?"

"Just another fisherman," I said, which was more relevant and less provocative than telling him I was a private investigator from San Francisco. "Have you been here long?"

"A little while. Why?"

"Alone?"

"That's right. But I heard *you* shouting to somebody."

"Nobody I know," I said. "A red-haired man I saw drag himself out of the slough a few minutes ago."

He stared at me. "What?"

"Sounds funny, I know, but it's the truth. He was fully dressed and he looked hurt; he disappeared into the tules. I put my boat in and I've been hunting around for him, but no luck so far. You haven't seen him, I take it?"

"No," the craggy guy said. "I haven't seen anybody since I put in after crayfish an hour ago." He paused. "You say this red-haired man was hurt?"

"Seemed that way, yes."

"Bad?"

"Maybe. He looked dazed."

"You think he could have had a boating accident?"

"Could be. But he also seemed scared."

"Scared? Of what?"

"No idea. You heard me shouting, so he must have heard me, too; but he still hasn't shown himself. That might mean he's hiding because he's afraid to be found."

"Might mean something else, too," the craggy guy said. "He could have gone back into the water and swum across to one of the other islands."

"I don't think so. I would have seen him if he'd done that anywhere off this side; and I guess you'd have seen him if he'd done it anywhere off the other side."

"He could also be dead by now if he was hurt as bad as you seem to think."

"That's a possibility," I said. "Or maybe just unconscious. How about helping me look for him so we can find out?"

The craggy guy hesitated. He was still wary; the

way a lot of people are of strangers these days—as if he were not quite convinced I was telling him a straight story and thinking that maybe I had designs on his money or his life. But after a time he said, "All right; if there's a man hurt around here, he'll need all the help he can get. Where did you see him come out of the water?"

I turned a little and pointed behind me. "Back there. You can see part of my boat; that's about where it was."

"So if he's still on the island, he's somewhere between here and your boat."

"Seems that way," I said. "Unless he managed to slip over where you were without your seeing him."

"I doubt that. I've got pretty sharp eyes."

"Sure." I thought I might as well introduce myself; maybe that would reassure him. So I gave my name, with a by-the-way after it, and waited while he made up his mind whether or not he wanted to reciprocate.

"Jackson," he said finally. "Herb Jackson."

"Nice to know you, Mr. Jackson. How about if we each take one side and work back toward my skiff?"

He said that was okay with him and we fanned out away from each other, me into the vegetation on the south side. We each used a switchbacking course from the center out to the edges, where the ground was boggy and the footing a little treacherous. Both of us kept silent, but all you could hear were the keening of the wind and the whispery rustle of the tules as I spread through them with my hands and Jackson probed through them with his fishing rod. I caught him looking over at me a couple of times as if he wanted to make sure I intended to stay on my half of the turf.

Neither of us found anything. The only things hidden among the rushes were occasional rocks and chunks of decaying driftwood; and there was no way anybody could have concealed himself in the sparse offshore grasses. You're always hearing about how people submerge in shallow water and breathe through a hollow reed, and maybe that's a possibility in places like Florida and Louisiana, but not in California. Tule grass isn't hollow and you can't breathe through its stalks; you'd swallow water and probably drown if you tried it.

It took us ten minutes to make our way back and down to where my rented boat was. I got there first, and when Jackson came up he halted a good eight feet away and looked down at the empty beach, into the empty skiff, across the empty slough at the empty levee on the far side. Then he put his butterscotch eyes on me.

I said, "He's got to be over where you were somewhere. We've gone over all the ground on this end."

"If he's on the island at all," Jackson said.

"Well, he's got to be." A thought occurred to me. "The outboard on your boat—do you start it with an ignition key or by hand?"

"Key. Why?"

"Did you leave it in the ignition or have you got it with you?"

"In my pocket," he said. "What're you thinking? That he might try to steal my boat?"

"It could happen. But it wouldn't do him much good without power. Unless you keep oars for an emergency."

"No oars." Jackson looked a little worried now, as though he might be imagining his boat adrift and in the hands of a mysterious redheaded stranger. "Damn it, you could be right."

He set off at a soggy run, bulling his way through the rushes and shrubs, slashing at them with whiplike sweeps of the rod. I went after him, off to one side and at a slower pace. He reached the blackberry bushes, cut past them onto the hump and pulled up near the drooping fan of branches on one willow. Then I saw him relax and take a couple of deep breaths; he turned to wait for me.

When I got up there I could see that his boat was still tied alongside the empty rock shelf. The channels beyond were a couple hundred yards wide at the narrowest point; you could swim that distance easily enough in fifteen minutes—but not on a day like this, with that wind whipping up the water to a froth, and not when you were hurt and so unsteady on your feet you couldn't walk without stumbling.

"So he's still on the island," I said to Jackson. "It shouldn't take us long to find him now."

He had nothing to say to that; he just turned toward the willow, spread the branches, looked in among them and at the ones higher up. I went over and did the same thing at the second tree.

The red-haired man was not hiding in either of them—and he wasn't hiding among the blackberry bushes or anywhere else on or near the hump.

We started down toward Jackson's boat, one on each side as before. Rocks, more pieces of driftwood, a rusted coffee can, the carcass of some sort of large bird—nothing else. The pepper tree was on my side, and I paused at the bole and peered up through pungent leaves and thick clusters of mistletoe. Nothing. The shoreline on this end was rockier, with shrubs and nettles growing along it instead of tule grass; but there was nobody concealed there, not on my half and not on Jackson's.

Where is he? I thought. He couldn't have just disappeared into thin air. *Where is he?*

The eerie feeling came back over me as I neared the rock shelf; in spite of myself I thought again of O'Farrell, the murdered Gold Rush miner, and his ghost that was supposed to haunt Dead Man's Slough. I shook the thought away, but I didn't feel any better after I had.

I reached the shelf before Jackson and stopped abaft the boat. She was a sleek little lady, not more than a year old, with bright chrome fittings to go with the green-and-white paint job; the outboard was a thirty-five-horsepower Evinrude. In the stern, I saw then, was a tackle box, a wicker creel, an Olympic spincast outfit and a nifty Shakespeare graphite-and-fiberglass rod. A heavy sheepskin jacket was draped over the back of the naugahyde seat.

When I heard Jackson come up near me a few

seconds later I pivoted around to face him. He said, "I don't like this at all."

Neither did I, not one bit. "Yeah," I said.

He gave me a narrow look. He had that rod slanted across the front of his body again. "You sure you're not just playing games with me, mister?"

"Why would I want to play games with you?"

"I don't know. All I know is we've been over the entire island without finding this redhead of yours. There's nothing here except tule grass and shrubs and three trees; we couldn't have overlooked anything as big as a man."

"I guess not," I said.

"Then where is he—if he exists at all?"

"Dead, maybe."

"Dead?"

"He's not on the island; that means he had to have tried swimming across one of the channels. But you or I would've seen him at some point if he'd got halfway across any of them."

"You think he drowned?"

"I'm afraid so," I said. "He was hurt and probably weak—and that water is turbulent and ice-cold. Unless he was an exceptionally strong swimmer and in the best possible shape, he couldn't have lasted long."

Jackson thought that over, rubbing fingertips along his craggy jaw. "You might be right, at that," he said. "So what do we do now?"

"There's not much we can do. One of us should notify the county sheriff, but that's about all. The body'll turn up sooner or later."

"Sure," Jackson said. "Tell you what: I'll call the sheriff from the camp in Hogback Slough; I'm heading in there right away."

"Would you do that?"

"Be glad to. No problem."

"Well, thanks. He can reach me on Whiskey Island if he wants to talk to me about it."

"I'll tell him that."

He nodded to me, lowered the rod a little, then moved past me to the boat. I retreated a dozen yards over the rocky ground, watching him as he untied the bowline from a shrub and climbed in under the wheel. Thirty seconds later, when I was halfway up to the willow trees, the outboard made a guttural rumbling noise and its propeller blades began churning the water. Jackson maneuvered backward away from the shelf, waved as he shifted into a forward gear and opened the throttle wide; the boat got away in a hurry, bow lifting under the surge of power. From up on the hump I watched it dwindle as he cut down the center of the southern channel toward the entrance to Hogback Slough.

So much for Herb Jackson, I thought then. Now I could start worrying about the red-haired man again.

What I had said about being afraid he'd drowned was a lie. But he was not a ghost and he had not pulled any magical vanishing act; he was still here, and I was pretty sure he was still alive. It was just that Jackson and I had overlooked something—and it had not occurred to me what it was until Jackson said there was nothing here except tule grass and shrubs and three trees. That was not quite true. There *was* something else on the islet, and it made one place we had failed to search; that was where the man had to be.

I went straight to it, hurrying, and when I got there I said my name again in a loud voice and added that I was a detective from San Francisco. Then I said, "He's gone now; there's nobody around but me. You're safe."

Nothing happened for fifteen seconds. Then there were sounds and struggling movement, and I waded in quickly to help him with some careful lifting and pushing.

And there he was, burrowing free of a depression in the soft mud, out from under my rented skiff just above the waterline where I had beached the forward half of it.

When he was clear of the boat I released my grip on the gunwale and eased him up on his feet. He kept trying to talk, but he was in no shape for that yet; most of what he said was gibberish. I got him into the skiff, wrapped him in a square of canvas from the stern—he was shivering so badly you could almost hear his bones clicking together—and cleaned some of the mud off him. The area behind his right ear was pulpy and badly lacerated, but if he was lucky he didn't have anything worse than a concussion.

While I was doing that he calmed down enough to be coherent, and the first thing he said was, "He tried to kill me. He tried to murder me."

"I figured as much. What happened?"

"We were in his boat; we'd just put in to the island because he said there was something wrong with the ignition. He asked me to take a look, so I pulled off my coat and leaned down under the wheel. Then my head seemed to explode. The next thing I knew, I was floundering in the south-side channel."

"He hit you with that fishing rod of his, probably," I said. "The current carried you along after he dumped you overboard and the cold water brought you around. Why does he want you dead?"

"It must be the insurance. We own a company in Sacramento and we have a partnership policy—double indemnity for accidental death. I knew Frank was in debt, but I never thought he'd go this far."

"Frank? Then his name isn't Herb Jackson?"

"No. It's Saunders, Frank Saunders. Mine's Rusty McGuinn."

Irish, I thought. Like O'Farrell. That figures.

I got out again to slide the skiff off the beach and into the slough. When I clambered back in, McGuinn said, "You knew he was after me, didn't you? That's why you didn't give me away when the two of you were together."

"Not exactly." I started the engine and got us under way at a good clip upstream. "I didn't have any idea who you were or where you'd come from until I looked inside Jackson's—or Saunders'—boat. He told me he was alone and he'd put in after crayfish. But he was carrying one rod and there were two more casting outfits in the boat; you don't need all that stuff for crayfish; and no fisherman alone is likely to carry *three* outfits for any reason. There was a heavy sheepskin jacket there, too, draped over the seat; but he was already wearing a heavy mackinaw, and I remembered you only had on a short-sleeved jacket when you came out of the water. It all began to add up then. I talked him into leaving as soon as I could."

"How did you do that?"

"By telling him what he wanted to hear—that you must be dead."

"But how did you know where I was hiding?"

I explained how Saunders had triggered the answer for me. "I also tried to put myself in your place. You were hurt and scared; your first thought would be to get away as fast as possible. Which meant by boat, not by swimming. So it figured you hid nearby until I was far enough away and then slipped back to the skiff.

"But this boat—like Sauders'—starts with a key, and I had it with me. You could have set yourself adrift, but then Saunders might have seen you and come chasing in his boat. In your condition it made sense you might burrow under the skiff, with a little space clear at one side so you could breathe."

"Well, I owe you a debt," McGuinn said. "You saved my life."

"Forget it," I said, a little ruefully. Because the truth was I had almost got him killed. I had told Saunders he was on the island and insisted on a two-man search party; and I had failed to tumble to who and what Saunders was until it was almost too late. If McGuinn hadn't been so well hidden, if we'd found him, Saunders would probably have jumped me and I might not have been able to handle him; McGuinn and I could both be dead now. I'm not a bad detective, usually; other times, though, I'm a near bust.

The channel that led to Whiskey Island loomed ahead. Cheer up, I told myself—the important thing is that this time, 120 years after the first one, the red-haired Irish bludgeon victim is being brought out alive and the man who assaulted him is sure to wind up in prison. The ghost of O'Farrell, the Gold Rush miner, won't have any company when it goes prowling and swearing vengeance on those foggy nights in Dead Man's Slough.

Who's Calling?

I.

Wednesday morning, late January.

The weather was good, clear and mostly warm, but with a nip in the air that reminded you there was still some icy wind and rain between now and spring. Nearly everybody on the streets was smiling, even the men cleaning up the last of the broken bottles, confetti and other litter from the celebration on Sunday and the victory parade to City Hall on Monday. About the only person who wasn't smiling was me.

The reason everybody was so cheerful was not the weather; it was the same reason there had been a two-day celebration on Sunday and Monday. The Forty-niners had just won the ultimate prize in professional football, the Super Bowl—San Francisco's first-ever national championship in any sport. I had watched the game myself on TV, and done some smiling and mild celebrating of my own when it was over. But I had celebrated alone, inside my Pacific Heights flat, instead of out on the streets where hordes of other people congregated.

I don't like crowds much, particularly the kind of crowd that keeps fueling itself on alcohol. Ninety-nine percent of the people are all right, even in a riotous mass of merrymakers. It's the other 1 percent you have to worry about. That 1 percent is made up of troublemakers and vandals, criminals looking for a chance to pick pockets or loot stores or commit armed robbery, and just plain loonies. Several people had been hurt during the festivities; dozens more had been arrested.

Well, any city of substantial size has its criminal element and its lunatic fringe; San Francisco was no exception. In a sense, the outlaws kept me in business—not that I was grateful to them for the privilege. I did not mind the crooks so much; for the most part they acted in predictable ways, and if you knew what you were doing, you could deal with them all right. It was the crazies who bothered me. I didn't often get a job that involved a crazy, and for that I *was* grateful. But every now and then, such a job comes along. And sometimes, in spite of my better judgment, I decided to take it on.

A job involving a crazy had come along this morning. I was probably going to take it on, too, because I needed the money. At least I had agreed to go and talk to the man who wanted to hire me, an attorney named Jud Canale.

And that was why, on this clear and mostly warm Wednesday morning three days after the

Forty-niners had won the Super Bowl, I wasn't smiling along with everybody else.

The corporate law firm of Tellmark, Graham, Canale and Isaacs was located in one of the newer high-rise office buildings on Montgomery Street, in the financial district. It occupied most of the fifteenth floor, and judging from the reception room the firm was doing very well, thank you. Oak-paneled walls, matching oak furniture covered in autumn-colored fabric, rust-brown carpeting and a decorative young lady behind the reception desk. The lady had auburn hair to match the motif; I wondered, a little cynically if that was why she'd been hired.

Jud Canale's office turned out to be similarly appointed, though his secretary was a little less decorative and had blond hair; the room was windowed on two sides, with the other two walls taken up with shelves of law books. Canale himself looked to be about my age, early fifties, and he had iron-gray hair and penetrating gray eyes. The three-piece pinstripe suit he wore, combined with that gray hair, gave him a dignified appearance. He was standing behind his somewhat cluttered desk when the secretary showed me in; beyond him, through the windows, I could see more than I cared to of the Transamerica Pyramid—a high-rise building that resembled an ice-cream cone turned upside down, as a local newspaper columnist had once aptly described it.

Canale came around the desk as I approached,

stopped with his face a few inches from mine and said in grave tones, "Thank you for coming."

"Not at all, Mr. Canale."

We shook hands. He was still standing close to me—one of those people who had a penchant, conscious or unconscious, for intruding on other people's space—and I could see the worry in his eyes; the skin across his cheekbones had a stretched look. I let go of his hand and backed up a step. My space was my own, and I did not want anyone else occupying it. Nor did I want to stand that close to another man's fear.

Canale nodded toward the nearest of two leather visitor's chairs, waited until I had seated myself, and then went around and plunked himself down in his own chair. He leaned forward with his hands flat on the desk blotter and looked at me as if I were a witness on the stand in court.

"There's been another call," he said.

"When?"

"Last night late. I called Lynn after I spoke to you, and she admitted it."

"Same sort of thing?"

"Yes. She wouldn't go into details."

"How is she?"

"She says she's all right, but I don't believe her. A thing like this . . ." He shook his head. "She's only twenty," he said.

"She's not alone today, is she?"

"No. One of her girl friends is staying with her at her apartment."

I was silent a couple of seconds before I said, "Mr. Canale, are you sure you want to go through with this—hiring me? As I told you on the phone, I don't know that there's much I can do in a case like this. The police department and the telephone company investigate hundreds of complaints about obscene calls every year—"

"I know that—"

"—but even with the manpower and facilities at their disposal, they aren't able to catch or even identify more than a handful of the callers. Besides, almost none of these crazies ever molest the women they call up. They're talkers, usually, not doers; according to psychological profiles, most of them are afraid of women. What they do is pick names out of the telephone directory, at random—"

"I know that, too," Canale said; "the police told me the same thing when I contacted them two days ago. But the man who keeps harassing Lynn is not a random caller. I think he knows her, and she knows him. In fact, I'm sure of it." He held up a hand as I started to speak. "I know what I said to you on the phone; I said it was a possibility that ought to be explored, and that was why I wanted to hire a detective. But now I'm convinced that's the case."

"What convinced you?"

"That call to Lynn last night. She had her number changed yesterday afternoon, at my insistence. Her new number is unlisted."

I said slowly, "I see."

"Yes. How could some anonymous crank find out a person's brand-new unlisted telephone number in less than twelve hours?"

"I doubt if one could. Unless he worked for the phone company, or knew someone who did."

"That strikes me as unlikely," Canale said. "No, it's someone Lynn knows well enough to have given her new number to. Or someone who got the number secondhand from one of her friends."

"Do you have any idea who it might be?"

"No."

"What does your daughter say?"

"She refuses to believe it's anyone she knows."

"Did she tell you who she'd given the number to?"

"No. She wouldn't talk about it, at least not to me."

"Why not to you?"

Canale smiled sardonically, without humor. "We haven't been close in the past couple of months," he said. "Ever since she became engaged to a young man named Larry Travers."

"You don't approve of this Travers?"

"No. And of course Lynn rebelled when I made my feelings clear to her."

"Is there any particular reason you don't like him?"

"I don't think he'll be good for her. Besides, she's too young to marry." He made a small suffering sound in his throat. "Father-daughter relationships can be difficult sometimes," he said. "Particularly when the father is the only parent. My wife and I were divorced when Lynn was a year old; neither Lynn nor I has seen her since."

I was not qualified to comment on any of that,

never having been either a husband or a father, so I remained silent.

Canale watched me for a moment. "So. Am I correct in assuming you'll investigate the matter for me?"

"Yes, sir," I said. "As long as you understand that there's only a limited chance of success on my part. All I can guarantee you is my time and an honest effort."

"That's all I ask of any man." He leaned back in his chair. "I expect you'll want to talk to Lynn right away."

"Yes."

"Good. I told her when I talked to her that I was hiring a detective, and I gave her your name as the probable man. She'll be expecting you."

He wrote me a retainer check, and I told him I would be in touch as soon as I had anything to report, and he showed me out. The check was for two hundred dollars, my daily rate; I took it out and looked at it again in the elevator on the way down. It made me feel a little more cheerful than I was when I got there.

II.

Lynn Canale lived in one of the apartment buildings in Parkmerced, near the San Francisco State College campus where she was a student. She had moved out of her father's house in the Forest Hill district two years ago, when she first entered school; Canale had told me on the phone earlier that she was strong-willed and self-sufficient, and that she had insisted on being on her own, rather than living at home, while she pursued a bachelor's degree in history. He had tried to talk her into moving back home with him when he found out about the calls, but she had refused. Stubbornness and a highly developed sense of pride were two other facets of her personality, Canale had said. I suspected she'd inherited them from him.

She had received the first call two weeks ago. There had been two others the first week, and since then she'd been getting them almost daily. She hadn't told her father about the calls until three days ago and then reluctantly, when he pressed her because she seemed tense and nervous at a family dinner. She hadn't offered any details of what the caller said to her; all she would say was that he made lewd suggestions and that his tone of voice frightened her.

I parked my car on Grijalva Drive, just down the street from Lynn's building. She lived in 3-C, and she buzzed me in immediately when I identified myself on the intercom above her mailbox in the entrance alcove. When I went upstairs to 3-C, I found that she was a slim, graceful girl with the fine-boned face that attracts fashion photographers and portrait painters. She had thick brown hair, worn long and straight, and brownish gold eyes under long natural lashes; the eyes told me she was as worried as her father, even though she was trying not to show it. She wore white slacks and a dark blue tunic.

The living room she led me into was small and over-furnished, so that it had a cramped feel. The window drapes were open, and the room was brightly lit by sunshine and by a hammered-brass curio lamp. Books and papers were scattered on a writing desk and on an old mohair sofa that looked as though it had come out of somebody's attic.

A little apologetically, she said, "I hope you don't mind the mess. I've been trying to study."

I thought about my flat, with the dirty dishes and the pulp magazines I collect strewn around, the dust-mice under the furniture; her apartment, compared to the home of a slob like me, was immaculate. "Not at all," I said. "Are you alone, Miss Canale? Your father said someone was staying with you."

"Someone is. Connie Evans, a friend from school. But she had a ten o'clock class, and this is the week final exams start for the fall semester."

"Will she be coming back?"

"Yes." She gave me a faintly defiant look. "I don't mind being alone, you know."

I didn't say anything.

"Well," she said. "Sit down, won't you?"

I sat in an armchair opposite the sofa; it was not very comfortable, but it was better than the only other places to sit—a couple of beanbag chairs. Lynn asked me if I wanted some coffee, and I said no, nothing. Then she sat on the sofa, tucked her legs under her and regarded me solemnly.

"I'm not sure this is a good idea," she said.

"What do you mean?"

"My father hiring a detective. I mean, lots of women get obscene telephone calls, don't they?"

"Yes," I said. "But in most cases, the calls don't keep coming as frequently as you've been receiving them."

"I'm not afraid," she said. "He's just a crank."

"Are you certain of that?"

She averted her eyes. "Oh, God, I wish he'd just go away and leave me alone."

"Maybe I can see to it that he does. Will you tell me about the calls?"

"Not what he says, no. I won't repeat that filth."

"Sexual suggestions, that sort of thing?"

"Yes. In great detail. It made my skin crawl, the first time I heard it."

"Has he threatened you at any time?"

"Not in so many words."

"Implied threats?"

"Yes. The things he wanted to do to me . . . well, they involved pain. You know, S and M stuff."

"Yeah," I said. "I know."

"He's an animal. Just . . . an animal."

"Is his voice at all familiar to you?"

"No."

"You're sure you've never heard it in person?"

"I'm sure," Lynn said.

"Is there anything distinctive about it? An accent, a lisp, anything like that?"

"Well, it sounds sort of adolescent . . . you know, high-pitched. And muffled, as if it's coming from a long way off."

"That might mean he's trying to disguise it," I said.

"I know, I've thought of that."

"Because if he didn't, you'd recognize who he was."

She pursed her lips. "My father thinks he's one of my friends. Is that what you think, too?"

"I don't know enough to think anything yet. But you did have your number changed yesterday; and you did get another call last night."

"I can't account for that," she said. "I don't *know* how he got my new number, or why he's doing this to me. All I know is, I want him to *stop.*"

I let a few seconds pass in silence; any more reassurances or solicitous comments would only have sounded empty. Or fatherly, which might be worse. When I spoke again I made my voice gentle. "How many people did you give the new number to?"

"Not many," she said. She sounded calm again. "My father. Connie. Larry. Tim Downs—"

"Wait, now. One at a time. Who would Larry be?"

"Larry Travers, my fiancé. We plan to be married in June."

"Congratulations. Have you known him long?"

"We met three months ago. He was going with Connie at the time, but I didn't know her very well then, not until after they broke up and Larry and I started dating. Anyhow, it didn't take long for both of us to know that . . . well, that we were in love."

"Does he also attend S.F. State?"

"No. U.C. He's a phys-ed major."

U.C. was the University of California, across

the bay in Berkeley. "Does he live in the East Bay?" I asked.

"No. Here in the city. On Potrero Hill."

"I'll need the address if you don't mind."

She told me a number on Missouri Street and I wrote it down in my notebook. "You mentioned someone named Tim Downs," I said then. "Who would he be?"

"A friend of Larry's."

"Also a student at U.C.?"

"No. He's an apprentice plumber. He lives near Larry and he's a sports nut; that's how they became friends. Larry is a sports nut, too."

"Why did you give Downs your unlisted number?"

"Because he's Larry's friend."

"Did he ask you for it?"

"No. He and Larry stopped over last night, on their way to another Super Bowl party; Larry wanted me to go along, but I had studying to do. While they were here I gave Larry the new number, and Tim, too, because he was standing right there."

I asked her where Downs lived and where he worked, and she told me. Then I said, "Is there anyone else you gave the number to?"

"No."

"Has anyone else been here besides Connie Evans? Anyone who might have seen the number on the phone itself?"

"No, I haven't had any . . . wait, yes I have. Joel Reeves stopped by yesterday while the man from the phone company was here. He only stayed a couple of minutes—Joel, I mean—but he might have noticed the number."

"This Reeves is a friend of yours?"

"Yes. Well, an acquaintance. He's a T.A. in the History Department at State."

"T.A.?"

"Teaching assistant. A graduate student who assists the professors. He lives in this building, up in Five-E."

"Why did he stop by yesterday?"

"He wanted to borrow a book of mine on Victorian poetry. The Victorian era is Joel's primary historical interest."

"Has he ever indicated any romantic interest in you?"

She laughed. "Joel? My God, no. All he cares about is history and old books."

"The serviceman from the telephone company," I said. "Had you ever seen him before yesterday?"

"No, never."

"Do you know anyone who works in the phone company?"

"No. You don't think—"

The door buzzer sounded. Lynn glanced at her wristwatch and said, "That's probably Connie. She said she'd be back after her exam."

It was Connie. "What time is it?" I heard her ask when Lynn let her into the foyer. "My damn watch stopped again."

"Five of one. You don't have another class today, do you?"

"No. I want to catch 'Another World.'" She

sounded relieved, as if missing an episode of a TV soap opera would have been a major blow to her. "The exam lasted longer than I expected."

"How do you think you did?"

"Not too bad." The two girls came into the living room, and Connie Evans and I saw each other for the first time. "Oh," she said. "You must be the detective Lynn's dad hired."

"Yes."

Lynn introduced us, and Connie came over and shook my hand somberly. She was about Lynn's age, not as attractive, with dark blond hair cut short, a Cupid's-bow mouth and a somewhat harried expression. Levi's and an S.F. State sweatshirt covered her angular body.

She asked me, "Do you really think you can find out who's making those calls to Lynn?"

"I'm going to try," I said.

"Well, if there's anything I can do to help . . ."

"I do have a couple of questions."

"Sure. Let me get a Coke first, okay? I'm dying of thirst."

"You and your Coke," Lynn said.

Connie disappeared into the kitchen. I asked Lynn, "Does anyone else besides you have a key to this apartment?"

"No, no one."

"Not even your fiancé?"

Faint color came into her cheeks; in this permissive age, it was nice to see that young girls could still blush, "Of course not," she said. "Larry and I don't have that kind of relationship."

Connie came back drinking from a can of Coca-

Cola, walking with her eyes closed and her head tilted back; only young people seemed able to perform that little trick without stumbling into something. When she lowered the can I asked her, "Did you give Lynn's new unlisted number to anyone?"

"No," she said. "Absolutely not."

"Did you mention to anyone that she had a new number?"

"No."

"Did you happen to call her for any reason while you were with someone else?"

"No. I've been here most of the time since—"

And the telephone rang.

The sudden sound of the bell had an effect on all three of us. Lynn bit at her lower lip. I stiffened. Connie had been lifting the can of Coke; she froze with it halfway to her mouth.

The thing ran again. Lynn said, "It's probably Larry. Or my father."

She went over to where the telphone sat on a driftwood stand; I followed her. She hesitated, and then, as it rang a third time, she caught up the receiver and said, "Hello?"

She didn't say anything else. Her face went white; a little sound came out of her throat that was half-gasp and half-moan. I plucked the receiver out of her hand. But I did not get to hear anything except a whirring click, then the buzzing of an empty line.

In a hushed voice Connie said, "Was it him?"

Lynn nodded convulsively as I cradled the handset.

"What did he say?" I asked her.

She shook her head; the fear in her eyes made them look enormous.

"Lynn, what did he say?"

"He said . . ." The words seemed to catch in her throat; it was a few seconds before she could get them out. "He said he's going to kill me."

III.

I spent another couple minutes in Lynn's apartment—the only other thing the caller had said was that if he couldn't have her, nobody would—and then left her with Connie Evans. Maybe the threat was meaningless, just another element of verbal abuse; but the bastard might also be crazy enough to mean it. There was just no way of telling yet. But it was my job to treat it as the real thing, and I felt a sense of urgency. The feeling was enhanced by the fact that talking to Jud Canale about the call and about what protective measures he might want to take, would have to wait; he had told me he would be in court all afternoon.

I took the elevator up to the fifth floor, found apartment 5-E and rapped on the door. Pretty soon a voice said from inside, "Yes?"

"Joel Reeves?"

"Yes. Who are you?"

I told him who I was, and what I did for a living, and that I was investigating the anonymous calls Lynn Canale had been receiving.

Reeves said, "Oh, well, just a second," and the

lock snicked free and the door opened on a chain. "I'd like to see some identification, please."

I showed him the photostat of my investigator's license. He studied it pretty good, and when he finished doing that he studied me for a couple of seconds. Then, satisfied, he took the chain off and let me come in.

"Cautious, aren't you?" I said as he closed and relocked the door.

"We've had burglaries in this building. And I own some valuable books."

He was in his mid-to-late twenties, dumpy, weak-chinned, with sparse black hair and watery green eyes behind Ben Franklin glasses. He had a studious, preoccupied air about him—the kind of kid who would grow into a tweedy, middle-aged stereotype of the college professor. Or so it seemed on the surface, anyway.

His apartment was similar in size and layout to Lynn's, except that the windows faced west, toward Lake Merced and the Harding Park golf course. It was neatly if unimaginatively furnished, with filled bookcases dominating two of the walls in the living room. When Reeves led me in there, I noticed the titles on a couple of the books. They brought me over to the cases for a closer look.

Nearly all of the books were from or about Victorian England; Lynn had told me Reeves was a budding Victorian scholar. But what she hadn't told me was that one of his particular interests was Victorian erotica. At least two shelves were jammed with such pornographic novels and "confessions" as *My Secret Life, May's Account of Her*

Introduction to the Art of Love, A Night in a Moorish Harem, Venus in India and *The Amatory Experiences of a Surgeon;* several bound volumes, dated 1879 and 1880, of an underground sex journal called *The Pearl;* and more than a dozen contemporary references, some scholarly and some designed to titillate.

I turned to face Reeves. "Nice collection of books you've got there," I said.

"Thank you. Some are quite rare."

"The erotica, for instance?"

"Oh, yes. Those bound volumes of *The Pearl* are worth . . . well, they're quite valuable."

"How do you happen to have them?"

"I bought them in London last summer." He gave me a prideful smile. "At auction. I outbid several antiquarian book dealers for them."

"You must be well off financially."

"What? Oh, no—not at all. My father left me a small inheritance when he died seven years ago, enough to put me through school and to finance the London trip and the book purchases."

"Then you must have wanted those volumes of *The Pearl* pretty badly."

"I did," Reeves said. "They don't generally turn up for sale."

I moved away from the bookcase. "Aren't you a little young to be so interested in erotica?"

"Young?" He blinked at me owlishly behind his Ben Franklin glasses. "What does age have to do with a person's interest in history?"

"Is that why you collect sex books—because of historical curiosity?"

"Of course. And for research purposes. The same reasons I collect Victoriana of all types. I'm doing my master's dissertation on popular and underground Victorian literature."

"Uh-huh," I said. But I was thinking that Lynn was an attractive young woman, and Reeves was an unattractive young man whose interest in erotica may or may not have been purely academic. He also seemed to be the obsessive type, judging from what he had told me about those volumes of *The Pearl*; if that type of man wanted a woman and he knew he could never have her, and if he was a little unbalanced to begin with, he might take the obscene-phone-call route.

Reeves said, "Has Lynn had more of those calls? Is that why you've been hired?"

"Two more. One last night, one this morning. The last one wasn't obscene, it was threatening."

"Threatening?"

"The man said he was going to kill her."

Reeves looked shocked. "Good Lord!"

"So I'm sure you can understand that I want to find out who he is as soon as possible."

"Yes, certainly. But I don't know how I can help."

"Just answer a few questions for me."

"Of course."

"Lynn said you dropped by her apartment yesterday, while the telephone serviceman was there. Did you happen to notice her new number?"

"No, I didn't."

"But you knew she was having a new phone put in?"

"Well, she didn't say so, but I assumed that was what the serviceman was doing there."

"How long did you stay?"

"Only a minute or so."

"Okay. A few other questions and I'll be on my way. Do you know Lynn's fiancé, Larry Travers?"

"I've met him, yes."

"What's your opinion of him?"

"I don't like the man," he said flatly.

"No? Why not?"

"He's arrogant and self-centered and not very bright. All he ever talks about are sports and how much beer he can drink without gaining weight. Lynn is intelligent and serious about her studies; I don't know how she could have chosen someone like Travers."

"Love is blind sometimes," I said.

He sighed. "Yes. So it is."

"Do you know a friend of Travers' named Tim Downs?"

"No, I don't think so. May I ask why you're so concerned with people Lynn knows? Surely you don't believe the man on the phone is one of her friends?"

"There's a good possibility he might be. The only people she gave her new number to are friends. And she's had those two calls since the new phone was installed yesterday."

"I see." He sighed again. "Poor Lynn. She must be very upset."

"She's bearing up. Connie Evans is staying with her."

"Oh yes, the computer woman."

"Pardon?"

"A computer science major." Reeves made a wry mouth. "I don't like computer science," he said.

"Why is that?"

"It's cold, dehumanizing. Computers, *machines*, are symptomatic of what's wrong with today's world; in fact, they may be at the root of the problem. That's why I prefer the past. It may be imperfect, but I would much rather have lived a century ago than today. And I would much rather live today than a century from now; the probable shape of the future horrifies me."

"Maybe it won't turn out as badly as you think," I said.

"Yes, it will. It certainly will."

I gave him one of my business cards, just in case, and then left him and left the building to pick up my car. The way it looked now, there were only three people on the list of suspects—Reeves, Larry Travers and Tim Downs. But would it stay narrowed down to those three?

I went looking for Travers and Downs, to find out.

IV.

Potrero Hill was an older section of the city, built on one of San Francisco's forty-three hills—residential on its upper slopes, industrial down at the base. It had become a fashionable "in" place to live for the young and ambitious among the city's population; there were a lot of old Victorian houses up there, and the young people had begun buying and fixing them up. The appearance and tenor of the neighborhood had improved markedly in recent years.

The address Lynn had given me for Larry Travers was a Stick-style Victorian—one of the tall, vertical row houses that had been the dominant architectural style in the 1880s. It had a false front adorned with a "French" cap, and it had been painted recently in two not very harmonious shades of blue. It also had a *Flat for Rent* sign, with the name of a Mission Street realtor on it, on the garage door under the big, rectangular bay window.

The pair of mailboxes on the porch told me that the building had been divided into two flats and that the upper floor belonged to Travers. I pushed the button alongside his name, listened to the bell ring inside. There was no response. And none when I rang the bell a second time either.

So maybe he was still in school; it was only three-thirty. But that *Flat for Rent* sign had me curious. I poked the bell beside the name on the second mailbox, Rodriguez, and pretty soon a thin, middle-aged woman opened the door to the downstairs flat. The look she gave me was full of annoyance.

"They only put the damn sign up an hour ago," she said.

"Ma'am?"

"The realtors. I told 'em people would start bothering me, even though it says right on the sign 'Do Not Disturb Residents,' and they said oh no, don't worry, that won't happen. Hah. It didn't even take an hour for it to happen." She glared at me. "Don't you read what it says on signs, mister?"

"I'm not here about the flat," I said.

"No? Then what do you want? If you're selling something, we don't want any."

"I'm not selling anything. I'm looking for Larry Travers."

"Oh," the woman said. "Well, I don't know if he's still here or not."

"Still here?"

"I saw him moving some of his stuff out this morning, but I don't know if he took it all. Maybe he'll be back."

"It's the upstairs flat that's for rent, then? Travers' flat?"

"Sure. My husband and me, we been here twenty-five years, and we'll be here another twenty-five if the government don't starve us out or blow us up."

"Do you know where Travers is moving to?"

"I didn't ask him. I don't care where he's going."

"Hasn't he been a good neighbor?"

"Too many loud parties," Mrs. Rodriguez said. "Different girls, booze, noise until all hours. Probably dope, too, for all I know."

"You mean he's brought different girls here himself, or his friends have?"

"Who knows? They came and they went; sometimes they stayed all night. Orgies, that's what he's been having up there, right over my head. I'm a respectable woman, I go to church, I pay taxes, I shouldn't have to listen to orgies in the middle of the night."

"Did you talk to Travers about these wild parties?"

"Sure, I talked to him, my husband and me both. He told us to mind our own business, the young snot. So we called the cops on him, twice, but what good did it do? The cops came and the party stopped, they went away and it started right up again. You'd think the cops could break up an orgy so decent people could get their sleep, wouldn't you?"

"Yes, ma'am."

"Cops," Mrs. Rodriguez said, and shook her head. Then a thought seemed to strike her and she frowned warily. "Say, *you're* not a cop, are you?"

"No, I'm not."

"Good. How come you're looking for Travers?"

"A private matter."

"Huh," she said. "He in some sort of trouble?"

"I don't know. Probably not."

"Well, it wouldn't surprise me if he was. Kids nowadays, they got no respect for nothing, not even the law. If you ask me—"

"Thanks for your help, Mrs. Rodriguez," I said, and left her standing there with her mouth open.

On the way back to my car, I did some wondering about Larry Travers. The fact that he was in the process of moving out of his flat didn't have to mean anything; people move every day for a hundred different reasons. But it seemed odd that Lynn hadn't mentioned it when she gave me his address. Maybe Travers hadn't got around to telling her about the move yet; but that was odd, too, if so. He and Lynn were engaged. Why wouldn't he tell her he was moving?"

Mrs. Rodriguez's diatribe about loud parties didn't have to mean anything either. The testimony of a complainer and a busybody wasn't always reliable, and the way she had kept using the word "orgy" made exaggeration another of her faults. Still, there was probably a fair amount of truth in what she'd told me. So was Travers playing around on Lynn Canale or wasn't he?"

The one person besides Travers who could give me the answer to that question figured to be Tim Downs. He might still be at work, but I seemed to remember that plumbers quit for the day at three-thirty. I decided to try his home first because it was closer than La Costa Plumbing and Heating, over on Harrison, where Lynn had told me Downs worked.

I drove up to De Haro. The building Downs lived in was also a Stick-style Victorian, in a somewhat shabbier state of repair, and like the one on Missouri it sat near the top of a steep hill; it would command a nice view of the city from its rear windows. I parked down the block, trudged uphill and climbed onto the porch.

Downs had the main-floor flat, and he didn't have it alone; a second name was written below his on the mailbox card; Pam Scott. Girl friend, probably. I rang the bell. No answer here either. I was just about to start back down the steps when a dark green Toyota pulled into the driveway below and a young guy dressed in a soiled work uniform and carrying a lunch pail got out.

He gave me a curious glance and then mounted the stairs, taking his time about it. He was a big kid, mid-twenties, built like a football player. His black hair hung to his shoulders, curling up on the ends, and he wore one of those bushy mustache-and-sideburns combinations that were popular back in the 1890s. Deep-set blue eyes studied me levelly when he reached the porch and stopped a couple of paces away.

"You looking for me?" he asked.

"I am if your name is Tim Downs."

"That's my name. What can I do for you?"

I told him who I was and more or less why I was there; I also showed him my license photostat. Nothing much changed in his blue eyes. He wasn't impressed one way or another. "Who hired you?" he asked. "Lynn's old man?"

"Yes."

"Yeah, that figures. He's the type."

"What type is that?"

"The Establishment type. Always overreacting."

"Why do you think he's overreacting?"

"Lots of women get obscene telephone calls," Downs said. "It's no big deal. San Francisco is full of creeps."

"Lots of women don't have their life threatened," I said.

"Is that straight? The guy threatened Lynn?"

"This morning. He said he was going to kill her."

"Christ. You think he means it?"

"Maybe. There's no way to tell without know-ing who he is. You wouldn't have any ideas, would you?"

He shook his head. And then he scowled and said, "Why ask me? I don't know anything about those calls."

"You're a friend of Lynn's, aren't you?"

"So? She's got a lot of friends."

"She had her phone number changed yesterday. Except for her father, you and Larry Travers are the only ones she gave the new number to."

"What the hell?" he said. There was hostility in his voice now, in the set of his mouth. "You think maybe I'm the one who called her up and threat-ened her?"

"Did I say that? I don't have any ideas about you one way or another; all I'm here for is to ask you some questions. You don't have to answer them if you don't want to."

"What questions?"

"Did you give Lynn's phone number to any-one?"

"No. Why should I?"

"Are you sure?"

"Sure, I'm sure. I didn't even tell Pam."

"Who's Pam?"

"Pam Scott, the lady I live with."

"Do you know if Travers gave the number to anyone?"

"No. Ask him, why don't you?"

"I stopped by his flat before I came here. He wasn't home."

"Yeah, well, he's been busy lately."

"There's a *Flat for Rent* sign on his building," I said. "The woman who lives below him said he's moving out."

"That's right, he is."

"Where to? Another place here in the city?"

Downs hesitated. "No. He's splitting."

"You mean he's leaving San Francisco?"

"This coming weekend, yeah."

"Where's he going?"

"San Diego."

"Why? He decide to change schools, or what?"

"Not exactly. He dropped out of U.C. at the end of last semester; he may stay out until the fall, sign up at San Diego State. It all depends."

"On what?"

"On whether this deal he's got going works out."

"What deal?"

Downs hesitated again. Then he shrugged and said, "Him and another guy are taking a boat down to Dago for the guy's old man. Guy he met over in Berkeley. The old man bought the boat when he was up here over Christmas, had it put in for some minor repairs; he owns a bunch of boats down south. Larry figures maybe he can get a regular job with him."

"Does Lynn know about this deal?"

Another shrug. "Maybe Larry didn't tell her yet. Ask him."

"He didn't tell her he'd dropped out of school either, did he? Or that he was leaving San Francisco?"

"So he hasn't told her, so what?"

"He's engaged to marry the girl."

"Yeah, sure," Downs said, and grinned crook-edly.

"What does that mean? He isn't going to marry her?"

"Larry's not the marrying type."

"No? Then why the hell did he get engaged to her?"

"Come one, man, why do you think?"

"You tell me."

"You met her, didn't you? She's a nice kid, but a little square; she's got old-fashioned ideas. Getting engaged was the only way Larry could score with her."

Anger clotted my throat; I didn't trust myself to speak for a moment. Some sweet guy, this Larry Travers. A girl like Lynn won't go to bed with him, so he tells her he loves her, promises to marry her and strings her along until he's had enough of her and her body. Then he drops her, shatters her dreams and away he goes without giving her another thought. A bum like that was capable of just about anything. Including a series of obscene and threatening telephone calls, for whatever warped reason of his own.

What I was thinking must have been plain on my face. Downs said, "Hey, man, why get so uptight about it? Lynn'll get over it; they always do. It's no big deal."

"It's a big deal to me, sonny."

His jaw tightened. "Don't call me sonny."

"I'll call you any damn thing I feel like calling you. Where can I find Travers?"

He glared at me without answering. I glared right back at him. He was half my age and in better physical shape, but the way I felt right now, I was ready to beat the crap out of him and Travers both. Maybe he saw that in my face, too; or maybe he just didn't feel like mixing it up with anybody on his front stoop. His eyes shifted away from me, and he muttered something under his breath and started past me to the front door.

I blocked his way. "I asked you a question. Where can I find Travers?"

"How should I know?"

"Where does he hang out when he's not home?"

"I don't have to answer your questions, man—"

"Not mine, maybe. How about the police?"

"You can't put the cops on me. I ain't done anything . . ."

"I can and I will. I used to be a cop myself; I've still got friends on the force. Now, do you want to tell me where Travers hangs out or don't you?"

He muttered something else under his breath that I didn't catch. Then he said, tight-mouthed and sullen, "Elrod's, on Eighteenth and Connecticut. He's there most days around five."

"He still living in his flat or not?"

"Some nights. Other nights he spends on the boat."

"Where?"

"China Basin. The Basin Boatyard."

"What's the name of the boat?"

"*The Hidalgo.*"

"All right," I said. "If you talk to Travers before I do, tell him I'm looking for him. Tell him I think he's one of those creeps San Francisco is full of."

I brushed by Downs and clumped down the stairs. And I didn't look back.

V.

Elrod's was a neighborhood tavern that had been outfitted to resemble an English pub—British and Irish beer signs on the walls, a couple of dart boards, a big fireplace with some logs blazing inside. From the look of the twenty or so patrons, it catered to the under-thirty crowd and was probably what passed for a singles bar on Potrero Hill. I was the oldest person in there by at least ten years.

The bartender was a young guy with a bright red beard. I ordered a pint of Bass ale and asked him if he knew Larry Travers. Sure, he said, but Larry hadn't come in yet today. A great guy, Larry. Drank beer like it was going out of style; drank beer for *breakfast*, once poured some on a bowl of cereal to prove it. A hell of a guy.

Yeah, I thought. A hell of a guy.

A dollar tip got the bartender to agree to point Travers out to me if he showed up. Then I took my ale into a telephone booth at the rear and called Tellmark, Graham, Canale and Isaacs. Jud Canale was back from court and in his office—it was almost five o'clock—and he came on the line immediately.

"A couple of things to report," I said, "neither

of them good." I told him about the call to Lynn this morning, the threat against her life. And I told him what I'd found out about Larry Travers. The only thing I didn't tell him was the reason why Travers had pretended to want to marry Lynn; I just said he'd been seeing other women all along and was backing out of the marriage by running off to San Diego. Lynn Canale's sex life was her own business, not her father's.

Canale let me tell it straight through without interrupting. When I was finished he said in a thin, angry voice, "Have you talked to Travers yet?"

"Not yet. I haven't been able to find him. I will, though. I'm calling from a place where he hangs out; he's liable to show up here sooner or later."

"Did you tell Lynn what you found out?"

"No. I didn't think it was my place."

"You're right, it isn't. It's mine. I'll drive over and talk to her right away."

"Whatever you think best, Mr. Canale."

He gave me his home phone number and asked me to call him again as soon as I talked to Travers. Then he rang off, and I went back to the bar and found a place to sit where I could watch the entrance. The place was full now and getting fuller—a more or less even mix of male and female kids in their twenties. I felt out of place among them; I felt old and anachronistic, a product of a different world that they could never really understand, any more than I could really understand theirs. Several of them gave me curious glances, and the look on one girl's face said that she was

wondering if I might be a pervert. It might have
been funny in other circumstances. As it was,
with Lynn Canale and Larry Travers on my mind,
it wasn't funny at all. It was only sad.

Five-thirty came and went. So did a second pint
of Bass ale. But Travers didn't come.

He still hadn't shown at six. I gave him another
twenty minutes, until the crowd began to thin out
for dinner and other activities, and when the
bartender came over and shrugged and said, "I
guess Larry's not coming in tonight," I decided it
was time to call it quits. I paid my tab and went
out into the early-evening darkness.

The wasted time had made me irritable, and the
ale and the noise and smoky atmosphere of Elrod's had given me a headache. I didn't want food;
I didn't want to go home yet. I was still fixated on
Travers.

I took my car back to Missouri Street. And there
was a light on in the Victorian's upper flat, Travers' flat, and parked in the driveway was a battered
old Triumph TR-3. Well, well, I thought. The
prodigal returns. But I couldn't find a goddamn
parking space anywhere on the block, and I did
not want to risk putting the car into somebody
else's driveway. It took me a couple of minutes to
locate a space a block and a half away.

When I came huffing and puffing up the hill,
the upstairs light in Travers' flat had been put out.
The sports car was still in the driveway, though,
and I could see a guy loading something into its
trunk. There was enough light from a nearby
street lamp to tell me that he was big, blond and

young. He heard me coming, glanced around and then straightened as I approached him.

"Larry Travers?"

"That's right. You're the detective, right?"

I nodded. "Your friend Downs tell you about me?"

"Yes." There was no hostility in his voice, as there had been in Downs's; he was playing it neutral. "I'm sorry you feel the way you do about me, I really am. But you just don't understand how things are."

"I understand how things are, all right," I said. "I also understand that somebody threatened Lynn Canale's life this afternoon. Or don't you care about that?"

"Sure, I care about it."

"How about her? Do you care about her?"

"Why do you think I don't? Because I'm moving to San Diego and I haven't told Lynn yet? That doesn't make me a bad guy; and it doesn't mean I'm trying to run out on her, or that we won't see each other again."

He sounded very earnest, and in the pale light from the street lamp his expression was guileless. He was a handsome kid: athletic build, boyish features, long blond hair and a neat blond mustache. But it was all on the surface. Inside, where it counted, he wasn't handsome at all.

I said, "Where were you at one o'clock this afternoon?"

"Why? Is that when Lynn got the threatening call?"

"Where were you?"

"I didn't make the call, if that's what you think," Travers said. "Lynn is special to me; the last thing in the world I want is to see her hurt. Why don't you go find out who did do it, instead of bothering me?"

I took a step toward him. "Answer my question, Travers. Where were you at one o'clock this afternoon?"

He didn't answer the question. Instead, he slammed the trunk lid, moved away from me to the driver's door and hauled it open. I went after him, but he was quick and agile; by the time I got around there, he was inside and he had the door shut again. He shoved the lock button down as I caught hold of the handle.

"Travers!"

But he wasn't listening. The starter whirred and the engine came to life; he ground gear teeth getting the transmission into reverse. I stepped back out of the way just before he released the clutch and took the Triumph, tires squealing, out into the street. A couple of seconds later, he was rocketing off down the hill. And a couple of seconds after that, he was gone.

There was no point in trying to follow him; my car was too far away. I swallowed my anger and made myself walk slowly down the steep sidewalk. Round one to Travers. But there would be a round two, and that one, by God, would be mine.

When I got to where I had left my car, I debated driving over to China Basin. But that might not be where Travers was headed; and, in any event, you couldn't get into a boatyard at night without a key or somebody letting you in. So I pointed the car in the opposite direction and went home to my flat in Pacific Heights. I had done enough for one day. As long as Lynn was in a safe place, Travers could wait until tomorrow.

I opened myself a beer, took it into the bedroom and dialed Jud Canale's home number. He wasn't in yet; there was a whirring click and I got his recorded voice on his answering machine. I left a brief message outlining my abortive talk with Travers and said I would get in touch again in the morning.

Dinner was leftover pizza and another beer. After which I took a 1935 issue of *Black Mask* off one of the shelves where I keep my collection of mystery and detective pulp magazines, and crawled into bed with it. I got halfway through an Erle Stanley Gardner story about Ed Jenkins, the Phantom Crook, but my head wasn't into it. I kept thinking about Lynn Canale, and about Travers, and about those calls.

I shut the light off finally and waited for my thoughts to wind down and sleep to come. I was still waiting two hours later . . .

VI.

Jud Canale got in touch with me in the morning, while I was having toast and coffee a few minutes past eight. He sounded tired and upset, and one of the reasons turned out to be that Lynn had refused to go home with him last night, or any night to come. She hadn't even spent the entire evening in her apartment; she had gone off with Connie Evans to a Drama Club meeting, because she said she couldn't stand staying cooped up. But she was all right so far. There hadn't been any more anonymous calls during the night, or any other disturbances. Canale had insisted that she phone him first thing this morning, to check in; she had done that a few minutes before he called me.

The second reason he was upset was that Lynn had also refused to accept the truth about Travers. Even if Travers had dropped out of U.C. and given up his apartment, even if he was going to take a boat to San Diego, even if he hadn't told her any of this yet, she was convinced he had his reasons and that he still loved her. She was certain he hadn't been fooling around with other women either. That sort of loyalty and trust was good to see in a young person like Lynn, but in this case it was tragically misplaced. When she did accept the truth, as she would have to sooner or later, it was going to go twice as hard for her. Love, like dreams and old beliefs, dies hard.

"What are you going to do about Travers?" Canale asked. "Talk to him again today?"

"Yes. I'm driving down to China Basin as soon as I finish my breakfast. Chances are he spent the night on the boat; he should still be there, this early."

"And if you can't get anything out of him? What then?"

"I don't know. I'll just have to play it by ear."

"All right. But tell him something for me, will

you? Tell him if he ever tries to see Lynn again, I'll kill him."

"Look, Mr. Canale—"

"Tell him," Canale said, and rang off.

I didn't want any more toast and coffee; the conversation with Canale had taken away my appetite. I got my coat, went out and picked up my car, and headed crosstown to Third Street and the waterfront.

China Basin was on the southeast side of the city, at the foot of the Embarcadero and not all that far from Potrero Hill. Back in the 1860s, the long deep-water channel had been the place where the "China Clippers" of the Pacific Mail Steamship Line berthed; that was how it had got its name. Today, incoming and outgoing freighters tied up at the industrial docks there, and there were boatyards and a military shipyard, and a few small waterfront cafés where you could sit at outside tables and watch what was going on in the basin and on the bay beyond.

The Basin Boatyard was on Channel Street, just down from the Banana Terminal where freighters carrying tropical fruit from South America were once unloaded. There was a good deal of activity in the area; trucks coming and going, strings of freight cars maneuvering on the network of rail tracks. Mornings were always the busiest time along the waterfront. Parking was at a premium, but I managed to find a place to wedge my car— and when I neared the open boatyard gates on foot, I noticed a battered black Triumph TR-3

dwarfed by and half-hidden behind a massive trac-
tor-trailer rig. Travers was here, all right.

I went in through the open gates. The boatyard
was fairly large, cluttered with wooden buildings
with corrugated-iron roofs, a rusty-looking crane,
a variety of boats in and out of the water, and a
couple of employees at their jobs. At the far end
was a moorage—a half-dozen slips extending into
the basin on either side of a rickety board float.
About half of the slips were occupied.

A beefy guy dressed in paint-stained overalls
intercepted me as I started toward the moorage.
"Something I can do for you, mister?"

"I'm looking for Larry Travers," I said.

"Haven't seen him this morning."

"His car's out front. Maybe he's still sacked in
on the *Hidalgo*."

"You a friend of his?"

"No. I've got business with him.

The guy shrugged. "Been here before?"

"No."

"*Hidalgo's* the sloop-rigged centerboarder in
the last slip out."

"Thanks."

I went the rest of the way to the moorage, out
onto the board float. The day was another clear
one, not too cold in the sun or in sheltered places;
but out here, with the wind gusting in off the bay,
it was chilly enough to make me shiver inside my
light coat. I bunched the fabric at my throat,
hunched my shoulders. Overhead, a seagull cut
loose with its screaming laugh, as if mocking me.

Until I came in sight of the *Hidalgo*, I had no

idea what a "sloop-rigged centerboarder" was. But it wasn't anything exotic—just a thirty-foot, cruise-type sailboat, the kind with an auxiliary inboard engine that makes it capable of an extended ocean passage. It was made out of fiberglass, with aluminum spars, and it had plenty of deck space and a low, squat cabin that would probably sleep four below deck.

I caught hold of the aluminum siderail and swung onto the deck aft. The fore cabin window was uncurtained, so I could see that the cockpit was empty. I moved around on the companionway that led below. A lamp burned down there; I could make out part of two quarter-berths and not much else.

"Travers?" I called, and then identified myself. "I want to talk to you."

No answer.

I called his name again; the only answer I got this time was another cry from a passing gull. All right, I thought. I went down the companion ladder, into the living quarters below. There was plenty of space, and all of it seemed to be deserted. On the port side, I saw a good-sized galley complete with sink, icebox, and stove, and ample locker space for food and utensils; to starboard opposite, there was an enclosed toilet and a hanging locker. A galley table set up between the two quarter-berths was littered with the remains of a McDonald's fast-food supper, some empty beer bottles and soft drink cans. And up forward, separated from the rest of the cabin by a bulkhead and curtain, were what figured to be the two remaining berths; I couldn't see in there because the curtain was drawn.

A vague, tingly feeling started up on the back of my neck. It was a sensation I'd had too many times before—a premonitory feeling of wrongness. I stayed where I was for several seconds, but it did not go away.

"Travers?"

Silence.

I took a breath, and my legs worked and carried me over to the forward bulkhead. I was still holding my breath when I swept the curtain aside; then my stomach kicked and the air came out between my teeth in a flat, hissing sound.

Travers hadn't gone anywhere; he would never go anywhere again. He was lying back-sprawled on the rumpled port-side bunk, one leg hanging off to the deck. Just above his right cheekbone was a blackened hole caked with dried blood. The gun that had evidently killed him was a .38 caliber Smith & Wesson automatic; it was in his right hand, with his fingers lax around it.

So it looked as though he'd shot himself— maybe because he was the caller who'd been deviling Lynn Canale and his conscience had got the better of him, maybe for some other reason. It looked like a simple case of suicide.

But I didn't believe it for a minute.

It was a case of murder, and it wasn't simple at all.

VII.

I called the Hall of Justice from a phone in the boatyard office. The man I asked for was Lieutenant Eberhardt, probably my best friend on or off the force, but it was his day off; I had to settle for potluck. It worked out all right, though, because one of the two Homicide inspectors who showed up was Jack Logan, whom I also knew.

He listened to my story, more or less sympathetically, and to my speculation that Travers had not died by his own hand: "The kid just wasn't the type to kill himself, Jack; he was too arrogant, too wrapped up in himself. And even if he was the type, he wouldn't have bothered to move out of his flat, make all his plans for the trip to San Diego, if he was going to do the Dutch." But Logan was a methodical cop, and he wasn't making any judgments of his own until he had all the facts. Not the least of which, he said, was a nitrate test on Travers' hands to determine whether or not he had fired the .38 automatic.

Logan had gone back aboard the *Hidalgo* to confer again with the assistant coroner and the lab boys, and I was standing out on the float, when Jud Canale got there. I had called Canale's office right after notifying the police, and he'd said he would come right down. His only reaction to the news of Travers' death had been to say, grimly, that the circumstances being what they were, he wasn't sorry to hear it.

The patrolman standing guard at the shore end of the moorage had been given Canale's name and let him pass. I went ahead to meet Canale halfway; I wanted a few words alone with him before he talked to the inspectors.

"Mr. Canale," I said, "how long did you stay at your daughter's apartment last night?"

He squinted at me. The wind had picked up and it was sharp enough to make his eyes water. "What does that have to do with anything?"

"Just answer the question, please."

"I was there until about six-thirty," he said.

"Then what?"

"I went home."

"You weren't home when I called your house at a quarter to eight."

"I stopped for a couple of drinks on the way; I felt I needed them."

He bent toward me, putting his face close to mine, intruding on my space again. "Why do you want to know where I was last night?"

I did not back away from him this time. "The assistant coroner says rigor mortis has already come and gone in Travers' body; he thinks Travers was shot sometime last evening. Before midnight."

"My God, do you think *I* shot him? I thought you told me he'd killed himself."

"I said it looked that way. But it wasn't suicide, Mr. Canale; it was murder."

"How do you know that?"

"I don't know it; I suspect it."

"Why would anyone murder Travers?"

"You've got a pretty good motive, for one," I said. "You told me this morning to tell him that if he ever went near Lynn again, *you'd* kill him."

"I didn't mean that literally. I was angry."

I just looked at him.

"Besides, I said that to you this morning. Why would I do that if I'd already shot Travers last night?"

"Smoke screen, maybe. To make you look innocent."

Canale made a disgusted sound. "This is ridiculous," he said, and gave me his courtroom stare. "I did not kill Larry Travers. I don't suppose that satisfies you, but it happens to be the truth."

"The ones you want to satisfy are the police," I said. "They'll be asking you the same questions pretty soon."

He'd had enough of me for the time being; he sidestepped me and went down to the *Hidalgo*. I watched him stop abaft of the boat and stand there stiff-backed against the wind, and I wondered if he was guilty after all. There was no question that he had a good motive—but then, he wasn't the only one. Somebody else had the same motive, just as strong and maybe stronger.

His daughter, the woman Travers had been about to run out on.

It was a little past noon before Logan gave me permission to leave the boatyard. Canale was still there; I asked him if he wanted me to continue my investigation into the calls, and he said, a little stiffly, that he hadn't decided yet, he wanted to see whether the police turned up anything that might identify Travers as the caller. I told him I would be available if he still wanted me.

I drove downtown to the building on Taylor Street where I have my office. A cup of coffee seemed like a good idea, so I took the office pot into the little side alcove, filled it from the sink in there, and brought it back and put it on the hot plate.

While I waited for the water to boil I switched on my answering machine. There had been only one call, but whoever it was had hung up without leaving a messsage; some people just do not care to talk to machines, not that I blame them much. I shut the thing off and started to go through my mail.

Machines . . .

And then I just sat there. Things had begun to happen inside my head. My mental processes worked that way; if you tossed enough scraps of information, enough impressions and other factors, into my subconscious, sooner or later something would act as a catalyst and they would start to connect up. And pretty soon the answer to whatever case or problem I was working on would emerge.

It took me fifteen minutes and most of a cup of coffee to get the answer to this one. And when I had it, it turned me cold and a little scared. I told myself that I could be wrong, that I might be misinterpreting the facts. But I wasn't wrong, any more than I was wrong about Larry Travers' death being murder and not suicide.

I knew who had shot Travers, and I knew who had made all those phone calls to Lynn Canale.

The proper thing to do was to call the police. But I had no proof; all I had were circumstantial evidence, and supposition, and the burning hunch that I was right. Calling Jack Logan, explaining it all to him, would take time . . . and maybe I didn't have much time. For all I knew—and this was what scared me—I might already be too late.

I hurried out of the office and out of the building, got my car and took it as fast as I dared out Highway 280 and into Parkmerced. In the foyer of Lynn Canale's building, I punched the doorbell button beside her name. But her voice didn't come over the intercom; nobody answered the bell.

That made me a little panicky. I pushed the button for 5-E, kept my finger on it. Joel Reeves was home, and when I identified myself and told him to let me in, he obeyed without question.

I took the stairs to the third floor, half-running, so that I was winded by the time I got to Lynn's door. I tried the knob; locked. Then I banged on the door, loudly, and called Lynn's name. All that got me was a woman poking her head out of a door down the hall and demanding to know what I was doing. I told her I was a cop, to save time, and asked her if she'd seen Lynn today; she said she hadn't.

I turned back to 3-C. Breaking the door down was an extreme measure; there did not have to be anything wrong inside. It occurred to me that someone on the premises might have a passkey, a building superintendent, somebody like that. I was just about to ask the woman when the door to the stairwell opened and Joel Reeves appeared.

"I thought this was where you'd gone," he said. "What's going on?"

"Where's Lynn? Have you seen her?"

"A little while ago, yes; downstairs in the lobby,

I was just coming back from school and she was on the way out. She seemed very upset—"

"Was she alone?"

"No. Connie Evans was with her."

"Did either of them say where they were going?"

Reeves shook his head. He could see the alarm in my face and he was frowning behind his Ben Franklin glasses. "But Lynn was carrying an overnight case," he said.

"Where does Connie Evans live?"

"Somewhere in the Sunset district, I think. Out near the Great Highway. Why are you so upset? Lynn's safe with Connie, isn't she?"

I ran for the stairwell without answering him. The hell Lynn was safe with Connie; the hell she was.

Connie Evans was both the anonymous caller and the person who had murdered Larry Travers.

VIII.

The directory in a public telephone booth near Lynn's building contained a listing for a C. Evans on Forty-seventh Avenue. That was the only C. Evans in the Sunset district, and the only Evans near the Great Highway. I had to take the chance that it was the right one; the address was only fifteen minutes from Parkmerced.

I barreled my car around the edge of the lake and down Sloat Boulevard past the zoo. Despite the fact that Forty-seventh Avenue was the closest residential street to Ocean Beach, it wasn't a particularly desirable neighborhood in which to live; the weather was foggy a good part of the time, and when the sea wind blew heavily it swept sand across the Great Highway, which paralled the beach for several miles, and slapped it against the building faces. It was like living in a sandblast zone, some days.

The address for C. Evans was an old-fashioned, shingled cottage tucked back between a two-unit apartment building and a crumbling stucco row house. There was a car parked in front; I pulled up behind it, blocking the row house driveway, and the hell with that. I pushed through a sagging gate, climbed onto a front porch littered with dying plants and rang the bell.

Nothing happened for several seconds. The palms of my hands were sweaty and my stomach was knotted with tension. I reached out to ring the bell again—and the door opened and Connie Evans stood there looking at me.

"Oh," she said in a dull voice, "hello. What do you—"

I hit the door with my shoulder, not lightly; it smacked into her, sent her backpedaling into the middle of the room. I went in and shut the door and glanced around. Living room. And we were the only two people in it.

"Where's Lynn?"

Evans stood rubbing her arm where the door had hit it. Her expression was as dull as her voice had been. Under her eyes were smudges so dark they looked like lampblack smeared on skin that was pale white, almost translucent. There was a zombielike quality about her, as if she had lost some of her grasp on reality.

I moved up close to her. "Answer me. Where's Lynn?"

"In the bedroom."

Two doors led off the living room. One was open and through it I could see part of the kitchen; the other one was closed. I hurried over to the closed one, opened it and went into a short hallway. The bedroom was at the far end, at the rear of the house.

The drapes had been drawn in there and the room was dim; Lynn Canale was a small, still mound under a quilted comforter on the bed. But she stirred when I pulled the comforter down and lifted one of her arms to check her pulse; and the pulse was strong and steady. I let out a relieved breath. Lynn moaned softly as I lowered her arm; she rolled onto her back, but she didn't wake up. Her face appeared puffy, the lips dry and cracked.

I covered her again and returned to the living room. Connie Evans was sitting curled up in an ancient morocco chair, sipping from a can of Coca-Cola. Her eyes were vacant, staring at something only she could see.

I went around in front of the chair. "What did you give Lynn?"

She focused on me. "What?"

"You gave her some kind of drug, didn't you?"

"Oh. Yes. Some sleeping pills."

"How many sleeping pills?"

"Two or three. She was very upset . . . about Larry being dead. She shouldn't have been, though; he wasn't worth it." Evans shook her head, as if she were still a little awed by the fact. "He wasn't worth it."

"How did Lynn find out about Travers' death? Did you tell her?"

"No. Her father . . . he called. He said he was coming over to take her home, but she didn't want to see him, she didn't want to go home."

"So you brought her over here."

"She asked if she could stay here tonight. It was her idea . . ." She drank some more of her Coke. "You know, don't you," she said.

"Yeah," I said. "I know."

"Everything?"

"I think so."

"How did you find out?" she asked, but not as if it mattered much to her.

I didn't answer right away. Most of the tension had drained out of me; Lynn was all right and I did not think Evans was going to give me any trouble. I backed away from her, over to where she had fashioned a work space in one corner of the room; I had noticed it when I first came in. There was desk and a couple of tables, arranged so that they formed a little ell, and on them was a variety of electronic equipment. A bank of stereo components—tape recorder, phonograph, AM-FM radio, VHS videotape deck, even an oscilloscope. An answering machine hooked up to the telephone. A small cassette recorder. And an Apple home computer with an oversized readout screen.

From there I said, "Yesterday, when Lynn got the threatening call while the three of us were together and I took the phone away from her, I heard the connection being broken. A whirring click. It didn't mean anything to me at the time, but it should have. There's always a click on the line when somebody hangs up, but you only get the whirring when a machine is involved. An answering machine, for example. I called Lynn's father last night; he wasn't home and I got his answering machine and there was the whirring click when it came on. The same thing happened when I checked my office answering machine this afternoon. That was what finally started me thinking and remembering."

I paused, but Evans had nothing to say. She just sat there looking at me, sipping from that damned can of Coke.

"There's another kind of machine that makes a whirring click," I said. "A machine that can de-liver messages, not just take them—a cassette recorder like this one here. If you've got the right equipment and some knowledge of electronics, you can tape a message on a cassette, hook up the recorder to the phone and to a home computer, and program the computer to *make* a call when-ever you want it to. Isn't that right, Connie?"

"Yes," she said.

"Sure. The computer opens the line at a preset time, 'dials' a programmed number and switches on the recorder so it can play the message you've taped. As soon as the message ends, the computer shuts everything off and breaks the connection . . . with a little whirring click." I tapped the recorder on the table. "What would I hear if I played this cassette? Or did you already erase the tape?"

"No." Another sip. "You know what you'd hear."

"Was yesterday the first time you used a tape to make one of those calls to Lynn?"

"Yes."

"Why? Because she told you her father had hired a private detective who was coming over to see her, and you thought that if you timed a call to come in while you were there, the detective would never suspect the truth? Or was it just that you wanted to see Lynn's face when you told her on the tape you were going to kill her?"

Sip. Sip.

But it didn't really matter. The facts were, she had timed the call for one o'clock, probably before she'd gone to her ten o'clock class to take her exam, but the exam had lasted longer than she'd anticipated, and on the way to Lynn's from the college she'd realized her watch had stopped. That was why she had asked Lynn what time it was the moment she arrived. It wasn't a soap opera program on TV she had been afraid she'd missed; it was the programmed call.

"I wasn't going to do it," Evans said after a time. "Kill her, I mean."

"No? Then why did you threaten her?"

"I wanted to hurt her even more. Inside, the way she'd hurt me."

"How did she hurt you?"

"She took Larry away from me. We were going together; I loved him and he said he loved me. We

were going to get married. Then Lynn came
along."

It was about what I had expected, but that didn't
make it any easier to listen to. I quit looking at
Connie Evans and looked out through the front
window instead. You could see across the Great
Highway to the beach and the Pacific beyond, and
because it was a clear day the shapes of the Faral-
lon Islands were outlined against the horizon.
They were a long way from here, thirty-two miles
west of the Golden Gate, and I wished I was a long
way from here, too.

She said, "I tried to get Larry back, but he
wouldn't have anything more to do with me. And
I kept seeing Lynn around school, always around.
I hated her, but I couldn't get her out of my mind.
So I started talking to her, I got to know her; she
thought we were friends."

"Why the obscene calls? Why pretend to be a
man?"

"She told me once she hated that kind of thing,
some man she didn't know talking to her like
that. She said it scared her more than anything. I
thought . . . I don't know what I thought. One
night I just picked up the phone and called her,
that's all."

And it hadn't been difficult for her to disguise
her voice, I thought, or to make it sound masculine. She'd had at least some actor's training; Jud
Canale had told me the Drama Club was where
she and Lynn had gone yesterday evening.

I said, "Everything changed last night. Why?"

Sip. "It was Lynn's father. I was there when he

came to see her. He asked me to step into the bedroom, but I listened anyway. He told her about Larry leaving her, going to San Diego; he called Larry a lot of bad names. At first I couldn't believe Larry would do something like that. Then I hoped it was true. I thought maybe I could talk him into taking me back, letting me go to San Diego with him."

"Is that why you went to the boatyard?"

She nodded; her head bobbed as if it were on a spring, like one of those little toys you see on the dashboard of cars. "Mr. Canale said the name of the place. I went to Larry's flat first, but he wasn't there; then I went to the boatyard. It was closed up and I couldn't get in. But Larry drove up just as I was about to leave. He let me in, and we went and sat in the boat. He had a Big Mac and some fries that he'd bought, but he didn't offer me any. He just sat there eating and drinking beer. I had to go out to a machine by the office to get some Coke for myself."

I remembered the empty bottles and cans on the galley table. Two people, Joel Reeves and the bartender at Elrod's, had told me how fond Travers was of beer; so the empty bottles on the table figured to be his. But beer drinkers never mix beer and soda pop, which meant the soft drink cans had to belong to whoever killed him. And Connie Evans was as fond of Coke as Travers had been of beer.

"We talked for a while," she said, "and then he wanted to go to bed. So we did. Afterward I asked him to let me go to San Diego with him, but he said no. I begged him, I told him how much I loved him; he just laughed. Then I saw how he'd used me, how wrong I'd been about him and about Lynn. He was running out on her just like he'd run out on me, and he would keep on doing the same thing to other women if somebody didn't stop him. I felt so ashamed. And I hated him."

Sip. "The gun . . . it was in one of the lockers. I saw it when I fist came on the boat; Larry told me it was for shooting sharks. So I got it while he was getting dressed and I pointed it at him. 'This gun is for shooting sharks, Larry,' I said. 'Isn't that what you told me?' Then I shot him. I don't know why I put the gun in his hand afterward. I don't remember much about what happened after he was dead."

Her voice was still as emotionless as when she'd started speaking; nothing had changed in her expression either. She took one last sip of the Coke and then put the can down carefully on the carpet beside her chair.

"I guess that's all," she said. "Except that I wouldn't have hurt Lynn anymore. I really wouldn't have." She folded her hands in her lap. "Are you going to call the police now?"

"Yes."

"That's all right. I don't care."

"They'll get you some help, Connie," I said.

"I don't care about that either. I hated him but I loved him so much longer. He's dead and so am I."

I looked away from her again, away from the emptiness in her voice and in her eyes. There was

no anger left in me, not toward her; there was
only pity and sadness. She wasn't to blame for all
of this. Neither was Larry Travers, when you
stripped it all to the bottom line. Blame it on the
kind of animals we poor humans are, the things
that drive us and obsess us. Blame it on a cosmos
that might not be so benevolent after all.

I picked up the telephone receiver and called
Jack Logan at the Hall of Justice.

IX.

Friday morning, late January.

The weather was still good, clear and mostly
warm. And people on the streets, I saw as I drove
to my office, were still smiling over San Francisco's surprising Super Bowl victory on Sunday. But
Lynn Canale, in seclusion at her father's home,
wasn't smiling; and Jud Canale wasn't smiling;
and neither was Connie Evans in her new home in
a prison hospital. Death, like life, goes on—and so
do mental breakdowns, and aberrant behavior, and
pain and tragedy and grief—even in the midst of a
week-long, city-wide celebration as jubilant as
any San Francisco has ever known.

And that was why, on this clear and mostly
warm Friday morning five days after the Forty-
niners had won the Super Bowl, I still wasn't
smiling along with everybody else.

Booktaker

It was a Thursday afternoon in late May, and it was gloomy and raining outside, and I was sitting in my brand-new offices on Drumm Street wishing I were somewhere else. Specifically, over at Kerry's apartment on Diamond Heights, snuggling up with her in front of her nice big fireplace. Thoughts like that seemed to come into my head all the time lately. I had known Kerry Wade only a couple of weeks, but it had already developed into a pretty intense relationship. For me, anyhow.

But I was not going to get to snuggle up with her tonight. Or tomorrow night either. She worked as a copywriter for Bates and Carpenter, a San Francisco advertising agency, and when I'd called her this morning she'd said she was in the middle of an important presentation; she was going to have to work late both nights in order to finish it to deadline. How about Saturday night? I said. Okay, she said. So I had a promise, which was better than nothing, but Saturday was two long days away. The prospect of spending the next forty-eight hours alone, cooped up here and in my Pacific Heights flat, made me feel as gloomy as the weather.

My flat wasn't so bad, but these shiny new offices left a great deal to be desired. They consisted of two rooms, one waiting area and one private office, with pastel walls, beige carpeting, some chrome chairs with beige corduroy cushions and venetian blinds on the windows. The bright yellow phone somebody in the telephone company had seen fit to give me looked out of place on my battered old desk. The desk looked out of place, too, in the sterile surroundings. And so did I: big hulking guy, overweight, shaggy-looking, with a face some people thought homely and other people—me included, when I was in a good mood—thought of as possessing character. Sort of like the late actor Richard Boone.

I didn't belong in a place like this. It had *no* character, this place; it was just a two-room office in a newly renovated building down near the waterfront. It could have been anybody's office, in just about any profession. My old office, on the other hand, the one I had occupied for better than twenty years before moving here two weeks ago, had had too much character, which was the main reason I had made up my mind to leave it. It had been located in a frumpy old building on the fringe of the Tenderloin, one of the city's high-crime areas, and with the neighborhood worsening, I had finally accepted the fact that prospective clients wouldn't be too keen about hiring a private investigator with that sort of address.

This place had been the best I could find for what I could afford. And so here I was, all decked out with a new image, and the phone still didn't ring and clients still didn't line up outside my door. So much for transitioning upscale and all the rest of that crap. So much for detective work in general.

I was starting to depress myself. What I needed was to get out of here the rest of today and all day tomorrow; what I needed was work. So why doesn't somebody come in? I thought. I looked out across the anteroom to the access door. Well? I thought. Come on in, somebody.

And the door opened and somebody came in.

I blinked, startled. It was enough to make you wonder if maybe there was something after all to the theory of solipsism.

My visitor was a man, and I was on my feet when he limped through my private office and stopped in front of the desk. "I don't know if you remember me," he said. "I'm John Rothman."

"Yes, sir, sure I do. It's good to see you again, Mr. Rothman."

I had recognized him immediately even though I hadn't seen him in more than a year; I have a cop's memory for faces. He was the owner of San Francisco's largest secondhand bookshop—an entire building over on Golden Gate Avenue near the Federal Building, three floors and a basement full of every kind of used book, from reading copies of popular fiction and nonfiction to antiquarian books, prints and the like. I had first met him several years ago, when pulp magazines were still reasonably cheap and there were only a few serious collectors like myself around; he had acquired, through an estate sale, about a thousand near-mint issues of *Black Mask*, *Dime Detective*, *Dime Mystery*, *Thrilling Detective* and other pulps from the thirties and forties, and because I happened to be fairly solvent at the time, I'd been able to buy the entire lot at not much more than a dollar an issue. Those same thousand copies today would cost more than I made most years.

On four or five occasions since then, whenever a new batch of pulps came his way, Rothman had contacted me. I hadn't bought much from him, what with escalating prices, but I had purchased enough to keep my name in his files and in his memory.

But it wasn't his profession that had brought him here today; it was mine. "I've got a serious problem at the bookshop," he said, "and I'd like to hire you to get to the bottom of it."

"If I can help, I'll be glad to do what I can."

I waited until he was seated in one of the two clients' chairs and then sat down again myself. He was in his fifties, tall and aristocratic-looking, with silvering hair and cheekbones so pronounced they were like sharp little ridges. His limp was the result of some sort of childhood disease or accident—he had once made a vague reference to it—and he needed the use of a cane; the one he hooked over the arm of the chair was thick and gnarled and black, with a knobby handle. Its color matched the three-piece suit he wore.

"I'll get right to the point," he said. "I've been

plagued by thefts the past few months, and I'm damned if I can find out who's responsible or how they're being done."

"What is it that's been stolen?"

"Valuable antiquarian items. Rare books at first; more recently, etchings, prints and old maps. The total value so far exceeds twenty thousand dollars."

I raised an eyebrow. "That's a lot of money."

"It is, and my insurance doesn't cover it all. I've been to the police, but there doesn't seem to be much they can do, under the circumstances. There seldom is in cases like this."

"You mean book thefts are a common occurrence?"

"Oh, yes," Rothman said. "Thieves are a thorn in the side of every bookseller. I lose hundreds, if not thousands, of dollars of stock to them each year. No matter how closely we watch our customers, the experienced thief can always find a way to slip a book into a concealed pocket or inside his clothing, or to wrap a print or an old map around himself under a coat. A few years ago an elderly gentleman, very distinguished, managed to steal a first edition of Twain's *Huckleberry Finn*, even though I can still swear I had my eyes on him the whole time."

"Do these people steal for profit—to resell the items?"

"Sometimes," he said. "Others are collectors who don't have the money or the inclination to pay for something they desperately want. A much smaller percentage are kleptomaniacs. But this is an unusual case because of the number and value of the thefts, and because of the circumstances surrounding them, and I'm fairly certain the motive is resale for profit. Not to other dealers, but to unscrupulous private collectors who don't care how the items were obtained and who don't ask questions when they're offered."

"Then you think the thief is a professional?"

"No. I think he's one of my employees."

"Oh? Why is that?"

"For several reasons. All of the items were taken from the Antiquarian Room on the third floor; a room that is kept locked at all times. I have a key and so do—or did—two of my employees; no customer has ever been allowed inside without one of us present. And after the first two thefts—a fine copy of T.S. Arthur's temperance novel, *Ten Nights in a Bar Room*, and an uncommon children's book, Mary Wollstonecraft's *Original Stories from Real Life*—I ordered the Antiquarian Room out of bounds to customers unless they were personally known to me. I also had a sensor alarm installed on the front entrance. You know what that is, of course?"

I nodded. It was an electronic gateway, similar to the metal detectors used in airports, through which customers had to pass on their way out. Any purchases they made were cleared by rubbing the items across a sensor strip. If someone tried to leave the premises with something that hadn't been paid for and cleared, an alarm would sound. A lot of bookstores used the device these days; so did most libraries.

"Three weeks later," Rothman said, "a six-teenth-century religious etching attributed to one of the pioneers of print-making, Albrecht Dürer, disappeared. It was one of two I had recently purchased, and extremely valuable; if it had been authenticated, it would be priceless. Even so, I was in the process of realizing several thousand dollars from a collector in Hillsborough when it van-ished." He paused. "The point is, I checked the Antiquarian Room that morning, before I went out to lunch, as I regularly do; the Dürer was still there at that time. But it had vanished when I checked the room again late that afternoon—and no customer had been permitted inside in the interim, nor had the door lock been tampered with."

"Did you take any further precautions after that theft?"

"Yes. I confiscated the other two keys to the Antiquarian Room. But that didn't stop him ei-ther. There have been four other thefts since then, at increasingly frequent intervals—all of them between eleven and two o'clock, evidently when I was away from the shop. The second Dürer etch-ing, two seventeenth-century Japanese color prints and a rare map of the Orient; the map disappeared two days ago."

"The thief could have had a duplicate key made before you confiscated the originals," I suggested.

"I know; I thought of that, too. Any of my four employees could have had a duplicate made, in fact, not just the two who had keys previously. On occasion those two gave their keys to the other two, when they needed something from the Antiquarian Room and were too busy to get it themselves."

"Did you consider changing the lock?"

"I did, yes. But I decided against it."

"Why?"

"As clever as the thief is," Rothman said, "I suspect he'd have found a way to circumvent that obstacle, too. And I don't just want to stop the thefts; I want the person responsible caught and punished, and I want to know how he's getting the stolen items out of the shop so I can take steps to prevent it from ever happening again. The *how* of it bothers me almost as much as the thefts themselves."

"Couldn't the thief have simply cleared the items through the sensor when no one was looking and walked out with them later under his clothing?"

"No. The only sensor strip is located at the cashier's desk, and none of my people had access to it on the days of the thefts except Adam Turner. Adam is the only one of my people I trust implicitly; he's been with me twenty years, and he's loyal and honest to a fault. He'd taken to guarding the sensor since the thefts began, and on at least two of the days he swears he never left the desk for even a moment."

"Do you deactivate the alarm system when you close up for the day?"

"Yes."

"Well, couldn't the thief have stashed the items

somewhere in the store and left with them after the alarm was shut off?"

Rothman shook his head. "I'm the last person to leave nearly every day. And when I'm not, Adam does the locking up. No one but the two of us has a key to the front door. Not only that, but each of the others has to pass through the alarm gateway on his way out, before it's shut off; that is a strict rule and there have been no exceptions."

I did some ruminating. "Is it possible the thief could have slipped out through another entrance during working hours? He wouldn't have to have been gone more than a couple of minutes; he could even have passed the stolen items to a confederate. . . ."

Rothman was shaking his head again. "All the other entrances to the shop—first-floor rear and fire-escape doors on the second and third floor— are kept locked and are protected by separate alarm systems."

"How many people have keys to those entrances?"

"Only myself. And even if one of the others managed to get hold of it and have a duplicate made, the alarm would still ring if any of the doors were opened."

"Where is the control box for those alarms located?"

"Behind the cashier's desk. But it's also kept locked, and Adam guards it zealously as he does the sensor strip."

"What about a window?" I asked. "Are there alarms on those, too?"

"No, but they are all securely locked and also painted shut. None of them has been touched."

I ruminated again. "I can think of one other possibility," I said at length. "Suppose the thief *hasn't* gotten the stolen items out of the shop? Suppose he hid them somewhere with the idea of making off with them later, because he *hasn't* figured out a way to beat the alarms?"

"I'm afraid that's not the answer either," Rothman said. "For one thing, Adam and I have searched the shop on more than one occasion; it's quite large, granted, but I'm sure we would have found the missing pieces if they were there. And for another thing, at least one item—the first Dürer etching—appears to have surfaced in the collection of a man named Martell in Chicago."

"You've heard rumors, you mean?"

"More than just rumors. After each theft I notified other antiquarian booksellers throughout the country and in Europe, as well as *AB Bookman's Weekly* and other publications in the trade; that's standard procedure whenever anything of value is stolen. A dealer in Chicago called me not long after I publicized the theft of the first Dürer, to say that he'd heard Martell had intimated to another collector that he had acquired it. Admittedly, that's secondhand information. But I know of Martell; he's a passionate collector of fifteenth- and sixteenth-century religious etchings, and he had a reputation of being unscrupulous about it. My colleague in Chicago knows Martell personally and says that if he has bragged about having the Dürer etching, he really does have it."

"Did you try to contact Martell?"

"I did. He denies possession, of course."

"Isn't there anything you can do to prove otherwise?"

"No. Without proof that he bought it, there is no legal way I can have his premises searched or force him to admit to its current ownership."

"So the only way to get that proof," I said, "is to find out who stole it from you and sold it Martell."

"That's correct."

"Do you suspect any one employee more than the others?"

"Not really. I've ruled out Adam Turner, as I told you; it could be any of the other three."

I had been taking notes as we talked; I flipped over to a clean page on my pad. "Tell me about those three."

"Tom Lennox has been with me the longest, next to Adam. Four years. He's quiet, intense, knowledgeable—a good bookman. He hopes to open his own antiquarian shop someday."

"So you'd say he's ambitious?"

"Yes, but not overly so."

"Is he one of the two who had keys to the Antiquarian Room?"

"Yes. Adam was the other. They both gave up their keys willingly."

"Uh-huh. Go ahead, Mr. Rothman."

"Harmon Boyette," he said, and spelled the last name. "He has worked for me a little more than two years, ever since he moved here from Seattle. He owned a bookstore there for several years, but he went bankrupt when his wife divorced him. He seems quite bitter about it."

"Do you consider him dependable?"

"Most of the time. But he does have an alcohol problem. Not that he drinks on the job—I wouldn't stand for that—but he comes in badly hungover on some mornings, and has missed days now and then."

"Does money seem to be important to him?"

"If so, he's never said anything about it. Nor has he ever said anything about wanting to go into business for himself again."

"And the third man?"

"Neal Vining. A Britisher, born in London. His father is a bookseller there. He married an American girl and came to San Francisco about eighteen months ago. I hired him because he has considerable expertise in English and European books, both antiquarian and modern. He learned the business from his father, and in a remarkably short time; he's only twenty-six."

"Is *he* ambitious, would you say?"

"Yes. He's eager, always asking questions, gathering more knowledge. His only apparent fault is that he tends to be a bit egotistical at times."

I took a moment to go back over my notes. "The thefts began how long ago?" I asked.

"Approximately five months."

"Were there many valuable items stolen in, say, the year prior to that?"

"Two books, as I recall." He frowned. "Are you thinking the same person might have stolen those, too?"

"It's possible," I said. "The man responsible could have started off in a small way at first and then decided to risk stealing items on a more regular basis. Particularly if he feels he has an undetectable method. Impatience, greed, a feeling of power—all those things could be driving him."

Rothman nodded speculatively. "Now that I think of it," he said, "an inscribed first edition of Henry Miller's *Black Spring* disappeared about three months after Neal Vining came to work for me."

"Lennox and Boyette are just as likely to be guilty, from what you've told me. Lennox could have been taking rare books off and on for four years, Boyette off and on for two."

"Yes, you're right." He ran spread fingers through his silvering hair. "How will you handle your investigation?"

"Well, first of all I'll run a background check on each of the three suspects. And it would be a good idea if I spent some time in the store, especially since the thief seems to be getting bolder; I might be able to spot something that'll tell us how he's doing it. You could introduce me as a new employee, give me some work to do and let me take it from there."

"Fine. Can you start right away?"

"This afternoon, if you like. But I think it would look better if I came in first thing in the morning. That way I can spend the rest of today making those background checks."

Rothman agreed. He gave me addresses for Lennox, Boyette and Vining, after which we settled

on my fee and I made out one of my standard
contract forms and had him sign it. We also settled
on what my job would be at the book shop—I
would come in as a stock clerk, which entailed
shelving books, filing customer orders and the
like, and which would allow me to move freely
around the shop—and on the name I would be
using: Jim Marlowe, in honor of Raymond Chandler. Then we shook hands, and he limped out,
and I got to work.

I called a guy I knew in Records and Identification at the Hall of Justice; he promised me he'd
run the three names through his computer and
the FBI hookup, to see if any of them had a
criminal record, and get back to me before five
o'clock. The next order of business was to get a
credit report on each of the three, so I called
another friend who worked for a leasing company
and asked him to pull TRW's on the trio. He also
said he'd have the information by five.

I got out my copy of the reverse directory of city
addresses and looked up the street numbers I had
for Lennox, Boyette and Vining. All three of them
lived in apartment buildings, which made things
a little easier for me. I made a list of the names
and telephone numbers of all the other residents
of those buildings; then I called them one by one,
telling each person who answered that I was a
claims representative for North Coast Insurance
and that I was conducting a routine check in
connection with a substantial insurance policy.
Human nature being what it is, that was a ploy

that almost always put people at their ease and got them to open up about their neighbors.

Two of Lennox's neighbors said that he kept pretty much to himself, had no apparent bad habits and seemed to be more or less happily married. A third person, who knew him a little better, had a somewhat different opinion of Lennox's marital status; this woman said that his wife, Fran, was a complainer who constantly nagged him about money matters. The woman also said that Lennox had a passion for books and that his apartment overflowed with them. She didn't know if any of the books were valuable; she didn't have time for such foolishness as reading, she said, and didn't know anything about books except that they were dust collectors.

Harmon Boyette's neighbors confirmed that he was a heavy drinker; most of his imbibing was done at home, they said, and he tended to be surly when he was tight. They didn't seem to like him much. Nobody knew if he had money to spend, or what he spent it on if he did. None of them had ever been inside his apartment.

Neal Vining, on the other hand, was friendly, gregarious, enjoyed having people in for small parties and was well liked. So was his wife, Sara, whose father owned a haberdashery shop in Ghirardelli Square that specialized in British imports; she and Vining had met during one of the father's buying trips to London. I also learned that Vining was the athletic type—jogged regularly, played racquetball—and that he liked to impress people with his knowledge of books and literary matters.

As with Lennox and Boyette, he didn't seem to have a great deal of money and he didn't spend what he had indiscriminately.

There was nothing in any of this, at least so far as I could tell, that offered a clue as to which of the three men might be guilty. I considered running a check on Adam Turner, even though Rothman had seemed certain of Turner's innocence; I like to be thorough. But I decided to let Rothman's judgment stand, at least for the time being.

The guy at R and I called back at four-thirty, with a pretty much negative report; none of the three suspects had a criminal record, and with the exception of Boyette, none of them had ever been arrested. Boyette had been jailed twice, overnight both times, on drunk-and-disorderly charges.

Just before five, my friend at the leasing company came through with the credit reports. Not much there either. Vining had a good credit rating, Lennox a not very good one and Boyette none at all. The only potentially interesting fact was that Lennox had defaulted on an automobile loan nine months ago, with the result that the car—a new Mercedes—had been repossessed. Up until then, Lennox's credit rating had been pretty good. It made me wonder why he had decided to buy an expensive car like a Mercedes in the first place; he couldn't have been paid a very hefty salary. But then, it might have been his wife's doing, if what I'd been told about her was true.

By the time I looked over everything again, reread the notes I'd taken during my talk with Rothman and put it all away in a file folder, it was five-twenty and I was ready to pack it in for the day. I was feeling considerably better than I had been before Rothman's arrival; I had a job, and I would not have to spend tomorrow sitting around this damned office watching it rain and waiting for something to happen and pining away for Kerry.

The telephone was ringing when I let myself into my flat an hour later. I hustled into the bedroom, where I keep the thing, and hauled up the receiver and said hello.

"Hi," Kerry's voice said. "You sound out of breath."

"I just came in. *You* sound tired."

"I am. And the way it looks, I'm not going to get out of here until nine o'clock."

"How's the presentation going?"

"Pretty good. I'll probably have to work Saturday morning, but I should be finished by noon."

"We're still on for Saturday night, aren't we?"

"We are. What did you have in mind?"

"Well, I've been wondering—"

"Oh, damn," she said. "Can you hold on a minute? I'm being paged by the boss."

"Sure."

There was a clicking noise as she put me on hold. I shrugged out of my damp overcoat, tossed it on the floor and sat down on the rumpled bed. While I waited I occupied myself by visualizing Kerry in my mind. She was something to look at, all right. Not pretty in any classic sense, but strikingly attractive: coppery hair worn shoulder-length; animated face marked with humor lines; generous mouth; greenish eyes that seemed to change color, like a chameleon, according to her moods. And a fine willowy body, with the kind of legs men stared at and most women envied.

I wondered again, as I had on several occasions, what she saw in me. I was fifty-three to her thirty-eight and not much to look at, but she thought I was pretty hot stuff just the same. Sexy, she'd said once. Which was all a crock, as far as I was concerned, but I loved her for feeling that way.

I *did* love her, that was the thing, even though we'd only known each other a couple of weeks. I'd met her during a pulp-magazine convention, which she'd attended because both her parents—Ivan and Cybil Wade—were ex-pulp writers who had been well known in the forties, Ivan for his fantasy/horror stories in *Weird Tales* and *Dime Mystery*, Cybil for a hardboiled detective series under the male pseudonym of Samuel Leatherman. The pulp angle had been part of my attraction to her in the beginning, just as part of hers for me had been the fact that, as a result of her mother's writing, she'd always been intrigued by private detectives. So we'd struck up an immediate friendship, and had become lovers much sooner than I could have hoped for.

Meanwhile, things had been happening at the convention that culminated in murder, and I had found myself in an investigation that had almost got me killed. When it was finished I had asked her to marry me, surprising myself as well as her. She hadn't said no; in fact, she'd said that she loved me, too, after her fashion. But she'd been married once, a bad marriage, and she just wasn't sure if she wanted to try it again. She needed more time to think things over, she said. And that was where things stood now.

Not for long, though, I hoped. I had never been as sure of anything as I was that I wanted Ms. Kerry Wade, she of the fine legs and the wonderful chamelcon eyes, to be my wife.

There was another noise as the line reopened, and she said, "You still there?"

"Would I hang up on a gorgeous lady like you?"

"Gorgeous," she said. "Hah. What were you saying about Saturday night?"

"I was just wondering," I said, "how you felt about snuggling up at your apartment in front of a nice hot fire?"

"Oh ho. So that's it."

"Yep. So how *do* you feel about it?"

"Well, I might be persuaded. Providing, of course, that you take me out first and ply me with good food."

"Done. How about Oaxaca's, over on Mission?"

"Mmm, yes. We could spend the afternoon together, too. Drinks in Sausalito, maybe?"

"Sounds terrific," I said. "Only I think I may be tied up during the afternoon. I picked up a job today." I told her about John Rothman and what he had hired me to do. "So unless I can wrap things up tomorrow, which doesn't seem likely, I'll be at the book shop all day Saturday. The place closes at six, though. I could pick you up around seven."

"Fine," she said. "Right now, I'd better get back to work. Call me tomorrow night? I'll be here late again."

"Okay. And Kerry . . . I love you."

"Me, too," she said, and she was gone.

Smiling, feeling chipper, I went out into the kitchen and opened myself a beer and made a couple of salami-and-cheese sandwiches. Kerry wouldn't have approved; she was of the opinion that my eating habits left something to be desired. Well, she could change them when she became my wife. I had been a bachelor too long to want to change them on my own.

After I finished eating I curled up on the couch in my cluttered living room—another thing Kerry disapproved of, and that she could change if she was of a mind to, was my sloppy housekeeping habits—with Volume One, Number One of *Strange Detective Mysteries*, dated October 1937. Norville Page's lead novel, "When the Death-Bat Flies," kept me amused for an hour, and stories by Norbert Davis, Wayne Rogers, Paul Ernst and Arthur Leo Zagat took care of the rest of the evening.

I got down to Rothman's book shop, dressed in a sports shirt and a pair of old slacks instead of my usual suit and tie, at five minutes to nine on Friday morning. The building, a big old structure with a Victorian facade, was sandwiched between an auction gallery and a Chinese restaurant. A pair of wide plate-glass windows flanked the entrance; behind them were display racks of books of various types. Both windows bore the same legends in dark red lettering.

J. ROTHMAN, BOOKSELLER
Fine Books—Used, Rare, Antiquarian

The front door was locked; I rapped on the glass panel. Pretty soon a stooped, elderly guy, coatless but wearing a white dress shirt and a bow tie, appeared inside. When he got to the door he peered out at me through rimless glasses and then threw the bolt lock and opened up.

"My name is Jim Marlowe," I told him. "I'm the new man Mr. Rothman hired yesterday."

"Oh, yes." He gave me his hand and I took it. "Turner, Adam Turner. Assistant Manager."

"Pleased to meet you, Mr. Turner."

He nodded, stepped aside to let me come in. While he was relocking the door I glanced around the main floor. The cashier's desk was on the left, flanked by the wide gateway for the sensor alarm; you had to go through the gateway both entering and leaving, because there was a six-foot-high partition on the right-hand side. Beyond, several long display tables filled with sale books and recent arrivals were arranged for easy browsing. Floor-to-ceiling shelves covered the side walls, and stacks with narrow aisleways between them took up the rear half of the room. Off to one side toward the back, a flight of stairs led up to the second floor and another down to the basement.

I let Turner precede me through the gateway. He looked to be in his mid-sixties, nondescript and mild, but his rheumy blue eyes were alert and intelligent, and I thought that they would not miss much.

I asked him, "Is Mr. Rothman here?"

"Yes. He's in his office, upstairs on the second floor. He asked me to send you right up; he'll show you around personally."

"Thanks."

Most of the second floor was given over to stacks; according to a number of neatly painted signs, all of the books here were used hardcover fiction—general novels, mysteries, Westerns and science fiction. Another flight of stairs led to the third floor, but there was a chain drawn across the bottom and a sign that said, *No Admittance*. A wider corridor than the aisleways between the stacks extended the length of the far wall, and when I got over there I saw three doors, the middle one standing open. I stopped in front of the open one. Inside was a good-sized office—Rothman's, probably, judging from the size of the desk and the big old-fashioned safe in one corner—but nobody was in it.

I was standing there looking in when I heard a toilet flush. Then the third door opened and Rothman appeared. He saw me, caught up his cane from where it was leaning against the wall and limped over to me.

"One of the signs of advancing age is a weak bladder," he said, and gave me a rueful smile. "Have you been waiting long?"

"No, I just came up."

"You spoke to Adam, of course. I didn't tell him

you were a detective; I thought it would be best if only you and I know your real purpose here."

I nodded. "Does he always come in this early?"

"Most days, yes. Sometimes he's here before I am, and I usually arrive by eight-thirty. His wife died a few years ago; he's lonely, and the shop is a second home to him."

"I see."

"Would you like to see the Antiquarian Room before I show you the rest of the shop?"

"Yes, please."

We went back to the stairs, and Rothman unhooked the chain and led me up to the third floor. There was a door at the top of the stairs; he unlocked it with his key, switched on the lights inside.

The Antiquarian Room was divided into two sections—the first and larger one containing several hundred books and pamphlets, the other one about a fifth as many prints, etchings, engravings, broadsides and maps. Half of the items were in glass display cases or inside glass-covered bookcases; the rest were openly shelved, most of those being sets of books; encyclopedias, histories, the collected works of nineteenth- and early twentieth-century authors. Refectory tables were set in the middle of each section, presumably so potential buyers could sit down and inspect whatever they were interested in. The good, musty smell of old books and old leather bindings was strong in the room.

I asked, "Are all the things in here valuable?"

"Comparatively, no." Rothman said. "Some are

worth less than fifty dollars; they're kept here because of their age and because they're of interest only to serious collectors. I transferred a dozen or so of the most valuable items to my office safe several months ago, but there are still quite a few here worth a thousand dollars or more."

"Are most of those prints and the like?"

"No. Books."

"But the prints and engravings and maps that were stolen were worth much more, weren't they?"

"Only in the case of the two Dürer etchings."

"Then why would the thief have taken prints and maps instead of the more expensive books?"

"I suppose because the people he's selling them to specialize in that sort of thing."

I moved around the room, examining the cases. Most of them were locked, but the locks were pretty flimsy; once the thief had got in here, it wouldn't have taken him long to break them open. The lock on one in the print section had scratches on it, as if it had been picked with a sharp instrument. That was the case, Rothman told me, which had contained the Orient map that had disappeared three days ago.

When I was done looking around, Rothman locked the door again and we descended to the second floor. He gave me a brief tour of the fiction section; took me down to the first floor, where most of the nonfiction was kept; and pointed out the location of the various categories. With the exception of a wall devoted to Western and regional Americana, and to travel books, the basement was full of trade and mass-market paper-backs of various types and back-issue magazines. There was also a stockroom down there, at the rear.

By the time we came back up to the main floor, it was a quarter to ten and the other employees were beginning to arrive. The first of the three to show up was Harmon Boyette. He was about forty, gaunt, with curly black hair, ascetic features and a bushy mustache. Judging from his bloodshot eyes and splotchy skin, the faint trembling of his hands, he'd had another rough night with the bottle.

Rothman introduced us. Boyette gave me a brief, appraising look, seemed to decide I was nobody he was much interested in and said he was glad to meet me without meaning it. He didn't offer to shake hands.

Neal Vining came in five minutes later. Rothman had excused himself and gone back upstairs to answer another call of nature, so it was Adam Turner who performed the introductions this time. Vining had brown eyes, lank brown hair, a bright smile with a lot of teeth in it and one of those lean, athletic bodies that make you think of long-distance runners. He was dressed in a sports jacket and slacks, very spiffy, and he looked older than the twenty-six Rothman had told me he was.

"Marlowe," he said, pumping my hand. "English name. But you don't look a bit English, I'm afraid."

"My mother was Italian," I said truthfully.

"Lovely people, the Italians. Have you ever been?"

"To Italy? No, I haven't."

"You should go someday, if you have the chance. Do you know books well, Jim?"

"Not as well as I'd like to."

"You'll learn them here, then. Won't he, Adam?"

"If he chooses," Turner said.

I did not get to meet Tom Lennox right away because he hadn't shown up yet when Turner hustled me down into the basement stockroom and put me work. There were a couple of hundred newly acquired paperbacks on a table; my job was to sort them into categories and shelve them alphabetically in the proper sections. I figured I had better complete that task, to make the proper impression, before I did any roaming around. It took me more than an hour, and the place was full of customers when I finally went back upstairs.

Vining was over in the Occult section, trying to sell a fat woman a book on witchcraft; I could hear him regaling her with esoteric information on the subject when I passed. Turner was behind the cashier's desk, and so was a short, stocky guy with not much hair who was talking on the telephone. I didn't see any sign of Boyette.

The stocky guy finished his conversation and replaced the receiver as I came up. He was around thirty, freckled, with sad eyes and the sad, jowly face of a hound; what hair he had was a dark reddish color. I thought he must be Tom Lennox, and Turner confirmed it when he introduced us.

"Good to have you with us, Mr. Marlowe," Lennox said. He had a soft, cultured voice that belied his appearance.

"Thanks. I'm glad to be here."

"You've had previous bookstore experience, have you?"

"Some," I said. "I'm also a collector."

"Oh? What do you collect?"

"Pulp magazines."

He wasn't impressed. Maybe he was a literary snob, or maybe he just had no interest in pulps; in any case, he said, "You have plenty of company these days. The prices tend to be highly overinflated."

"I know," I said. "Supply and demand. That's why I collect the more inexpensive variety."

Lennox nodded and turned away. So much for me, and so much for pulp magazines.

Turner asked me if I'd finished shelving the paperbacks, and I told him I had. Then he said, "Harmon is upstairs working in hardcover fiction. I'd like you to go up and give him a hand."

When I got upstairs I found Boyette in the mystery section, weeding out the stock—evidently to make room for new acquisitions. Books were stacked on the floor to one side.

"Mr. Turner sent me up to give you some help," I said.

"I don't need any help."

"Well, those were my instructions."

He ran a hand over his splotchy face; he was sweating and he looked sick. "All right, then. Take that stack of books downstairs and put them out front in the bargain bins. But make sure you stop at the desk first."

"Why is that?"

"So Turner can clear them before you go out. They told you about the alarm, didn't they?"

"Oh, right. I guess that's a pretty good safeguard, the alarm system."

"Is it?"

"It prevents thefts, doesn't it?"

"Sometimes," he said. "Not always."

"You mean people can still manage to steal books? I don't see how."

"There are ways."

"What ways?"

"Didn't anybody tell you about the thefts we've been having?"

"No," I said. "What sort of thefts?"

"Valuable items from the Antiquarian Room upstairs. A half-dozen over the past few months. Nobody knows how it's been done." His mouth turned sardonic. "Rothman thinks one of us is responsible."

"One of the employees?"

"That's right."

"Is that what you think, too?"

"I don't get paid to think," Boyette said. "Personally, I don't give a damn who's responsible. Whoever it is can steal Rothman blind for all I care."

"You sound as though you don't like Mr. Rothman much."

"Maybe I've got reason not to like him."

"He seems like a decent sort to me . . ."

"He is if you suck up to him. I've got five times as much bookselling experience as Lennox and Vining, but I'm the one who gets all the scut work around here. That's because I don't brownnose anybody."

"But Lennox and Vining do?"

"Lennox goes to garage sales, buys books and resells them to Rothman for a few cents apiece. Vining gives him fancy presents from his father-in-law's men's store. All I give him is a good eight hours of work."

"That ought to be enough."

"It isn't," he said bitterly. He narrowed his eyes at me. "What about you, Marlowe? Are *you* a brownnoser?"

"No."

"Then we're in the same boat. But I wouldn't care if you were. I wouldn't even care if you went to Rothman and told him everything I just said."

"I wouldn't do that—"

"He could fire me tomorrow and I wouldn't give a damn. I don't like him and I don't like this place and I don't like being under suspicion all the time."

"If you feel that way, why don't you quit?"

"That's just what I intend to do. As soon as I can find another job."

A customer came clumping up the stairs just then and over into the aisle where we were, and that put an end to the conversation. Boyette said, "Go ahead and take those books downstairs," and returned his attention to the shelves.

I carried the stack of books down to the cashier's desk, waited while Turner cleared them across the sensor strip and then took them outside to where two rolling bins of bargain items were set in front of the display windows. When I got back to the second floor I tried to talk to Boyette again, to see if I could get anything else out of him, but he had lapsed into a moody silence. He didn't have more than a dozen words to say to me over the next two hours.

Rothman went out for lunch at twelve-thirty, Vining around one and Boyette at one-thirty. Lennox and Turner ate brown-bag lunches on the premises, Turner right there at the desk. I also ate lunch in the shop—I'd made myself a couple of sandwiches before leaving my flat that morning—up on the second floor where I could watch the stairs to the Antiquarian Room. Rothman had told me that all of the thefts had occurred between eleven and two; I didn't want to leave, even for a half-hour, and risk missing something.

But there was nothing to miss. Nobody went near the Antiquarian Room and nobody did anything else of a suspicious nature, at least as far as I could tell.

Boyette came back at two-fifteen. He no longer looked quite so sick; his face was flushed and his eyes were a little glassy. I was downstairs when he came in, working in the section marked *Belles Lettres.* Lennox happened to be nearby, and I moved over to him as Boyette climbed down the stairs to the second floor.

"Looks as though Harmon drank his lunch," I said.

Lennox made a disapproving noise. "He generally does."

"An alcoholic?"

"That's rather obvious, isn't it?"

"I guess it is. He seems to be a pretty bitter man, from some of the things he said to me this morning."

"Don't pay any attention to him," Lennox said. "The man has a chip on his shoulder. He thinks he deserves better than his present lot, and he can be damned unpleasant at times."

"Do you think he's honest?"

Lennox frowned. "What sort of question is that?"

"Well, he told me about the thefts from the Antiquarian Room," I said. "He says Mr. Rothman believes one of the employees is responsible."

"He had no business talking to you about that," Lennox said stiffly. "The thefts are none of your concern."

"Maybe not, but I do work here now—"

"Yes. And if you want to continue working here, you'll do well to tend to your work and mind your own affairs."

He stalked away toward the cashier's desk. As he did, Neal Vining appeared around the corner of the neat stack and came up beside me; he had a fat book on archaeology in one hand. "Harmon isn't the only fellow who can be unpleasant," he said. "Tom's a bit tight-assed himself, you know."

"You overheard?"

"Accidentally, yes."

"What's Lennox's problem?"

"Oh, he takes himself and his work much too seriously. One would think *he* owned this shop, the way he acts."

"Those thefts do seem pretty serious," I said.

"They are, of course. Nasty business. I expect we're all on edge because of them."

"Do you agree with Mr. Rothman that someone who works here is responsible?"

He shrugged. "So it would seem, given the circumstances."

"Who do you think it might be?"

"I really don't have any idea," Vining said. "For all *I* know, Mr. Rothman himself could be slipping out with the spoils. Not that I believe that's the case, you understand," he added hastily. "He's quite above reproach. The point is, the thief could be anyone."

"Even Adam Turner?"

"Adam? I hardly think so. But then, two of the missing items were etchings attributed to Albrecht Dürer, and Adam does have considerable expertise in that area. He once wrote an article on Dürer's work. He was also the person who arranged for Mr. Rothman to purchase the two etchings from the estate of a private collector."

"Oh? How was he able to do that?"

"The collector was an acquaintance of Adam's," Vining said. "They struck up a correspondence when the article was published."

Lennox returned and called Vining away to the telephone, so I didn't have a chance to press him for any more information. But what he'd told me was food for thought. If Turner was the guilty

party, there was no real mystery in how he'd
managed the thefts. He could have cleared the
stolen pieces through the sensor at any time,
working as he did on the cashier's desk, and
walked out with them hidden in his clothes. Or
he could have simply arrived early in the morning,
as Rothman had told me he did periodically, and
removed them from the store before Rothman
showed up.

I decided that on Monday I would run a background check on Turner, after all.

The rest of the afternoon passed uneventfully. I
spent most of it on the main floor, with occasional trips upstairs to check on Boyette. He was
still uncommunicative, and by four o'clock, when
the drinks he'd had for lunch had worn off, he had
turned surly; he snapped at me and at a customer
who asked him a question about a book. When
closing time rolled around, he was the first one
out the door.

I stayed until six-fifteen, making myself look
busy; Vining and Lennox were gone by then.
When Rothman came down he sent Turner and
me on our way so he could shut off the sensor
alarm and lock up as he usually did. I waited
around for him outside. The rain had stopped and
there were patches of clear sky among the clouds
to the east; with any luck, the weather would be
good for my weekend with Kerry.

Rothman came out a couple of minutes later.
"Where's your car?" he asked when he finished
locking the front doors.

"In the lot two blocks down."

"That's my direction. We can talk as we walk."

He set off at a brisk pace, in spite of his game leg. I asked him, "Everything okay in the Antiquarian Room?"

"Yes. I checked it this morning, and again tonight before I came down. Nothing's been touched. Have you found out anything so far?"

"Nothing specific, no," I said. I saw no purpose in telling him about Boyette's references to him, in making trouble for Boyette, unless it turned out to have some bearing on my investigation. And I didn't want to press him on Turner until I ran the background check. "I'm afraid this is the kind of job that may take some time, Mr. Rothman."

"I don't expect you to perform miracles," he said. "Time isn't important to me; finding out which of them is guilty, and how he's doing it, is what matters."

We had gone a block, and when we crossed the street Rothman stopped in front of a building that bore a sign reading *Pacific Health Club*. "This is where I'm going," he said.

"You belong to a health club?"

He smiled. "I don't lift weights or play racquetball with Neal Vining, if that's what you're thinking. Mostly I use the Jacuzzi; it helps me relax and eases the pain in my leg."

"Oh, I see."

"You can join me if you like. Guests are permitted."

"No, thanks. I think I'll head home. I like to do my relaxing with a cold beer."

He glanced at my protruding belly. "So I see," he said, but gently, without censure.

We said good night, and he entered the building and I went and got my car and drove home. I drank two cans of Schlitz—the hell with health clubs and the hell with my belly—and then called Kerry at Bates and Carpenter. But she was busy and couldn't talk more than a couple of minutes. She did say that the presentation was going according to schedule and that she still expected to be done with it by noon tomorrow.

"Is it all right if I stop by the book shop when I'm finished?" she asked. "I like bookstores; and I'd love to see you shlepping books around."

"I don't see why not. As long as you don't tell anybody I'm really a private eye on a case."

"I'll try to restrain myself. See you tomorrow, then."

"Lovely lady, I'll count the minutes."

"Phooey," she said, and rang off.

I made myself something to eat, read for a while and turned in early. It had been a reasonably productive day and I was satisfied with it. I had learned a few things; maybe I would learn a few more tomorrow that would establish some kind of pattern. Maybe tomorrow would turn out, I thought, to be an even more productive day.

Saturday was a productive day, all right.

The thief hit the Antiquarian Room again, and he did it right under my damn nose.

It happened, as before, sometime between eleven-twenty, when Rothman checked the room before going out for an early lunch, and two o'clock, when he went up to check it again. I was on the main floor talking to Kerry at the time he made the discovery. She had been there about a half-hour, browsing, looking terrific in a black suit and a frilly white blouse; she was about to buy a book she'd found—a scarce old one of her father's, one of his early novels—and she was telling me how pleased he was going to be because he was down to only two file copies of that particular title.

I didn't like Ivan Wade—Ivan the Terrible, I called him—any more than he liked me; he was overprotective of Kerry, supercilious, humorless and something of a jerk. So I said, "I'm thrilled for him."

"Now don't be that way," she said. *The Redmayne Horror* really is a scarce book. And they only want fifteen dollars."

"*The Redmayne Horror* is a dumb title," I said.

"It was a pulp serial, originally. That was the kind of title they put on weird fiction back in the forties, in the pulps and in book editions; you know that."

"It's still a dumb title."

"Oh, stick it in your ear," she said, and made a face at me. "Can't you see I'm excited about this? I almost knocked over a man with a cane upstairs when I found it."

"That would be Mr. Rothman. Nice going."

"Well, I'm sorry. But I—"

And that was when Rothman appeared on the stairs and beckoned to me urgently. I left Kerry and followed him up to his office, and as soon as he shut the door he told me about the latest theft.

"It was another rare map," he said. His face was flushed and his knuckles showed white where they gripped the head of his cane. "A sixteenth-century map by the Flemish cartographer and geographer Gerhardus Mercator."

"Valuable?"

"Very. Damn, I should have put it in my safe months ago."

"Where was it kept?"

"In one of the glass display cases. The lock was broken, just as in the other thefts."

"Whichever of them it is, he's bold and he's quick," I said. "I've been on this floor off and on ever since you left for lunch. He couldn't have spent much time up here; he had to know exactly what he was after."

"What do we do now?"

"What did you do after you discovered the other thefts?"

"Asked the customers to leave, closed up shop for the day, then gathered my people together and questioned them."

"All right. Do the same thing this time, only let me get rid of the customers. When you start the questioning, ask everybody if they mind being searched. If any of them refuses, press him on it. Then designate me to do the searching."

"Do I tell them you're a detective?"

"No. We won't get anywhere by blowing my cover. Just say you want me to do the searching because I'm new and you don't have any reason to suspect me."

"The thief won't have the map on his person," Rothman said grimly. "He's too clever for that."

"I know. But I want to see how they react and what they might be carrying in their pockets. I don't think he'll have the duplicate key on him either—he's probably got it stashed somewhere in the shop—but it's worth checking for."

"And if none of that does any good?"

"Then you'll have to let them go home. And you and I'll search this place from top to bottom. If none of them can leave with the map, then it's still got to be here somewhere."

We went downstairs together. Kerry was still waiting, when I joined her she said, "What's the matter? You look upset?"

"Trouble. Another theft. You'd better go now; we're closing the shop."

"Oh boy. Will you still be able to make our date tonight?"

"I hope so. If I can't I'll call you."

It took twenty minutes to clear the store of customers and to get the front door locked. Turner and the others knew right away what was going on; none of them had much to say at first, and I could see them giving each other faintly mistrustful glances. Lennox looked aggrieved, as if he took the thefts personally and the money was coming straight out of his pocket. Boyette seemed more angry than anything else, but it was a put-upon kind of anger; he was suffering another hangover and his bloodshot eyes said the last thing he wanted to deal with was another crisis. Vining was subdued, the set of his face grave and concerned. Turner wore an expression of mingled agitation and worry—the look of a loyal company man whose boss is in trouble. None of the four seemed nervous. Or any more guilty, on the surface, than I was.

The six of us were gathered near the cashier's desk. Rothman started off by explaining what it was that had been stolen this time. Then he asked if anyone had seen anyone else go up to the Antiquarian Room; nobody had. Had anyone seen anything of a suspicious nature between eleven-thirty and two o'clock? Nobody had. Who had left the store during that time period? Boyette had, and so had Lennox. But Turner had seen them both leave, through the alarm gateway as always, and nothing had happened.

Rothman said then, "I'm sorry, gentlemen, but these thefts have become intolerable; getting to the bottom of them calls for extreme measures. Do any of you object to being searched?"

The only one who did was Boyette. "Why the hell should I stand for that?" he said. "Even if I were guilty, I wouldn't be stupid enough to have the map on my person."

Lennox said, "Then you shouldn't object to being searched."

"I've had enough of this crap. Thefts, suspicion, body searches—pretty soon it'll be accusations. I won't stand for it; I'm leaving right now and I'm not coming back."

"If you do, Harmon," Vining said, "it will make you look guilty, you know."

"I don't care," Boyette said. He looked mean and belligerent; there was a pugnacious thrust to his jaw. "Is anyone going to try to stop me?"

Rothman glanced at me, but I gave him a faint headshake. I had no right to restrain Boyette, or to search him, without some proof of guilt; if any of us tried, it would leave us open to a lawsuit.

"All right, Harmon," Rothman said coldly. "Consider your employment terminated. I'll mail you what I owe you in salary. Adam, let him out."

Turner went through the gateway and unlocked the front door. The alarm was still operational, and when Boyette stomped through after him the bell didn't go off. It was still possible that he was guilty, but he wasn't walking out of here with the Mercator map.

When Turner relocked the door and came back to join the rest of us, Rothman said, "Does anyone else feel the same way? Or will you all submit to a search?"

There were no more objections. Rothman designated me to do the searching, as we'd agreed, and I frisked each man in turn. Turner first, because I knew he wasn't carrying the map; he'd gone through the gateway just as Boyette had. Then Vining, and then Lennox. No map. All three men had keys—no loose ones, though; they were all on rings or in cases—and Rothman examined each one stoically. His silence told me that none of the keys was the duplicate to the Antiquarian Room door.

There was nothing to do then but let the three of them leave, too. Turner was the last to go, and he went reluctantly. "If you're planning to search the shop, Mr. Rothman," he said, "I can help. . . ."

"No, you go ahead. Marlowe will help me this time."

As soon as Turner was gone, Rothman and I began our search. We started with the Antiquarian Room; it wasn't likely that the thief would have hidden the Mercator map in there, but we gave it a good going-over just the same. No map. We went down to the second floor and searched the stacks, the storage room next to Rothman's office, the bathroom. No map. We combed the first-floor stacks and shelves, the display tables, the cashier's desk, even the window displays. No map. In the basement we searched the paperback sections, the Americana and travel shelves, the stockroom. No map.

We covered every inch of that building, from top to bottom. There was no way the map could have been gotten out, and yet there was no place an item of its size and fragility could have been hidden inside the shop that we had overlooked.

So what *had* happened to it?

Where the hell was the missing map?

It was ten of seven when Rothman and I finally called it quits, left the shop and went our separate ways. I was almost as frustrated as he was by then. On the drive home to my flat, I kept gnawing at the question, the seeming impossibility of the theft, like a dog gnaws at a bone. And the more I gnawed, the more I felt as if I were close to the marrow of the thing.

The answer was something clever and audacious, yes, but I also sensed that it was something simple. And that I had heard enough and seen enough the past three days to put it all together— a lot of little things that just needed to be shifted around into the right order. Damn it, I could almost taste the marrow. . . .

I gave Kerry a brief call, to tell her I would be late, and then showered the bookstore dust off me and put on my suit. Dusk was settling by the time I got up to Diamond Heights. The weather had cleared and the view from up there was spectacular; you could see both bridges, the wide sweep of the bay, the Oakland hills and the Pacific Ocean in the opposite direction. It was too nice an evening, I told myself, to let my frustration spoil things with Kerry, and as I parked the car in front of her building I decided I wouldn't let that happen.

I went into the vestibule and rang her bell, and she buzzed me in right away. When I got upstairs she was waiting for me in a shimmery green dress with plenty of cleavage—a dress designed to knock your optic out, as the pulp private eyes used to say.

"Sorry I'm so late," I said, admiring her. "It was some afternoon."

"That's okay. Did you catch the thief?"

"No. He swiped another rare map and managed to get it out of the store again, past the alarm system. I ought to be able to figure out which one of them it is and how he did it, but I can't seem to do it."

"Uh-oh. Does that mean you're going to be moody tonight?"

"No. I am not going to be moody tonight."

"You're *already* moody," she said.

"Bah. Let's go eat."

We went down and out to the car. Kerry said, "I'm starved. You must be, too."

"Yeah. They do a fine chorizo-and-peppers dish at the Oaxaca, very hot and spicy."

"So of course you have to drink a lot of beer with it."

"Sure. What's Mexican food without cold Mexican beer?"

"You put away more beer than any man I've ever known," she said. "I swear, sometimes I think you've got a hollow leg."

I leaned forward to switch on the ignition. Then I stopped with my hand on the key and stared over at her. "What did you say?"

"I said sometimes I think you've got a hollow leg. What's the matter?"

"That's it," I said.

"What's it?"

"The answer."

"I don't know what you're talking about. . . ."

I waved her quiet, started the car, switched on the headlights—it was full dark now—and pulled away from the curb; I tended to think more clearly while I was driving. By the time we approached Diamond Heights Boulevard, I had most of it put together. And when we were headed down the steep, curving boulevard, nearing Glen Canyon, I had the rest of it. All I needed was confirmation of one thing, and Kerry herself could give me that.

But before I could ask her about it, there was a roar of noise outside and the interior of the car was bathed in the bright glare of headlights. Another car had come boiling up behind us, so close that its lights were like huge staring eyes framed in the rear window. Damn tailgater, I thought, and took my foot off the accelerator and tapped the brake pedal gently, just enough to let the other driver see the flash of the brake lights.

Only he didn't slow down; he just kept coming. And his front bumper smacked into my rear bumper, hard enough to jolt the car and almost wrench the wheel loose from my hands.

Kerry twisted around on the seat. "My God! What's the matter with him? What's he *doing*?"

"Hang on!"

The other car jarred into us again, harder than before, shattering one or both of the taillights. Even though I was ready for it, I had to fight the wheel and feather the brakes to keep my car from fishtailing into a skid. The tires made screaming noises on the pavement; I could smell the burning rubber and the sudden sour odor of my own sweat.

The road had steepened and hooked over toward the long, narrow, tree-choked expanse of Glen Canyon; for a stretch of maybe five hundred yards, Diamond Heights Boulevard paralleled the canyon's eastern rim. In the reach of my headlights I could see that there was no guardrail, just a sidewalk and some knee-high brown grass on a strip of bank and then the drop-off, sheer, almost straight down. If we went off there, there wasn't much chance that we'd survive.

And that was just what the driver of the other car wanted, all right. It wasn't a drunk back there, or kids playing dangerous games; it was somebody bent on mayhem.

Downhill to the left, on the other side of the curve, a residential street cut away uphill. I yelled at Kerry again to hang on and got set to drop the transmission lever into low gear so I could make a fast, sharp left-hand turn into the other street. There was nothing else I could do with the trailing car hanging on my bumper the way it was.

But the driver saw the street, too, and before I got close enough to make the turn, his headlights flicked out to the left, into the uphill lane. In my side mirror I could see the bulky shape of the car outlined behind the glare; then he accelerated and pulled up abreast. I glanced over at him, but all I could make out was one person, his face a white smear in the darkness. Then I put my eyes back on the road and kept them there, muscles tensed, hands tightened on the wheel, because I sensed what he was going to try to do next.

It was only a couple of seconds before he did it, just as I started onto the wide left-hand curve along the rim of the canyon; he pulled slightly ahead and then whipped over into me, hard along the front fender. There was a crunching sound, and Kerry cried out, and the car shimmied and the right front tire scraped against the curb on that side. But I was able to maintain control, even though we were still crowded together and he was trying to use his momentum to shove us up and over the bank.

I came down hard on the brake pedal, bracing myself, throwing my right arm out in front of Kerry to keep her from flying into the windshield. The tires shrieked again; we bucked and slid through the curve, losing speed. The other car glanced off, with another tearing-metal noise, yawing at a slight angle in front of me. Then the driver got it straightened out and braked as I had, swinging back full into the other lane so he could try ramming us again.

He would have done it, too, if it hadn't been for the third car that came sailing around another curve below, headed uphill.

I saw the oncoming headlights sweep through the scattered eucalyptus that grew inside the canyon further down, but the other driver was too intent on me to notice them because he didn't try to swing back into the downhill lane. Frantically I stood on the brake and got ready to yank on the emergency brake, if that was what it took to bring us to a stop; it seemed sure there would be a collision and all I could think was: Kerry might be hurt, I can't let her get hurt.

There was no collision. The driver of the third car saw what was happening, leaned hard on the horn, and managed to swerve up onto the sidewalk and across somebody's front lawn. But the guy who'd tried to kill Kerry and me had run out of luck. He saw the third car in time to swerve himself, back into the downhill lane, only he did it too sharply; he missed the third car, all right, by at least twenty feet—and he missed hitting mine by the same distance when he veered in front of me—but the rear end of his car broke loose and he wasn't able to fight through the skid and pull it out.

His car went out of control, spun all the way around, and then hit the curb and bounced up into the air like something made out of rubber. Its headlights sprayed the trees as it hurtled toward them, sideways. In the next second it was gone, and in the second after that the explosive sound of buckling metal and breaking glass and splintering wood erupted from inside the canyon.

I managed to bring my car to a stop. When I took my hands off the wheel they were as wet as if I'd dunked them in water.

"God," Kerry said in a soft, trembly voice.

"Are you all right?"

"Yes. I . . . just give me a minute. . . ."

I touched her arm, and then opened the door and got out. People were spilling from houses in the vicinity, running toward the canyon; the driver of the third car, a heavyset woman, was slumped against her front fender, not moving, looking dazed. I ran up onto the sidewalk and ahead to where the other car had gone over. It was wrapped around one of the eucalyptus about a third of the way down the slope; the upper part of the tree had been sheared off and was canted at a drunken angle. From the mangled appearance of the wreckage, I didn't see how the guy inside could have survived.

But I was wrong about that. When I got there along with a couple of other people, and we dragged him out, he was alive. Unconscious and pretty badly cut up, but unless he had internal injuries, it looked as though he'd make it all right.

It did not surprise me when I saw who he was. Because he was the same person who had committed the thefts in John Rothman's book shop—the same clever, greedy, *stupid* young man.

Neal Vining.

Three hours later, I was sitting in a room at the Hall of Justice with Kerry, John Rothman and an inspector I knew named Jack Logan, who had been the investigating officer when Rothman first reported the thefts. Vining was in the hospital under police guard. He'd already been charged with attempted vehicular homicide, and had been coherent enough and frightened enough to confess to that, and when I got done with my explanations he would also be charged with several counts of grand larceny.

I was saying, "I knew even before Vining tried to run us off the road that he was the thief. And I know how he got the stolen items out of the store, too. It was a combination of things I'd seen and heard; and when Kerry made a comment about me having a hollow leg, because I like to drink beer, it triggered an association that put it all together."

"Hollow leg?" Rothman said. "I don't understand what—"

"You'll see what I mean in a minute. The whole

thing is really pretty simple; it was Vining himself, in fact, who told me how he pulled off the thefts, either without realizing what he was saying or, more likely, because he was so sure of himself that it was his way of bragging. He said yesterday, 'For all I know, Mr. Rothman himself could be slipping out with the spoils.' "

They were all staring at me, Rothman with a look of incredulity. "Are you saying *I* took the items out of the shop for him? That's preposterous—"

"No, it isn't," I said. "You took them out, all right; that's the beauty of this scheme. He made you an unwitting accomplice?"

"How could he possibly have done that?"

"By putting the stolen items inside your cane," I said.

"My *cane*?"

"Vining gave it to you, didn't he? Some months ago? Harmon Boyette told me Vining was in the habit of giving you presents from his father-in-law's haberdashery."

"Yes, but . . ." Rothman seemed a little nonplussed. He reached for the cane, propped against the side of his chair, and gawped at it as if he'd never seen it before.

Logan said, "You mean the cane's hollow?"

"Yes. That's the significance of Kerry's hollow-leg comment. And that's why Vining stole only etchings, prints and maps, instead of books that were more valuable, since you installed your alarm system: they could be rolled up and inserted inside the cane. They still make canes like that over in England; people keep money and other small valuable items inside them—as a safeguard against theft, ironically enough. It wouldn't have been difficult for Vining to have one imported through his father-in-law's store."

Rothman was running his fingers over the thick barrel of the cane, peering at it. "How does the damn thing work?"

"I don't know. But it shouldn't take us long to find out."

It took us about two minutes. The catch was well concealed, and so was the long hinged opening; you couldn't see either with the naked eye, you couldn't feel the grooves with your fingers and it wasn't likely that you could open it by accident. Fine British craftsmanship. Logan was the one who finally found the catch, and when the hinges released I saw what I expected to see: the hollow interior contained a rolled-up length of parchment.

Rothman took the parchment out and unrolled it gently. "My God," he said, "the Mercator map."

"Right where Vining put it this afternoon," I said, "after he stole it from the Antiquarian Room."

"But I keep the cane with me at all times; I need it to get around for any distance. I don't see how—"

"You don't take it into the bathroom with you, Mr. Rothman. When I got to the store yesterday morning, and went up to talk to you, you were in the bathroom; the cane was leaning against the wall outside. I remember you taking it from there when you came out."

Rothman nodded. "You're right, of course; I never took the cane into the bathroom because it was too cumbersome in that little cubicle. I always left it against the wall outside."

"And you used the bathroom fairly often during the day, didn't you? Because of your bladder problem?"

"Yes."

"So it was easy enough for Vining to put the stolen items inside the cane. He committed each of his thefts while you were out to lunch or otherwise away from the store in the early afternoons so he could be sure you wouldn't catch him red-handed. Then he either hid the pieces somewhere, or kept them inside his clothes, until you returned and he saw an opportunity to put them inside the cane while you were in the bathroom and there was nobody else in the vicinity. It only took him a few seconds each time.

"The whole idea was to beat the sensor alarm. Everyone who left the store after one of the thefts had to pass through the alarm gateway *except you*; you were always the last one to leave on those days, and you always switched the alarm off before you went through the gateway yourself to lock up. The *only* person who could have taken the items out of the shop was you."

"But how did Vining retrieve them from the cane after I'd left?" Rothman asked. Then I saw understanding come to him and he answered his own question. "Well, I'll be damned. The Pacific Health Club."

"Right. Vining is a member, too, isn't he?"

"Yes, he is. How did you know?"

"You told me so yourself, last night. You said you didn't go to the health club to lift weights or to play racquetball with Neal Vining; you wouldn't have phrased it that way unless he was also a member."

Logan asked, "How did Vining get the stuff out of the cane at the health club?"

"I go there every night to use the Jacuzzi," Rothman explained. "It's right off the locker room, so I've never taken the cane in there with me; there's no place to put it near the Jacuzzi."

"You left it inside your locker, is that it?"

"Yes. The locker has a combination lock, but I don't suppose it would have been difficult for Vining to get the combination. I remember him standing there talking to me on more than one occasion while I was opening it."

"So all he had to do," I said, "was to wait for you to go into the Jacuzzi and then open up your locker, transfer the stolen items from the cane to inside his clothing and walk out with them. Simple as that."

Rothman shook his head wonderingly. "The only other question I have," he said, "is why did Vining try to kill you and Miss Wade tonight?"

"He slipped up this afternoon at the store, while he was putting the Mercator map inside the cane. He'd been careful not to let anybody see him in the past; this time he wasn't so careful and somebody did see him."

"Me," Kerry said. "Well, I didn't exactly see him putting anything inside the cane; I just saw him with the cane in his hand."

"How did that happen?" Logan asked.

"I was browsing in the stacks at the rear of the fiction section. In the W's, along the rear wall directly behind the last stack, near what must be the bathroom. I guess he didn't see me when he looked down the aisles, so he didn't think anybody was around. I found an old scarce book of my father's—he's been a writer for forty years, you see—and I was excited about it; I grabbed it off the shelf and hurried into the last aisle, and a man was standing there with that cane in his hand. I bumped right into him."

"She told me about that a few minutes later," I said. "At the time I naturally assumed the man she'd bumped into was Mr. Rothman. But later, I realized it could have been Vining. And it was."

"Then it was Miss Wade he was after tonight?" Rothman asked. "Because he was afraid she'd seen him put the Mercator map inside the cane?"

"Not exactly," I said. "Vining was trying to kill both of us. He was afraid Kerry had seen him with the map, yes, and he wanted to know who she was; from what he told the police at the hospital a little while ago, he hadn't formed any definite plans about her at that time. He'd followed her downstairs and overheard her talking to me, about the date we had tonight. So he knew we were friends. After he left the shop he waited around until I left at seven o'clock and then followed me until I led him to Kerry's apartment building. I was so preoccupied when I went inside to get her that I left my car unlocked. Vining looked inside and found out from the registration that I'm a detective. That really unnerved him. So when I drove away with Kerry a little while later, he followed us again—maybe with the intention of committing murder, maybe not. He said he didn't plan to try forcing us off the road; he just did it on impulse. Whether it was premeditated or not is up to a jury to decide."

And that was about it. Rothman still had the problem of recovering the other stolen items, but with a full confession from Vining—and it seemed probable the police would get one—he would know to whom they had been sold, and the chances were good that he would be able to force their return.

Saturday night may have been a bust as far as my date with Kerry had gone, but early Sunday morning at her apartment was something else again. Early Sunday morning was terrific.

"I love to watch you work," she said once. "You're a pretty good detective, you know that?"

"Well," I said modestly, "I do the best I can."

"Yes, you do. No matter what you're doing."

"The fire's getting low. Shall I get up and put another log on?"

"The heck with the fire," she said.

Neither of us noticed when it finally went out.

*Turn this book over
for more mystery
and adventure with*

THE "NAMELESS DETECTIVE"

WE HOPE YOU HAVE ENJOYED THIS
KNIGHTSBRIDGE BOOK.

WE LOVE GOOD BOOKS JUST AS YOU DO,
SO YOU CAN BE ASSURED THAT THE
KNIGHT ON THE HORSE
STANDS FOR GOOD READING, EVERY TIME.